BEDSIDE MANNER

Laurel took a chair near the head of the bed and reached for *Waverley,* which lay upon the coverlet.

In admonitory accents she said, "In all the times that I have been here we have not advanced a dozen pages. I cannot think you want to hear this book."

"But I do!" he declared fervently. "Dr. Dodd has *prescribed* it as necessary to my cure." He reached boldly for her fingers and, holding one hand firmly, as once before, he so distracted her that she let Mr. Scott drop on his head on the carpet with a faint thump.

"May I speak in confidence?" he asked softly.

She nodded, and this time did not snatch back her tingling hand.

The Beaux of Bayley Dell

Dorothea Donley

ZEBRA BOOKS
KENSINGTON PUBLISHING CORP.

ZEBRA BOOKS are published by

Kensington Publishing Corp.
850 Third Avenue
New York, NY 10022

First Printing: April, 1995

Printed in the United States of America

One

On the evening of the Ides of March, Sir John Eland, Bart., dozed in his usual indolent fashion in a wing chair to the right of the drawing room fire. Above the mantel portraits of his parents looked benignly on the scene. Across the room his two sisters and his daughter chatted. That is, the older ladies spoke softly, though indignantly, while Laurel nodded her understanding, if not her agreement.

"You should have made your bow two years ago!" declared Miss Frances.

"Yes, indeed," said Miss Mirabelle fretfully.

"John is failing his duty as a father."

"So he is."

"I've said this over and over to him."

"Indeed you have."

"And look at him! He prefers to sleep."

"As usual."

"Am I wasting my voice?" asked Miss Frances.

"Oh, no!" Miss Mirabelle responded. *"Someone* must convince him!"

"He will wake up when tea comes in," Laurel pointed out with a slight smile. She was a very pretty girl with absolutely no vanity. Her ringlets were golden-brown and her eyes were a rich brown that sometimes seemed as bright as amber.

Anyone overhearing the aunts' dialogue would suppose Miss Frances to be the dominant sister. It was true that she was the more verbal, as well as the younger and plumper.

Laurel, however, knew that Miss Mirabelle in her quiet way was the organizer of the household and the Keeper of Accounts. Twenty years' acquaintance with the two aunts had made her love both wholeheartedly because she always received from them *double* the love that a mother might have provided.

"I'm sure," said Miss Frances, "that if John were not so very generous to us I would bash him with the butter churn."

Sir John had come into his title a dozen years earlier, when his brother perished in a madcap curricle race to Dover. His patrimony virtually ended with him, and debts resulting from his profligate style fell upon Sir John, who had no choice but to sell all unentailed property. The present house in the hamlet of Bayley Dell and the family manor, whose entrance was immediately across the road, were all that remained in the baronet's control. Without repining, Sir John leased the manor to an affable cit, Mr. Hanger, who wished to try his hand at farming, and invited his sisters to share home and income with him and his motherless child.

The generosity that Miss Frances mentioned was not great, for Sir John's income required careful disbursement by Miss Mirabelle as long as there were still their brother's debts to be paid. Fortunately, all members of the family were content with simple comforts. The ladies busied themselves with the affairs of the village; only the two elder ones had any ambition, and that was focused upon Laurel. Perhaps the girl had secret dreams; if so, they did not trouble her unduly, as the future seemed remote to one who was only twenty. All proceeded smoothly. Sir John was cosseted in the most agreeable way and was able to enjoy an interesting assortment of nebulous ailments.

As a younger son, Sir John Eland had not been raised to indulge in any great Expectations. His nature was tranquil, his wife—when he married one—undemanding. A sti-

pend from his father kept the couple contented in a sweet
wee cottage on the Eland manor until the young wife died
of a fever soon after Laurel was born. At that time John
moved back into the manor house, where his mother and
two unwed sisters were happy to fondle and spoil the infant.

Fortunately, Laurel's disposition was a combination of
her parents'. She did not suppose herself cheated by Fate,
the victim of a spendthrift uncle. *His* death, following three
reckless years after the death of Laurel's grandparents, and
the subsequent shift to the small house in Bayley Dell, did
not disturb the child. As heir apparent to her father's
shrunken holdings (whatever were his to dispose of), she
was assigned the front chamber, across from her father's,
which received the cheerful morning sunlight and had a
pleasant view of the avenue to the manor house.

Her father had taught her to read and encouraged her to
study the small yet excellent assortment of books that he
had brought there from the manor house, and as the great
writers of the centuries were contained in them, she became
as knowledgeable as her Papa in eternal verities. The two,
father and daughter, enjoyed conversations that made the
aunts shake their heads in disapproval. *They* did their part
in other ways: both teaching frugality, Miss Frances impart-
ing social graces—for which there was lamentably little call
in Bayley Dell—and Miss Mirabelle teaching bookkeeping
and taking her niece regularly to church.

Miss Frances made a habit of talking "presentations" and
"come-outs" regularly, though she was not surprised when
her brother dismissed them. He was a smallish man, with
hair just beginning to turn gray. Like his sisters, he had
straight brows and rounded cheeks. A small gray mouse
ornamented his upper lip. Dapper he was, yet in no way
extravagant in his clothes. He was a rare creature—one perfectly satisfied to live within his means; a London season
for anyone named Eland was out of the question.

In consideration for their ancient, tottering butler, Fane,

Miss Mirabelle had dispensed with the great heirloom silver service and substituted a four-cup china pot. When she heard his footsteps in the hall she rose serenely to open the door: she had been doing this for so long that no one considered it the least strange, not even Fane, whose pride was just about all he had to keep him functioning.

"John! Tea!" said Miss Frances piercingly.

Sir John blinked and had only enough time to say "Eh?" when the knocker sounded. A visitor at nine thirty?

Laurel relieved Fane of the tray so that he might answer the front door. His quavering voice mingled with a youthful one.

"Why, it's the boy from the inn," Laurel exclaimed. "They must have a problem. Come in, Del."

The young male who entered was hardly a "boy," as he topped Sir John, but his cheeks shone beardless and his eyes were anxious. Evidently he was glad to see Laurel, for he addressed her: "We've an injured man, miss, and me mum sent me for the doctor, but *he's* abed with fever, so I come here."

The older ladies immediately cried, "Dr. Dodd *sick!*" It was plain that they did not think he should be allowed to take to his bed at any time. Sir John was all curiosity about the doctor's symptoms, but Del could supply no details.

It was not surprising that Del had come here. After all, they were next door to the doctor, and Laurel was known to assist him in treating village children.

"Mum's that upset," Del said urgently.

"I'll come, of course," Laurel replied. Already Fane was bringing her shabby woolen cloak. She darted under the steps to seize a scuffed black satchel. "I may only be moral support," she muttered, as Fane laid the cloak about her shoulders.

"Mum'll thankee," Del said. "It's a stranger. Hurt bad."

Directly, they went down into the street and turned right. Sir John's charming house was the central one of three brick dwellings built in the same period by someone with a good eye for proportions. Several stone steps led up to a door that was flanked by columns. Inside was a formal parlor with a dining room behind and a rear ell for a kitchen, down three steps. Across the hall was a sunny gold-and-white drawing room. On the second floor were four comfortable bedchambers, which were all the Elands needed as they had no acquaintances to invite to visit. The cook and a maid-of-all-work had quarters in a light and airy attic that very likely was less desirable in winter than Fane's warm cellar. Well, chilblains were nothing new to anyone in Bayley Dell.

Beyond Sir John's place another good brick house was dropping slowly to ruin over the unwary heads of two elderly ladies living there. "Maintenance" meant nothing to them. They were disintegrating themselves and cared only about sitting in the bow window, which *their* house boasted, to watch everything that occurred along the street.

Along Laurel's and the boy's route, a small garden separated Dr. Dodd from Sir John. The house was very much the same, except that parlor and dining room had been converted to office and waiting room, a side door having been cut to the doctor's driveway. Crowded behind his house was a shed, for naturally the doctor required both gig and saddle horse in his work, which covered several neighboring villages.

Next came the churchyard and church, an Everything Shop, several timbered cottages, and at last the inn.

Although it was near the end of a very long day, Mrs. Patten received Laurel wearing a tidy mobcap and an unmussed gray frock. "Mercy on us—hurt and fainting," she chattered anxiously, leading Laurel upstairs to her best guest chamber. "Patten and the ostler got him up here. There!" she whispered in tones of relief. Her pale blue eyes were apprehensive.

Full of misgivings, Laurel walked to the bedside and stared down at a most comely young gentleman. His nose and mouth were modeled like a Grecian statue; his eyes were closed, his complexion extremely pale. She scrutinized him carefully, knowing she would have to carry details to Dr. Dodd.

"Patten says the right arm is broken," offered Mrs. Patten.

Laurel moved to the far side of the bed to examine the arm. Someone had cut away the sleeve. She probed gently.

"Patten is right, I think. In any case we must bind it up to prevent more damage if he moves. Let us see if we can get off his boots . . . such good boots. Who is he?"

Mrs. Patten shrugged helplessly. "No purse, no cards. He rode in about seven, asking for some supper, which I served him. He had money *then*. Rode off toward Wells an hour later. Then he came back on foot and collapsed as he came in our gate."

They soon removed the boots, and Laurel sent Mrs. Patten off to fetch a slat and strips of fabric to immobilize the arm.

Patten returned with his wife to help bind up the stranger. They could not determine whether he was unconscious or too deep in pain to make any effort at response.

"Poor chap," said Mrs. Patten. "Best he sleeps whilst he can. I'll have the boys to keep watch over him tonight."

Laurel nodded. "I know Del will help, but Roddy is only twelve, isn't he, and might not be—"

"Ar," exclaimed Mrs. Patten. "Better nor any."

The innkeeper added, "Allus doctorin' creatures in the village. Be a rare treat for 'im to nurse a 'uman."

Del and Roddy were summoned to help Patten undress and wash the patient, while Laurel and Mrs. Patten descended to discuss sending to the next town for a doctor. Both preferred their own physician, whom everyone at Bayley Dell considered infallible, so they decided to wait to see what other hurts Patten might have discovered.

"He has the appearance of a gentleman. Will it be possible to find his family?" Laurel said. "What can you tell me about his horse? Was there a special horse that might be traced?"

Mrs. Patten said she had not seen the beast, adding indignantly, "And I can tell you this, if the creature tossed this fine young chappie, it better never come around me again! A curricle went through earlier that may or mayn't be his. I didn't notice it particular. He had no baggage with him."

When the burly Patten came down to the Pattens' private sitting room, where the ladies waited, he had a long face and a gruff manner. Under thick brows, his eyes were troubled.

"Had a bad time," he verified. "I'm afraid we hurt 'im some. Ought to recover, but there're a lot of nasty bruises all over that don't look like a simple toss. Expect you didn't see a 'orrid bruise on the corner of 'is jaw."

The two ladies gasped.

"Didn't feel cracked," he continued, "but I don't think 'e'll want to chew anything for a few days . . . maybe not even talk."

Laurel said she had not felt any fever in him. "Tell the boys to check every hour. If it starts to climb, then—"

"—bathe him with cool wet cloths. Yes'm," finished Mrs. Patten.

All three smiled ruefully at their own inadequacy.

"I will come to check on our patient first thing in the morning and then report to Dr. Dodd to see if he has anymore instructions for us," Laurel promised. "I hope you—and he—can have a peaceful night."

Mrs. Patten bobbed an abbreviated curtsy. "Thankee, Miss Laurel. Patten will just walk home with you to be sure you're safe."

Laurel knew every man, woman, child, dog, cat, horse, and cow in Bayley Dell, and had tramped every inch of it in all sorts of weather. Like a true lady, however, she graciously accepted Patten's escort for eight hundred feet to her home.

On the steps, with Fane waiting at the open door, Patten grumbled, "Place on the jaw looks like the kick of a boot."

Laurel moaned, "Oh, dear!" and flew into the house, where its six inmates were waiting to hear the gruesome details.

Sir John, in particular, was eager to know if the "fellow" had a knot on the head like the one *he* had received when a bottle of his best port fell from a rack in the cellar.

Because her patient was so beautiful and so vulnerable, and because she felt a burden of responsibility, all the questions seemed positively ghoulish. She was very short in her answers to them.

"Laurel is tired," said Aunt Frances sapiently.

"She needs her bed," agreed Aunt Mirabelle.

Fane took away her cloak and satchel. Her papa said, "Go to bed, dearest."

Three faithful servants watched her make her way upstairs. It was possible there were some wishes floating around that the stranger might be a prince in disguise. Or if not a prince, at least a duke.

As for Sir John, he was revitalized by the aspect of his daughter as a Healer of the Sick. "Next thing," he called after her, "you'll be setting out your shingle!"

"Perfect," retorted Miss Frances, following to see Laurel tucked in bed. "In that case you need not call on Dr. Dodd when your toe throbs."

"Perfectly outrageous," corrected Miss Mirabelle. "Pray remember Laurel is a *lady,* John."

The adoring aunts climbed the stairs, conferring with each other, saying, "Isn't it strange? . . . Who can he be? . . . Of course it was Christian of Laurel to help the poor gentleman. . . . Dr. Dodd will approve."

Already they had made the stranger into a gentleman.

While Miss Mirabelle hung away Laurel's clothes, Miss Frances helped her into a warm gown embroidered around the collar with pink rosebuds and brushed her hair soothingly. There was a merciful lack of rivalry between the sisters. They were an unconscious team, treating her as if she was theirs, when actually, if she belonged to anyone, it was Papa.

Laurel thought how dear they were to ask no questions when they must be bursting with curiosity, so she explained, "I am not physically tired—just cast down to see such a fine gentleman so battered. I felt helpless to make him comfortable."

"Did he thrash?" asked one, "and moan?" asked the other.

Aunt Frances's thick hair was escaping from her lace cap as she shook her head and clicked her tongue.

"No," Laurel answered. "He was still. Too still. I did not know what to do for him. We needed Dr. Dodd, although I could tell the man had no fever and that seemed a good sign."

Miss Mirabelle clasped her hands to her bosom. "You do not mean to say you *touched* him!"

"Well, to be sure I did. How else was I to tell about fever? I bent over close to listen to his breathing, too. As near as I could tell, he was breathing evenly, though not deeply—as in a gentle sleep, you might say."

Mirabelle looked shocked. "I hope you were properly chaperoned, Laurel."

"Oh, I was perfectly safe."

"But you are so pretty, dearest, and pretty girls sometimes attract unwanted attentions."

"Yes, so you have told me, Auntie Mirabelle, but as he never opened his eyes to see my charms, I could not have been safer. I do not know much about rakes and dandies, never having met any, but this man had none of the obvious marks. There was nothing exaggerated about his clothes— well tailored, you know, and not extreme in style or hue. I fear the riding coat is done for. He was very pale. I did not see his eyes, but I am guessing blue because his hair is blond."

The aunts chorused: "But where did he come from? Who is he?"

Laurel admitted that no one seemed to know. "Apparently he stopped for something to eat, then rode on in the direction of Wells. An hour or so later he staggered into the innyard and crashed at Patten's feet."

The aunts looked suitably horrified. "What did Patten do?"

Laurel rolled her eyes. "How do I know? Called his groom to help him carry the man inside, Mrs. Patten said, and then I suppose, manlike, he told Mrs. Patten it was a case for her to deal with. Whether it was he or his wife who sent for the doctor I do not know. At any rate, they got me, and I will admit that the whole situation made me decidedly uneasy. Who am I to make decisions in such a matter?"

"Poor girl . . . so brave," Miss Frances murmured, and her sister said gravely, "We must pray that he gets through the night."

Laurel said, "I think he will. I hope he will."

"Lord willing," added Miss Mirabelle with a sigh.

"Naturally I must look in on him in the morning, and then have a talk with Dr. Dodd about what to do next." Laurel sank back against her pillows, looking exceedingly young and fragile (although she was actually a healthy girl).

"But, Laurel," objected Miss Mirabelle, "you can't visit with the doctor when he is ill in *bed.*"

"Oh, yes, she can," said Miss Frances. "That is to say, she must—if the man is to have adequate care. We don't want his death on our conscience! *I* will accompany her."

Miss Mirabelle suggested, "Do you think—perhaps John should go—"

"*I* shall take her myself. You must know, Sister, that no one will criticize my chaperonage."

Miss Mirabelle did indeed know that. "While you are gone I will make a broth," she decided, "a very *nourishing* broth for the poor man. Mrs. Patten won't have time for such special things. What would you say to some hot milk laced with brandy?"

"Not brandy, if he is light-headed," objected Laurel.

Miss Frances said, "Very true."

"Broth will be best," agreed Miss Mirabelle amiably.

They patted the bedclothes around their niece, kissed her, blew out the candles, and departed, leaving Laurel to her anxious memories of the battered young man. Although it was well past their bedtime, the ladies went down the stairs again to regale their brother with what they had been able to glean in Laurel's chamber.

"You must not be afraid, John," said Miss Frances, "that we will let Laurel be compromised by visiting at a gentleman's bedside—Dr. Dodd's *or* the stranger's. I will chaperone her."

"And I will make some broth," added Miss Mirabelle.

Having perfect confidence that his sisters could cope with park-saunterers, rattles, rakes, and roués, Sir John nodded approvingly and said, "I may take a look at the fellow myself. And I will have a word with Dodd—though not, of course, until he is over his fever, for you know how susceptible I am to infection."

His sister Frances felt it was a splendid opportunity to point out that Laurel should never have been thrust into such a situation.

To which Sir John replied, "Surely she is safe in Bayley Dell!"

"Much too safe," said Miss Frances, turning the word back on him. "How can she be suitably settled if she does not meet eligible gentlemen? There isn't a single male in our village except the cit at your manor!"

"Forty if a day," inserted Miss Mirabelle.

"Forty-three," admitted Sir John. "He told me last week."

"And Laurel is only *twenty*," Miss Frances continued. "Could be Mr. Hanger's child!" Then, realizing she was defeating her own purpose, she added hastily, "She is at her years of greatest beauty and could have made a proper marriage before now if only you had let her have a come-out."

Sir John looked dashed. "It isn't a matter of 'letting' her make a bow to society. I am sorry to say that I haven't the funds. Mirabelle can tell you. *She* knows."

"I could sell Mama's diamond earrings," Frances offered.

"And I Mama's pearls'," said Miss Mirabelle quickly.

He shook his head ruefully. "Not enough, I'm afraid. She would need ball gowns, and all sorts of dresses and fripperies. An abigail. A carriage. A rented house in London. A reception, if not a ball. It just isn't possible."

"Not even Bath or—or *Wells?* They have public balls, I think."

He shook his head again and looked so woebegone that his sisters rushed to kiss him and insist that they thought he was the best and most generous of brothers.

"I won't say no to Wells if you think Laurel would meet gentlemen at dances there. Daresay we could hire Patten's carriage to take us."

Miss Frances returned happily to the contest. "If they have dances, the ladies must certainly have partners. They would undoubtedly think our Laurel charming."

"To be sure, they would," Sir John allowed. "Still, how can *you* be sure the gentlemen at the dances are eligible? The only man with whom I am acquainted at Wells is one who operates a stockyard and who sometimes furnished our manor with excellent manure for the poorer fields."

The ladies could not be certain that he was teasing. Miss Mirabelle came to the rescue, saying, "I have an old school friend at Wells, remember. Mrs. Walden is a lady of the first stare. She can be relied upon to steer us right."

So it was settled. All three being tolerably satisfied, they retired to bed.

Two

Although Sir John Eland was only forty-seven, his leisurely existence allowed him to indulge in naps during the course of a day—midmorning, afternoon at variable hours as fitted events, and between dinner and late tea. For this reason it was his habit to awaken early, which he did the morning after the crisis at the inn.

He was lying cozily under a heap of blankets when Fane entered with a cup of coffee—to invigorate his blood—and shuffled to draw back draperies at the windows on the street.

"Morning, Fane," said the baronet cheerfully, sitting up to sip his coffee.

"Morning, sir," returned the old man, who evidenced a fondness for Sir John that he had never accorded the elder brother. He laid out his clothes meticulously.

Both knew the lean and white-headed butler should have been pensioned off long ago. They also knew there had been no funds to do this when the manor was let to Mr. Hanger. To stay for a stranger—an outsider—would have broken Fane's heart, and he had no family of his own, so he had willingly stepped down to butler-valet-factotum at the house in the village.

"A nice day, sir," reported Fane, looking into the street. "I see the Pattens' boy coming this way."

"Something about the invalid," said Sir John, throwing back his covers. "Pray, see what it is." He began dressing with unusual haste.

Across the hall, Laurel heard the knocker sound and shot
out of bed to dive into a dressing gown and run to the top
of the stairs. Her heart was thumping in alarm. Had the
man died without a proper doctor?

She heard Fane ask, "What is it, Del?"

Sir John came from his room to join his daughter. They
heard Del answer cheerily, "The gent's awake. Mum thought
Miss Laurel would want to know."

"Oh, I do!" called Laurel softly. "Please tell your mother
I will come as soon as I have dressed."

"Frances will not be awake this early," Sir John observed.
"It will take an hour to get her on the road. I'll escort you,
love. By the time we return your aunt ought to be ready to
accompany you to Dr. Dodd."

"Thank you, Papa," said Laurel, returning to her room.
"You *might* have time for a half cup of coffee."

"I've had my cof—" he began, but her door had closed.
He continued quietly down the stairs and allowed Fane to
adjust his cravat with a proprietary air.

"Who says nothing happens in our village?" Sir John
asked.

"Not I, sir," replied Fane. "If it is not a stranger, it is
twins in one of the cottages."

Sir John smiled. "Then tell me: Is the doctor in better
health today?"

"Not up yet, sir."

Sir John said, "I knew you would know. When I see him
I shall ask if he takes his own nasty medicines."

"Fluids and bed rest only, is my understanding, sir."

When, presently, Laurel descended, she was slightly
flushed, and her gold-brown hair tumbled entrancingly from
the hood of her emerald green cloak.

"When your patient sees you," murmured her father
fondly, "it will kill him or cure him," to which Laurel re-
monstrated, "Oh, *Pa*-pa," but her tone implied that she was
not ill pleased.

The village was waking up as they went along the street. Two dogs ran homeward, hungry for breakfast after an early morning romp. On the steps of the Everything Shop a tiger cat was washing its face diligently, having nicer manners than the dogs.

Patten's inn rejoiced in the improbable name of The Nesting Dove, but in Bayley Dell it was regularly called "the inn." It was a small hostelry having on the lower story only one private parlor, plus a combination taproom and dining room. Overhead were two chambers for overnight guests. It was not a posting house.

Patten's groom could be seen watering a horse.

Sir John opened the door for his daughter, and they entered to find Patten sweeping the hall. He set aside his broom, saying, "Your man's awake, Miss Laurel. Remembers nothing."

"Nothing?" cried Laurel.

"Well," added Patten, "when 'e asked me where 'e was and I said Bayley Dell, 'e remembered *that,* all right."

"We will go up," said Sir John, taking matters in hand.

Mrs. Patten met them at the top of the stairs. "I'm right glad you've come," she said with some relief. Opening the door, she announced playfully, "Sir, here is your doctor."

The stranger in the bed turned uncertain blue eyes first to Sir John, which was a natural mistake for him to make.

"No, no," said Sir John with a slight laugh. "Not I. My daughter is your medical apprentice."

The eyes then shifted to Laurel for a long, assessing look before closing. The provoking creature said not a word.

Had he fainted? His color was better than it had been the night before. Not much of him was visible, however. She saw only his head and braced arm, the covers being tucked over the rest of him. As his upper portions had been somewhat raised on pillows, the flesh of his face fell into more normal lines, and he looked less like Hermes or Apollo and more like an Englishman with a sore head.

"What sort of night was it?" she asked Mrs. Patten.

The landlady cocked her head benignly at the stranger. "Not so bad. He made no trouble, though he woke several times. The boys say he complained of his knee. Would you be wanting to see it?"

Laurel said reluctantly, "I expect I must." If the fellow was pretending unconsciousness, this would wake him up for sure, Laurel thought with an inward chuckle.

The patient remained immobile.

Sir John made no comment as the ladies went around the bed. In fact, he followed closely to see what new injuries were revealed when Mrs. Patten raised the covers from the member in question.

They were rewarded with a view of shapely male leg, distorted by a swollen and multicolored knee. Sir John clicked his tongue, and Laurel whispered, "Oh, *dear!* That must hurt."

She touched the knee gently. "Feverish."

"Yes," agreed the landlady. "We've been using cool cloths."

Laurel nodded. "No way to tell if it is a fracture or a simple wrench . . . or a not so simple one." She watched the patient's face, which remained unchanged. "I *do* hope Dr. Dodd is mending! How thankful I am that you are in charge here, Mrs. Patten."

The landlady smoothed the covers into place. "Poor chap," she said softly. "Well, I daresay he will recover. Between a husband and two sons, I have seen a lot of the trouble that males can bring upon themselves by taking risks."

"Has the fellow taken any nourishment?" asked Sir John suddenly.

"Some sips of tea, sir," she said.

"Ah! Well, that is a start. Miss Mirabelle is making broth. I'll see it gets to you as soon as it is ready."

"Just the thing, thankee," said Mrs. Patten. "Now, Miss Laurel, dearie, don't you fret. I'll stay right here until the boys have had their breakfast and stretched their legs. Roddy is certain *he's* indis—indispen—needed."

"Thank *you,* Mrs. Patten," Laurel returned. "I will get to Dr. Dodd as soon as I can." A last look told her that the stranger had not stirred.

When Laurel and her father left the inn they encountered Mr. Hanger, who boomed, "Good-day," as he whipped off his beaver hat and stood with the chill early morning breeze ruffling his red hair. He was a large, ruddy man of perpetual good humor. "I'll be bound you've been to see your patient, Miss Eland," he said. There was no reason to be surprised that he knew about the stranger, since he had as many avenues of information as he had servants.

Laurel nodded civilly, while Sir John replied that the patient seemed in better frame, though in some discomfort from a badly swollen knee.

"Swollen, eh? Then he'll need ice on it. We cut some ice this winter and I think we have some left. I'll send it down."

"It would be most welcome, Mr. Hanger," Laurel said warmly, appreciating Mr. Hanger's kindness to one who could mean nothing to him. Even after twelve years, her aunts avoided the rich "upstart" who occupied their ancestral home. For this reason she always made it a point to be gracious to him.

He was not to blame for their lack of funds. In fact, the rent he paid for the manor kept them solvent. He might talk over-loudly and informally, yet he was never rude or crude. He seemed consistently kindhearted. Everything interested him. He had hired an excellent bailiff for the manor and consulted tactfully with Sir John about each improvement, of which there were many. As years passed, he devoted less and less time to his affairs in London and more to Bayley Dell. He was generally liked in the village, only Sir John's sisters holding themselves aloof.

"Is your patient awake this morning, missy?" Mr. Hanger asked.

"It is difficult to say for sure," Laurel admitted with a smile. "As soon as we arrived, he shut his eyes, and he still had not reopened them when we left."

Mr. Hanger said he would go along and see what he could do for the fellow. "I shall tell him what a pretty picture he will see if he keeps his eyes open next time you come," he promised with a burst of laughter.

"The point is to keep him quiet," reminded Sir John.

"Mayhap he's been struck dumb already by a glimpse of missy," Mr. Hanger suggested genially.

One could not be cross with such an amiable fellow, Laurel thought. She and her father returned to the street and Mr. Hanger bounded into the inn, still carrying his hat.

"He seems a kind man," Laurel said, meaning Mr. Hanger, which Sir John understood without difficulty. "Why are my aunts so critical of him?"

Sir John allowed himself to walk a few paces in thought. "Actually, it isn't criticism. They feel the loss of their home greatly, and our brother is not here for them to blame. They feel diminished, I think. Not to be the Misses Eland of Bayley Manor makes them feel they have been *robbed,* that in some way Hanger has stolen their 'place.' "

"Robbed! Stolen!"

"No, of course not, dearest. It is not what they think; it is what they feel. Too bad, really. I have been exceedingly fortunate to get someone of such honest and generous nature to be my tenant. We deal comfortably together."

"You aren't a bit alike, Papa."

"True. Nevertheless, we think alike about the land—and the house—and the village. His being rich certainly isn't a flaw of character!"

By this time they had reached home. They went in to find Miss Frances just rising from her breakfast. While her aunt went to fetch her cloak and bonnet, Laurel watched her father fill a plate at the sideboard.

"Did Mr. Hanger have a wife, Papa?" she asked hesitantly.

"Naturally he did, silly girl. You know he has a son who is off at Harrow and of whom he is very proud. Mrs. Hanger died soon after coming here. I don't suppose you remember. You were only eight or nine."

There was a pause during which Sir John seated himself at the head of the heirloom table that just did squeeze into the dining room.

"Why does Mr. Hanger never call here? Is it because my aunts never called at the manor?"

Sir John swallowed a bite of toast. "That's it," he admitted. "Shame. But there it is."

Laurel passed him apple jelly with a somber look upon her face.

"Do not take it to heart, child. Hanger understands. I visit *him* more than my sisters know. We have fine talks. I've learned to respect his mind and attitudes."

Mulling over what he said, Laurel allowed her father to eat a few forksful of his breakfast. As men go, he was not a big eater—would not have such a trim figure if he was. His sedentary life would have turned him fat before now, for strolls about the village could not count as exercise.

Presently she said, "He is good-natured. Isn't he lonely here?"

Sir John laid down his fork. "So serious this morning, dear one? Hanger could be lonely, but I do not think he is. Would not stay here if he were. I, myself, would be excessively lonely in the city, where one is insignificant among thousands!"

"Why, Papa, you would have a place in the *ton*."

He made a wry face. "Lose your money and you lose your place."

"Oh, surely you would always have a *place*, Papa."

"To be truthful, there might be a spot for me," he allowed, "but I do not have sufficient funds to occupy it."

She asked, "Will you ever be free of my uncle's debts? Tell me. I ought to know."

"Another four or five years of rents from Hanger and we ought to be clear," he said soberly. "That may not seem long to a young person like you, but I will be well into my fifties and your Aunt Mirabelle almost there. By that time we may not *care.*"

Laurel looked indignant. "Now, Papa, I won't permit you to be maudlin! It isn't like you. I forbid it!"

Sir John laughed and dropped his serviette. "You forbid it? Well, well. You know I never mope."

It was true; he never did. Laurel kissed the top of his head, where the hair was a wee bit thin, and left him to finish his meal in peace. She heard Aunt Frances descending the stair.

Sir John was not immediately destined to enjoy peace or mopes, for Aunt Frances, in a practical brown pelisse and plain villager bonnet, swept Laurel back into the dining parlor to witness to her commands for her brother. As usual they were contradictory—drink no more tea or coffee, remember to stay near the drawing room fire and avoid chills, get plenty of fluids, and not fail to see if the footbridge behind the church was rotting. Her brother remained calm, intending to follow his own inclinations.

"Oh, get along," he said, "and entertain the doctor in *his* boudoir for a change!"

Such a nonsensical remark made Miss Frances laugh. She beckoned Laurel and they departed. No sooner had they gone than Miss Mirabelle appeared from the kitchen to disturb her brother's tranquillity with a sample of broth.

"I was awake before anyone," she announced. "My broth for the poor stranger is almost done. We had an end of roast, so I boiled that. Men prefer beef, don't they? Here;

taste it and see what it needs." Her hair was rather flyaway and her face serious as she handed him the cup.

Her brother was not expected to criticize, and generally Miss Mirabelle's dishes were excellent. To her surprise, this most undemanding of brothers said at once, "Needs salt."

"Oh, not for an invalid," she objected. "You know sick people are not supposed to have spicy food."

"The man is not sick," Sir John said reasonably. "He broke his arm. Start him on some tasty broth, if you like, and if that rests well on his stomach, then Mrs. Patten can tempt him with a kidney pie or some such thing. . . . Shall I deliver the broth for you?"

Too hot, she told him; she would carry it to the inn later herself. "I want to see the stranger. They say he was going toward Wells when he was attacked. If his home is there, perhaps he will be an acquaintance for Laurel when we take her to balls."

"So much talk of balls . . ." he grumbled.

She retrieved the empty cup. "It will be a change for us. Do you good."

"Do *me* good? I don't dance. Haven't for a decade. Or longer."

She protested that he had been "sitting out" with books too long already. "The least you can do is present your own child as if you were proud of her!"

"I am proud of her."

His sister said that he must show it, and banged back into the kitchen, where the soup was on a slow boil of its own.

Meanwhile, Miss Frances and Laurel had gone a dozen steps along the street without talking when the elder lady suddenly said, "It was bad of John to imply things about Dr. Dodd and my boudoir. Everyone knows I am healthy as a horse. John is the one who is always having symptoms and calling for the doctor." It was true.

They reached the doctor's door and knocked. The man-

servant who answered seemed surprised to discover lady
callers with the hour not yet nine o'clock.

"I don't know," he mumbled vaguely.

"Pray see if Dr. Dodd will receive Miss Eland and Miss
Laurel," Aunt Frances commanded.

There was some general confusion in the village about
who—or which—of Sir John's household was "Miss Eland."
The title must rightly go to Mirabelle, as her parents' elder
unmarried daughter, which labeled the younger one forever
"Miss Frances." But Laurel, as *her* father's eldest (and only)
daughter was also properly "Miss Eland." Generally the villagers applied the title to whichever lady they happened to
be addressing.

The servant permitted them to enter the hall. He sped up
the staircase, and they could soon hear rumbles from the
doctor's chamber. Then the doctor himself appeared at the
top of the steps, dressing gown clutched about his shoulders
and hairy legs showing below his nightshirt.

"Good God, Frances Eland, what are you doing here?"
he demanded.

"Chaperoning my niece," she promptly snapped. "Have
you lost all concern for the Sick?"

"I am trying to keep this one in bed, if you don't mind!"

Miss Frances said she did not mind; they would come
up to him.

"No, you will not," he thundered. "Take a seat in the hall.
Laurel can come up if it is about the bloke at the inn."

"Alone?" shrieked Miss Frances.

"Didn't I bring her into the world?"

Laurel made a stab at peacemaking by saying mildly,
"We don't want to send Dr. Dodd into a relapse, Auntie.
Do sit. The doctor must return to bed. I will go up and
stand in the open door, and I promise to scream at the first
sign of attack."

Miss Frances gasped as her niece suited action to words,

and Dr. Dodd wheeled toward his room, roaring with laughter.

"Plain speaking," he approved, crawling under his covers. "Not missish, thank God. What's wrong with the fellow besides a broken wing?"

"A lot of scrapes and bruises—a particularly horrid black-and-blue one on his jaw."

"Broken?"

She shook her head. "Patten doesn't think so. I do not know."

Dr. Dodd shifted on his pillows. "Well, if it is broken there is nothing you or I can do today. *Almighty God, the jaw is up to you. I'll thank you to mend it. Amen.* Now, what about the knee?"

"Do you already know everything? The knee is only wrenched, I hope," she answered.

"Is it true he cannot tell his name? Or won't?"

Laurel admitted that no one seemed to know who the man could be. "It was strange," she said. "When my father and I went into his room this morning he took one look at me and shut his eyes! I don't know if he fainted. We got no response from him, even when we examined his poor knee."

"Oh, that's simple," Dr. Dodd replied. "He was hiding."

"Hiding!"

"My dear, just think how embarrassing for the fellow. A fine creature now in mortifying condition. Cannot disguise himself. Cannot disappear. So-o-o he closes his eyes and *you* disappear. When he is feeling more the thing he will be eager to see a pretty damsel." He beamed at her.

Laurel found herself smiling. She pushed back a curl and said that she thought he was gulling her even when he sounded most reasonable. "Tell me what I must do next."

He answered promptly: "Tie him in the bed, if necessary. He must stay off that leg until I see him in a day or two.

Maybe tomorrow, if I don't have any more visitors. *Do you hear me, Frances? Stay out of bachelors' houses."*

Miss Frances must have heard, for she cried, "Tyrant!" and was wearing a pixieish expression when Laurel descended.

The doctor would have the last word: "Tell that man of mine that if he admits any more females, I will personally decapitate him!"

Miss Frances and Laurel did not look at each other as they continued toward the inn.

Mrs. Patten met them at the door, saying, "Mr. Hanger has sent a valet to take charge of the patient. The boys are willing, but there's a lot they don't know, and Patten and I have our own duties to keep us hopping from morn to night, so we're right glad to have Blunk."

"Oh, Blunk," acknowledged Miss Frances, recognizing the name of her cook's brother. "Tell Mrs. Patten what the doctor said, Laurel."

Obediently, the girl explained that Dr. Dodd was worried about the bad knee and ordered the patient to be kept to his bed until the doctor was out of *his* and could see to matters himself.

"Will Blunk be able to keep him quiet?" she asked anxiously.

"Aye," said Mrs. Patten. "He's not as big as Patten, though I daresay he's a match for an invalid. Will ye come up now?"

They found the patient awake. He had been shaved, combed, and propped up, so it was evident that Blunk had matters in hand.

Laurel introduced her aunt, who asked if he was feeling more the thing.

"A bit," replied the patient. He did not close his eyes this time, although he did avoid meeting the eyes of either lady. Two words in a decent accent were hardly enough to determine the fellow's place in society; nor were there clothes to lend a clue. However, Blunk said, "The gentleman is somewhat easier after the taste of laudanum that Mrs. Patten offered."

If Blunk recognized the man as a gentleman, the chances were that he was one, Laurel thought, for well-trained servants had a sense about things like that. She looked to Aunt Frances, who gave a very slight nod, obviously thinking the same thing.

"I suppose small doses of laudanum will be all right," she allowed. "Dr. Dodd is concerned about that knee and wants the gentleman to remain immobile until he sees him in a day or two." To the patient she said, "Can you tell us who you are?"

"No, I cannot," he replied. The eyes closed for a moment, then reopened as he piteously addressed Miss Frances: "So confusing . . ."

"Poor gentleman!" she commiserated. "I expect all will turn out well if you rest quietly."

Laurel smiled to see her aunt won over so easily by a handsome man in distress. "I charge you, Blunk, to keep him still as a stone."

"Aye, miss. Mrs. Patten is having a cot found for me. I won't leave the gentleman unattended, you can be sure." With that, he retired to a rear corner, where his dark green livery merged with the shadows.

While both ladies turned their attention to the servant, the patient had studied them without their being aware. What he thought about them, as about other matters in his head, his facial expression did not reveal.

"My sister will be bringing some broth later, Blunk," Miss Frances said as she and Laurel departed.

Thus warned, the invalid was conveniently "asleep" when a third lady invaded his room. Miss Mirabelle assured Blunk that her offering was revitalizing and tiptoed away, leaving the patient to waken two minutes later to enjoy the soup.

Three

The Onslow ladies, next door to Sir John, were always early in their bow window. They had spied unusual traffic to and from his domicile, and when they saw Miss Eland travel down the street with something wrapped in a heavy cloth and return without it, this was too much to be borne. Miss Onslow, being the more agile (though elder), promptly put on a cloak and darted to the Eland home.

By this time the Elands were gathered around their drawing room fire. They received their neighbor kindly, assuring themselves that she was not chilled for having come seventy feet and asking if she would care for tea to warm her. She declined, throwing off her cloak and revealing a black dress strangely hung with fringe.

What she wanted was information.

"Oh, it is the most shocking thing," Miss Frances told her eagerly. "A stranger is lying abed at the inn. He was set upon on the road to Wells and most horribly beaten—black and blue, don't you know?"

As Miss Onslow never traveled to Wells, danger on the route did not alarm her. "But how did he reach the inn?" she asked reasonably. "Can he not say who he is?"

"That is the most distressing part," Miss Frances answered with a concerned knitting of her straight brows, which turned them at right angles above her nose. "He cannot remember a *thing*."

The visitor gave an appreciative little gasp, and Laurel,

watching in amusement, was not surprised when Miss Mirabelle added embellishments: "Such a handsome young man.
So sad. A terrible discoloration of the jaw."

"A broken arm!" inserted Frances.

"Yes, and a damaged *knee.*"

Nothing to equal this had ruffled the waters of Bayley
Dell for a long time.

"My sister will be so concerned," the visitor assured
them. "May we hope that he will recover?"

"Oh, yes," Frances replied quickly, before her sister
could do so. "He is young. His *body* will mend. About his
mind we cannot be sure."

There was a moment of respectful silence. Then Mirabelle said confidently, "If he does not remember who he
is, John will locate his family."

"I *will?*" ejaculated Sir John, surprised to find himself
the focus of all eyes.

"Well, of course, sir," said Miss Onslow, ever the syco-
phant. "You are chief gentleman of the village."

Sir John sank between his shoulders, and the conversation would have languished had not Mirabelle announced
proudly, "I have made a rich broth to speed the poor gentleman's cure."

Miss Onslow vowed that nothing could be as strength-
ening as that. "I know your broth, dear Miss Mirabelle—is
it beef this time? Oh, that will nourish him! It has been a
long time since you sent some to Sister and me, but I remember we enjoyed it."

"Then you must have some today," said Mirabelle
promptly. "There is some remaining."

"How kind! If you can spare it—I will accept it for Sister, as she is feeling a mite low today."

"There is enough for you, too," said Mirabelle, rising to
her feet with a smile.

"That much? . . . But you will want it for your own family."

Miss Frances brought an end to the wavering by saying, "John will not tolerate broth unless he is ailing, and you can see for yourself that he is in prime twig. We are all most healthy now that the winter is ending. You will please Mirabelle by accepting the soup."

"That is true!" said Miss Mirabelle, heading for the door. "You will be doing me a favor. We are all so interested in your sister's well-being. I will fetch the broth right now, as I know you do not want to be absent long from home. Your sister must wonder what news you have to bring."

"May I go for you, Aunt?" asked Laurel. "Or carry the jar for you, Miss Onslow?"

Both ladies replied, "Thank you, no."

Soon the visitor was sent happily on her way, having been bowed out by Fane as if she were the titled lady she would like to be.

"Miss Onslow buys her groceries with compliments," observed Miss Frances tartly.

"Yes," agreed her sister. "It was little enough for us to give. I sometimes think they would rather starve than ask for help."

"You are right," said Miss Frances quickly, "and gentler than I."

Sir John cleared his throat and said that Mr. Hanger sent down supplies from time to time.

Surprised, Frances averred, "Now that is real Charity!"

After nuncheon Sir John retreated to his chamber for a long nap, having missed his morning one due to interesting events. He was not sure he would sleep now, he warned his sisters, as excitement still had his pulse jumping.

The Eland ladies settled around the hearth again with assorted darning duties. Talk was preferable, however. There were all the details of Laurel's come-out at a Wells ball to be considered. Before long they went upstairs to examine each wardrobe.

They began in Mirabelle's room, eldest first, on the theory that they might not only choose her outfit, but also see what was available to hand down to her niece. Mirabelle's newest—that is, least old—evening gown appeared in good condition when taken from a protective muslin bag. It was a rich shade of purple, with lines simple enough to fall into any style.

"Beautiful," declared Laurel, who had never seen her aunt dressed thus grandly.

"Twelve years old," said Mirabelle with a wry smile.

"But elegant. No one will guess its age if you remove that lawn draped into the neckline," Laurel said daringly.

"So *low*," cried the aunts with one voice.

And why not? Mirabelle had the dignity to carry it off, Laurel told them. With Grandmama's pearls she would look distinguished. And Frances nodded in approval, saying, "We have been on the shelf for a long time, but after all you are only forty-four, dearest Mirabelle, and have a degree of countenance and a good name."

"Who in Wells has heard the name of Eland?" bleated Miss Mirabelle.

"Your old school friend, Mrs. Walden, for one. You must write to her at once. If no one knows our name, she will present us, will she not? And I daresay Sir John Eland is not unheard of there."

Laurel laughed and said, "Auntie Frances, I salute you! Now we will go to your room and rummage in *your* wardrobe."

Most of Frances's dresses, like her sister's, were years old, yet well kept. She was younger by three years, which meant she was only forty-one. Though she was a bit more curvaceous than she should be, and though her blond hair had darkened in recent years, she would be lovely with a bright frock to complement her vivacious manner. Mesmerized by her niece's sudden determination, she agreed to try on an apricot gown that fit without straining at the seams.

"The color is perfect," said Laurel.

The aunts were unable to contradict her; Frances looked glowing.

"But the sleeves are wrong," Laurel decided. "I will remake them for you. Long ones are so—so chaste. Better little ones just covering the shoulders."

Miss Frances protested that it sounded shocking—leaving so much skin bare.

"You must show the pretty dimples at your elbows," her niece declared, and so surprised were the older ladies by her assertiveness that they behaved like ewe lambs.

The aunts posed before Frances's mirror, liking what they saw, remembering their youth—dancing—houseguests—tea parties—strolls through shrubbery at Bayley Manor. It was so long ago. . . .

"Now you must let me do something about your hair, Aunt Frances," Laurel said. "I am no expert, but if you are to wear Grandmama's diamond earrings, which you showed me years ago, then your ears must be exposed." She reached for a brush and started drawing back Miss Frances's luxuriant hair and swirling it into a soft knot at the nape of her neck.

Secretly, Laurel resolved to apply a little rouge to the aunts' cheeks . . . if she could get some. Perhaps Mrs. Walden would help with that.

Her own situation Laurel knew to be pitiful. She had never owned a ball gown. In Bayley Dell? Where would she have worn it? She had hoped that one of her aunts' frocks might be alterable for her to wear—she was not too proud to accept used garments if the fabric was good—but their wardrobes had revealed nothing suitable for her.

Aloud she said, "Aunt Mirabelle's hair is perfect."

"It *is?*" squawked Mirabelle in astonishment. For convenience she wore it short, as it seemed to have a will of its own. Although threads of gray were showing amid the brown, it curled naturally.

"Just a few snips and it will be a modish *à la Titus,*"

Laurel told them. "I forbid both of you to wear turbans."
By this time the ladies were melting like butter in the sun.
"Now, what can be done about me?" she asked, throwing
out her hands in frustration.

The aunts looked at each other and came down to earth.

"Buy cloth," said Miss Frances.

"Stitch it up," said Miss Mirabelle.

"Green, I think."

"Yes, spring green."

"Shop at Nord Cross."

"Take Patten's carriage."

Laurel sank down on her aunt's bed. "But the money!"
she said anxiously.

"Eat *broth* for a week," suggested Miss Mirabelle happily.

They began to laugh and laugh until tears flowed.

"It has been so long since you taught me to dance," Laurel
reminded presently. "I may have forgotten my steps."

The next thing, Miss Frances had seized her hand, and
while Miss Mirabelle sang *tra*-la-la-*tra*-la-la, they swooped
mirthfully up and down the carpet.

A tap at the door went unnoticed. The door opened, and
Sir John exclaimed, "Good God! What on earth is going
on?"

"Come to the ball, Papa," urged his prettily flushed
daughter, who continued to dance with her aunt, though the
"music" had ceased. "Dance with Aunt Mirabelle."

"You are mad!" said Sir John, but his eyes were twinkling. "Practicing for your ball?"

Mirabelle said preemptively, "John, you must engage
Patten's carriage to take us to Nord Cross at once. I know
it is a week early for my marketing, but we need fabric for
your daughter. While we are there I will buy what foodstuffs
we will want for the remainder of the month, so there need
not be an extra trip."

Looking slightly overwhelmed, Sir John said, "I see. That

is, I don't exactly see, but as I can generally count on you to be reasonable, I will agree. Do you wish to go at once? Tomorrow?"

Tomorrow would be fine, they told him.

"Well, then," he said, "I will toddle down to the inn and speak to Patten. Do you wish to visit your patient, Laurel?"

In spite of her desire for Laurel to come to the attention of suitable gentlemen, Miss Frances vetoed that idea immediately, saying in an authoritative voice, "Twice in one day is enough."

When Sir John had put on a comfortable old jacket, found his hat, and departed, the ladies went down to the drawing room, where they had more space to practice and where Mirabelle could play the piano for the dancers.

Fane came in to ask if they wanted the rug rolled back, but as that would mean his huffing and puffing and creaking to bend, they said, "No, thank you, Fane, but have some tea ready in half an hour."

While the Eland ladies cavorted with unusual abandon, Sir John made his way to the inn, where he found Patten conversing in the stable yard with Mr. Hanger, who was mounted on a fine black horse.

"Ho!" said Mr. Hanger jovially. "Come to check on Miss Laurel's patient, have you?" His mount shifted its feet, but he steadied it with a firm hand.

"Well, I will do that while I am here," replied the baronet, "but what I came for was to tell Patten that my ladies have taken a fancy to shop in Nord Cross tomorrow and would like his carriage then instead of next week."

Patten shook his brindled head regretfully. "Sorry, sir. Tell the ladies I'm sorry. Looks to be a crack in a rear wheel, and the wheelwright's coming to see to it—but not until Thursday. Should be done in time for Miss Eland's regular shopping next week."

"Dear me!" exclaimed Sir John. "I fear I will be most

unpopular if I go home with news like that. There is something about a ball gown for my daughter. . . ."

"Nothing more important than that!" laughed Mr. Hanger. "Wouldn't want the ladies disappointed! They are welcome to my chaise. What time?"

Knowing his sisters' reservations about Mr. Hanger, and feeling sure they would not want to be indebted to him, but appreciating the kindness of the offer, Sir John demurred awkwardly, "So generous . . . but they would not wish to impose . . . tire your horses."

"Rot!" said Mr. Hanger genially. "Overeating hay. Need a run. Besides, they're *your* horses."

But this made Sir John indignant. "They are not mine! I sold them to you."

"Well, well," returned Mr. Hanger placatingly, "so you did. But they are getting lazy, and I'd thank you to make use of them. Groom, too. He's almost asleep on his feet for lack of something to do. I shall send it at nine." He glanced at the innkeeper. "Patten won't feel cheated of a fare. Take Miss Eland for groceries next week, if she wants."

It being impossible to decline without giving offense, Sir John thanked his tenant, and Mr. Hanger cantered away. Faced with annoying his sisters instead, Sir John delayed his return home by entering the inn and ascending to visit Laurel's patient.

He tapped gently, so as not to disturb a sleeper, but was promptly admitted by Blunk, who said, "Come in, Sir John. The gentleman is feeling brighter."

The patient did not look *that,* although having been enlightened as to Sir John's title without offering his own name, he managed to be tolerably civil, thanking the baronet for his kindness and concern and sending thanks to the young lady.

"I will tell her," said Sir John easily. "Won't be down tomorrow, I daresay, as her aunts are taking her to buy a ball gown for the assembly next week."

"Oh," said the patient more alertly. "Do they have balls in this small place?"

Sir John corrected, "No, no. Wells. Her aunts are taking her to Wells so she will meet—that is, have a little gaiety." He frowned cogitatively. "Do you remember Bayley Dell?"

"I remember having supper at a small inn which was this one, they tell me. Is Bayley Dell its name?"

"Bayley Dell is the village," said Sir John. "The inn is called The Nesting Dove. You rode off toward Wells. Can you remember if that was your destination?"

"N-no," answered the patient slowly. "I cannot be sure. Perhaps it was another place. Did I have a horse?"

"Patten says you did."

"All is so foggy."

"Well, well," replied Sir John reassuringly, "it will come, I'm sure. Dr. Dodd will be down before long."

Blunk stepped forward to say that the doctor had sent word he would come around in the morning.

"There you are. Just the one you need, although—" Sir John smiled "—not as pretty as my daughter."

The stranger grinned and winced. His jaw was royal purple now, and obviously giving him discomfort. "But no leeches!" he warned.

"I expect you are spotted all over like a leopard," Sir John said, and Blunk nodded, saying, "That 'e is, sir."

"But tamer," the patient declared with a grimace. "What color dress?"

"Dress?"

"Ball gown."

"Ah! I wouldn't wager. Something my sisters think will dazzle the beaux and make the other ladies green as grass. You must be feeling better if you are wondering about female finery. What about your own?"

The man in the bed made a rueful face. "Blunk showed me my coat. I cannot leave here in that!"

"Well, let us not worry about that now. Time enough when you know where to go."

Blunk said he had some hopes for the breeches. "I will work on them when the gentleman is feeling better and doesn't need me standing by every minute. The boots are scuffed but will polish up tolerably."

The patient rolled his eyes at the idea of scuffed boots being acceptable, which marked him as—not a popinjay exactly—as a meticulous gentleman.

Sir John eyed the long frame beneath the bedspread. "Nothing of mine will fit you. Well, well, it will be time to think of clothes when you are feeling better. It does not look as though you will be dancing any time soon. By then you may have remembered who you are. Already I can tell your mind is clearer."

The patient winced again and said his head still ached.

"Most understandable," Sir John assured him.

Blunk reminded him that a taste of Mrs. Patten's laudanum from time to time would help.

"I don't wish to be drugged," the patient asserted with some vigor.

"Miss Eland approved small doses," Blunk said, thereby revealing the family name, which, however, was not one the stranger recognized.

The baronet remarked that it sounded reasonable. "Say the word if we can aid you . . . or notify anyone." He descended to find the lower floor deserted except for two ancient laborers nodding before the taproom fire. Just as he was about to step from the building, Patten appeared from the kitchen, and Sir John thought to ask if he could describe the stranger's horse.

"Not well, sir," said Patten with a shake of his head that made his jowls tremble. "We was busy and I hardly noticed. It was black or bay. I remember the gentleman, seeing as I served 'im. Mayhap my groom could tell you more."

Sir John thanked him and went out a side door to the

stable yard, where the groom (good with horses but not very bright) said the same— black or bay—with no distinguishing marks.

He walked homeward slowly.

At the house Sir John found his three ladies in the drawing room where they were sorting laces and ribbons happily.

Miss Mirabelle looked up and asked eagerly, "Did you book Patten's chaise? What time?"

"Nine o'clock," he replied, answering the second question first and delaying the other for the space of two words. "The inn's chaise is not available due to a bad wheel, but Mr. Hanger has offered his carriage to you. It will take you up at nine."

For a moment there was a silence like a pall.

"Sir John!" began Miss Frances indignantly. "Surely you know we don't wish to be beholden!"

Laurel smiled faintly as her father replied, "I thought your chief interest was in turning out your niece in prime style."

"Yes, but—"

"But you cannot travel to Nord Cross on three wheels."

The aunts exchanged dubious looks, and Miss Mirabelle said what mattered was Laurel's ball gown, not *their* mortification.

"Besides," added Sir John encouragingly, "you will be riding behind the horses that once were mine."

It was not the best argument, so Laurel inserted quickly, "Mr. Hanger is very kind to provide for us. Surely we must not snub kindness!"

While Miss Frances hesitated, her sister reminded them what the vicar taught: not only must one do good but also permit others to do the same.

Sir John looked approving, and Laurel laughed in relief and said she was grateful to be the recipient of so much help from so many people. They all remembered that the vicar was the Soul of Kindness himself and therefore an expert in doing good.

"Mr. Appleton is an example to all," Sir John pointed out, to which Mirabelle nodded her agreement. Frances looked not ill-pleased, and even went so far as to say that the horses would give her some comfort as she recalled their smooth gait. How she could remember this after so many years no one asked.

At dinner that night the ladies resumed their discussion of ball gowns while their brother ate peacefully.

"You would like a green gown, would you not, Laurel?" queried Miss Frances.

"Yes. You know it is my favorite color," the girl replied.

"And very becoming to you," agreed Miss Mirabelle. "Not everyone can wear green."

"Strictly speaking," admitted Miss Frances, "she probably should be wearing white like other debutantes."

"Well, you like the idea of green as much as I," Miss Mirabelle reminded. "After all, Laurel is twenty. Who is to know in Wells that she hasn't had a London season?"

"I *feel* extremely green," Laurel confessed.

"No, no," objected her father, patting his mustache. "Very poised young lady. Practicing physician, you know."

"We won't repeat *that*," cried the aunts. "It could ruin everything!"

Four

Although Sir John slept innocently through the night, his three ladies rested less well, Miss Mirabelle fretting over how much they dared spend of her brother's inelastic funds, and Miss Frances regretting the borrowed coach.

Cinderella wavered between delight in a ball gown and worry about her patient. Would Dr. Dodd be able to reach the bedside? Was she deserting a sacred trust? Would the patient suddenly recover while she was away and leave Bayley Dell without a civil "good day," never to be seen again? Despite what the doctor had said about the patient's enjoying a pretty face, his reception of her had been more than cool; downright uninterested. Really, she knew very little about beaux and must prepare herself for all sorts at the ball at Wells. Perhaps no one would ask her to dance! The ball gown would be wasted and the aunties crushed.

On the dot of nine Mr. Hanger's elegant chaise arrived at the door, escorted by Mr. Hanger himself, sitting easily on the powerful black horse that he favored. Sir John was there to hand his ladies into the carriage.

They heard Mr. Hanger say cheerfully to him, "Never fear! I shall not let them buy you into Newgate."

The ladies exchanged rueful glances; it was obvious that Mr. Hanger intended to accompany them!

Off rolled the carriage without a jerk, and they had left Bayley Dell behind before Miss Frances ventured to suggest, "Surely he will not follow us into the draper's and modiste's."

"Oh, no!" breathed Miss Mirabelle.

"How could we discuss prices?"

"We could not."

"Most embarrassing."

Laurel endeavored to convince them that they were worrying without cause. "There is a vacant seat in this chaise. He might have ridden with us, but he brought a horse for himself. Does that look encroaching?"

The aunts had to admit it did not.

"Besides," continued the girl, "he has been so considerate of us—of the stranger—and the Onslow ladies. I cannot think he would be thrusting himself upon us."

"That is true," allowed Miss Mirabelle. "The vicar says Mr. Hanger has helped the church in ways that no one knows." She began to look more cheerful. "Perhaps he has come along for our safety—remembering the stranger's sad experience on the Wells road."

Miss Frances protested their road was more heavily traveled and in full sunlight. There had never been brigands on this stretch. "He may have business of his own in Nord Cross and did not wish to crowd us. I hope that is it."

Laurel said soothingly, "Papa would have come with us if he thought there was any danger. He seemed to think we would need room for our purchases."

It was a happy choice of words, for the ladies forgot their worries and began to discuss petticoats and plumes. Mr. Hanger had dropped back some distance to avoid their dust, and they ceased to speculate about him.

Most traffic was flowing in their direction, though more swiftly, as their groom had instructions to maintain an even trot that would keep them comfortable—no swaying to make anyone the least bit queasy. Speeders passed, yet in a little over an hour they were entering the market town and pulling into the yard of Drake's Inn.

Mr. Hanger swung from his saddle and handed over his mount without a backward look, to spring to the carriage door and address the Elands with a beaming face, hat in hand, and sweat marking his head where the hat had sat snugly. "Will this location meet with your approval, ladies? Say the word and I'll deliver you anywhere else that pleases you."

The aunts looked out at the oak-shaded town green around which the nicest shops were assembled. A street, churned by traffic, circled it, and from each corner, like spokes, ran roads to each direction, north, east, south, west. They had come in from the south, and across the green could be seen the wide entrance to the agricultural market, with a stone cross at its center.

As it was possible they would stick their noses into all the shops here, Miss Mirabelle said, "This is excellent."

One by one they debarked, supported by Mr. Hanger's firm hand and arm.

"Let me see," he said, examining a pocket watch. "Just ten past ten. You ladies will find more shops than you can visit in a morning. Suppose you return here at noon. I will order a nuncheon to refresh you. Have you dined here recently? No? The food is very good. If you have not found all you require for Miss Laurel to dazzle Wells, then you can browse again this afternoon."

So he was not to dog their footsteps! But they could think of no polite way to refuse his invitation. Feeling embarrassed by her aunts' hesitation, Laurel said warmly, "How kind of you to devise so pleasant a plan. We will come at twelve. Thank you so much."

Mr. Hanger bowed and disappeared into the inn, leaving the ladies to begin their circuit of the green.

For so small and provincial a town, Nord Cross held a tolerably good collection of shops. Some, of course, would not attract ladies—a tobacconist, two barbers, a wine dealer, and a "news" shop, although they did stop before the window of the last to examine the latest caricatures from London.

None were persons known to them. Miss Mirabelle spoke for the three when she said, "How viciously these attack! I am glad we are not persons to attract attention of this sort."

Scattered among the stores were several ancient and charming private houses; quite a noisy and *un*private place to live! "The Misses Onslow would enjoy this situation," observed Miss Frances.

The most pleasing features of Nord Cross were two—not just one!—drapers' shops. With heightened anticipation, they entered the first, where they were greeted by a courteous, gray-haired clerk. Mirabelle asked for bolts of green.

"For the young lady," Miss Frances explained.

Recognizing the elder ladies and regarding Laurel with interest, the clerk said, "Yes, green would be perfect with Miss Eland's coloring. Will you be seated, ladies? We have some splendid bolts that are just being unpacked. Let me see what I can find."

Pleased to be remembered, the shoppers drew chairs to the counter, while the clerk hurried to a rear portion of the premises. There was a whole wall of shelves to tantalize them—velvets, silks, lawns, muslins, and lace. Laurel knew her gown was sure to be muslin, yet her eyes feasted on the variety of fabrics and the riot of colors.

Meanwhile the woman had sought out her employer and announced the arrival of the three Misses Eland.

"Ah!" said Mr. Finkleshaff. "They want green for the girl? Bring that and that . . . oh, yes and *that*. They do not come here often, but when they buy they pay promptly. I will see them myself."

He led the way into the front room and greeted the ladies effusively. "My dear Miss Eland, I am glad to see you. And Miss Frances, how well you look. And this must be Sir John's daughter—her mother came from here, you know, and I can see the resemblance clearly. Miss Laurel, is it?"

The ladies could not resist such a warm welcome. To be treated with an excess of courtesy, in spite of their meager purchasing power, was wonderfully flattering; their confidence in the round, white-haired cherub of a draper increased immensely. And it was not misplaced. When they turned their eyes to the green selections the assistant was spreading before them, they breathed in concert: "Oh!"

All were lovely, but one was perfect. Not Pomona green or *Pistache*. A sheer muslin such as they had never seen, like sunlight on a shallow sea at a coral reef. Laurel reached out to touch it delightedly.

"Yes, yes," approved Mr. Finkleshaff. "Most unusual." He motioned for the woman to take away the other bolts, and he, himself, unfolded a length to drape across Laurel's bosom and shoulder like a shawl. There were no other customers in the shop at that time. He was free to devote himself to these impecunious ladies, to estimate what price he might ask that would bring him profit and that they could afford.

"What is it called?" asked Miss Frances.

"Southern Sea," he invented immediately. "Very new. You will not meet yourself, Miss Laurel. As a matter of fact, not many ladies could wear such a color so well."

It was true that Laurel's amber eyes were like sunlight on the sea. Her creamy complexion was exactly right.

Miss Frances murmured hesitantly, "I had thought of ivory for an underdress."

"Just the thing," agreed the merchant, seeing the sale almost made. "Perhaps a flounce on the dress, lined with ivory, to give the appearance of surf when she dances."

It sounded original and delightful.

The clerk handed Laurel a mirror, then turned without instruction to lift down two bolts of cream for the ladies' consideration.

There was no question of looking farther for Laurel's gown. The Elands were in complete accord, and they trusted the draper to keep them from making a mistake. There was a search for suitable thread, new needles, tiny buttons, and several yards of ribbon. Unfortunately, there was no matching Southern Sea ribbon, so they bought ivory just in case ribbon was needed. Mr. Finkleshaff promised to have their treasures delivered to Drake's Inn within the hour. Mercifully, his price did not exceed their budget.

He named and recommended two seamstresses of the town, and Miss Frances repeated them as though committing them to memory. They had no inclination to confess to the merchant that they would make Laurel's gown themselves, as he might jump to the mortifying conclusion that they were purse-pinched.

When Miss Mirabelle rose to depart her sister and niece realized they must buy no more. They, too, stood.

A chorus of cordial "Good days" sped them on their way.

"I wish we had bought fabric for you, aunties," Laurel said regretfully when they had stepped out to the walkway.

Aunt Mirabelle replied that *they* did not matter, and Aunt Frances added, "We will enjoy your success, dearest."

So touched was Laurel that she gave no thought to the spendthrift uncle who had brought them to such a pass.

As they walked, Aunt Frances suggested that the other draper's shop might by some lucky chance have green ribbon to match their cloth, but Aunt Mirabelle advised not risking the charms of other fabric when by now Mr. Finkleshaff might have already cut their purchase. So they strolled along, buying headache powders from a chemist and looking into windows, until a clock at a jeweler's shop told them it lacked five minutes of noon. Mr. Hanger would be waiting! Lifting their skirts to escape the dust, they crossed the roadway to the village green, where smudge-faced children were playing, and from there to the opposite road, on which Drake's Inn stood.

Mr. Hanger was waiting at the door. He held it open with no sign of impatience while they stamped their feet free of dirt.

"Good day, Mr. Appleton," they heard him say cordially.

"I would expect to find you in Bayley Dell or Hammish or Mendle, not here."

A middle-aged gentleman in clerical garb had come up behind them and was alive with pleasure. "Ladies, Hanger," he said. "How delightful to meet you." It was their own dear vicar, whom they shared with the villages of Hammish and Mendle. His expression, as always, was sweet and his eyes warm brown. The hair on his head had receded a bit above the temples without destroying the good looks of a benign lion. "I had to visit the aged parent of one of my Mendle parishioners . . . need a bite to eat before returning home."

The ladies would have liked to ask the vicar to join them, but as they were obliged to be guests of Mr. Hanger, they could not feel free to do so. Happily, in his genial fashion, Mr. Hanger immediately said of course Mr. Appleton must be one of their party.

"I have engaged a private room. Come this way."

How well things had worked out, thought Laurel. Mr. Hanger could be as generous as he pleased, the aunts would not be oppressed by the lone company of a man they disdained, and Mr. Appleton would have a bounteous free meal.

They found a round table awaiting them, to which another chair was added. With aplomb, Mr. Hanger seated the elder Miss Eland at his right, the vicar to her right, Miss Frances next, and Laurel between Miss Frances and himself. This excellent plan placed Frances Eland where she could be most comfortable (farthest from himself) and adjacent to the vicar. That it put Laurel beside her host may or may not have been his particular design.

Mirabelle and Mr. Appleton were soon deep into a discussion about the pruning and weeding needed in the churchyard at Bayley Dell, and Laurel fell into conversation with Mr. Hanger about the identity of the stranger at The Nesting Dove. This left Frances Eland to her own thoughts. The light from a window behind her left her face somewhat shadowed, while illuminating her host. She saw nothing of his appearance or manners to criticize. Nor could she feel neglected. A plate of golden-brown roasted chicken was placed before her, and assorted root vegetables (it was early for fresh ones) offered by a servant. Mr. Hanger passed gooseberry preserves for her bread and Mr. Appleton from time to time included her in his talk with her sister.

"I suspect that your patient is malingering," Mr. Hanger said quietly to Laurel.

Startled, she turned toward him wide-eyed. "Surely not that! I have seen his scars myself."

"I meant his convenient loss of memory," he explained. "His eyes were bright enough when I stopped in to see him this morning."

"Well, they are bright *blue,* of course," she admitted, "and if the room was well-lighted, they might seem to . . . sparkle."

Mr. Hanger said he was not talking of color and sparkle. "There was a sort of awareness. He was careful to think before he spoke."

As her host passed a basket of warm, crusty bread when he made this observation, Laurel accepted a piece without thinking and then discovered a half-eaten chunk on her plate. She gestured helplessly, and Mr. Hanger extended the basket again for her to return it. She hoped the aunts did not notice.

"Why would he pretend suffering?" she demanded.

Mr. Hanger shrugged his broad shoulders. "Oh—could be one of a dozen reasons. Perhaps he wishes to promote free lodging and food."

"He paid for his dinner the evening of the attack!"

"True."

"His clothes are good."

Mr. Hanger nodded. "Yes, Blunk has told me so. Do you not think it odd that he traveled without changes?"

Laurel said, "Y-es. Could he be between homes?"

"Aye."

"After all," she persisted, "he had a fine horse."

"How do you know it was fine?" her host asked reasonably.

Laurel looked chagrined. "I don't, of course."

"All we *know* is that he *had* a horse and a purse—full or empty," Mr. Hanger pointed out. "I will keep my eye on him. If he turns out to be destitute, what then?"

"Then," said Laurel firmly with a mocking smile, "you will find him work in your factory—or storehouse—or whatever your business is!"

Mr. Hanger laughed heartily and declared it would behoove him to see the fellow left Bayley Dell as soon as possible.

The sounds of merriment caused Mr. Appleton and the aunts to glance their way with curiosity, whereupon Mr. Hanger had the inspiration to urge the bread basket on Miss Mirabelle, which distracted all of them.

Soon the vicar and Miss Mirabelle resumed their conversation, this time about curtains in the cottage reserved for Mr. Appleton's use at Bayley Dell. This was a stone building behind the church, only two rooms (parlor-kitchen and bedchamber), yet dry and cozy.

The church custodian, who was called the "verger," to make up by title what was lacking in pay, had his sleeping quarters in the attic, and tended house as well as sanctuary.

Mr. Appleton scarcely noticed the splitting curtains of his two-day dwelling. Only when Miss Eland asked if anything needed to be mended did he remember them.

Nothing could have made Miss Eland happier. The women of the village would be *delighted* to stitch new curtains. "Just simple muslin ones. We all want you to be comfortable," she said earnestly.

The vicar's face radiated gratitude, and he said how kind she was.

Miss Frances spoke little, which was unlike her, but she ate with apparent appetite and did not seem disgruntled. Laurel noticed that she watched Mr. Hanger unobtrusively.

Besides being well dressed, he talked and ate with excellent manners. His flaming hair had been neatly combed and no longer showed the ring of perspiration. It was strange to Laurel that her amiable aunts should scorn such a gentlemanly person even if his origin was obscure. Her papa liked him. Of course, Papa was almost as unworldly as Mr. Appleton; never puffed up by his title, always willing to think well of anyone who respected books.

Papa had told her that Mr. Hanger was no scholar. He also had told her with obvious approval that Mr. Hanger was keeping the library in good order—had paid with his own money for a chap from London to come and revise its catalog and another to make repairs! So the fold of his cravat and the fit of his breeches did not suit Mirabelle and Frances? At least he respected books.

Laurel set down her fork. The aunts had already done so.

Mr. Hanger cast an eye around the table. "I see we are ready for a sweet now." He rang for a servant and ordered the dessert brought in.

The older ladies said, "Not a sweet, too!" and "How can we ever . . ." The vicar, who had been doing most of the talking with Miss Mirabelle, hurried to polish off his plate.

"You will not spurn the trifle that I have had made for you," Mr. Hanger told them firmly.

"Oh, I must not—" began Frances, but he overruled her.

"To be sure you must. I know ladies fancy a figure like a blade of grass, but gentlemen, let me tell you, find a few curves more—er—enticing. You do not want to be scrawny, do you?"

Though Frances was shocked speechless, she knew she didn't wish to be *that*. When the trifle, made with whipped cream and the landlady's own strawberry preserves, was passed she accepted a portion and enjoyed it. Coffee followed.

When the unprepossessing but faithful clock on the mantel registered almost two, Mr. Appleton reminded himself aloud that he must be on his way, thanked Mr. Hanger, bid the ladies farewell, and called for his horse. Like the doctor, he had both saddlehorse and gig but preferred the horse, and was no mean rider.

The draper's parcel had been delivered. By this time clouds were interfering with the sunshine.

"Perhaps it will rain. Should we leave now?" asked Miss Mirabelle.

Mr. Hanger said, "Just as you please. Horses do not mind rain, and the groom has a heavy cloak. Maybe you would like to shop another hour, say?"

"But if you wait for us, you may be drenched," said Miss Frances, surprising herself.

"I will await you here by the hearth with a newspaper— and perhaps a nap. Must see you safely on your way," he said. "If the rain is too much for me, I will spend the night here. My groom can be relied upon to take you home. There are no fords or steep hills."

It was seldom that they had such a treat. The Everything Shop in Bayley Dell was nothing to compare with the ones of Nord Cross, and the sky was not even black. So the Eland ladies succumbed to temptation, although they had no more shillings to spend. In the window of a modiste that Mr. Finkleshaff had mentioned they saw a rainbow of plumes and lovely white gloves but resolutely decided Laurel would wear her Aunt Frances's best gloves, and *she* would wear Aunt Mirabelle's second-best.

The allotted hour had not elapsed when they returned to the inn. Mr. Hanger saw them safely bestowed in his carriage. The last to enter, Frances Eland astounded her relatives by saying graciously, "It was a delightful day. Thank you so much. You must come to call sometime soon."

Mr. Hanger, with the poise of a prince, said that he would be charmed. He fastened the door, and they departed.

No more than a few sprinkles were encountered by horses, groom, or Sir John's admirable tenant.

Five

The house seemed singularly empty when Sir John Eland reentered it after the ladies drove away. There were no particular calls upon his time, except for Frances's previous command to inspect the footbridge over the ravine behind the church, and he had decided to ignore that until the path that way was drier.

Collecting Mirabelle's letter to Mrs. Walden, he clapped on his head the disreputable cap that his sisters always decried when they saw it. March was treating them kindly this year, with milder weather than usual. As he described a scalloped track down the village street, the sun smiled upon him—and the cap. First stop, Dr. Dodd's house, where he learned the doctor had already gone to the inn. Next stop, the Everything Shop, where he left the letter to be picked up by the post. Then a last scallop to The Nesting Dove, where he found Dr. Dodd, with kindest intentions, ferociously laying down the law to Laurel's patient.

"But I am sick of lying here," the man in the bed was complaining as Blunk admitted Sir John.

"You'll be sicker if you don't," replied the doctor, giving Sir John a nod. "Daresay you'd rather have Laurel quacking you than me, but if you think females like white faces and glassy eyes, you're dead wrong. They may go all pudding-soft over a suffering male, but they haven't an ounce of interest in *specters*."

"How about a book?" suggested Sir John mildly.

The patient made a wry face. "Fine . . . except how am I to hold a book and turn pages with only one hand? And what book would be suitable in this damnable situation?"

"Don't discount Sir John's collection," retorted the doctor. *"He's* well-read. I suppose you rollicked your way through Oxford or Cambridge and consider yourself educated. Sir John knows what education really is!"

Obviously the young stranger was boiling with indignation, which somehow seemed to please the doctor, for he said, "There now! Perking up. You'll do."

Sir John advanced the theory that books can comfort one. "Do you care for history—or science—or novels?"

"Oh, any of those," the man answered without much interest.

"What he wants," said the doctor, "is Laurel to read to him. Well, why not? Just ask her, Sir John."

The baronet said he would do so. "Her aunts will insist on a chaperone, I expect."

Dr. Dodd shrugged. "Is a man with one leg and one arm dangerous? With Blunk dancing attendance? Well, let Miss Mirabelle or Miss Frances tag along if they want. For that matter, can't stop them."

"I would not feel such a nonentity if I were not laid out like a corpse," said the patient. "May I sit up?"

"In bed. In bed," said the physician. "Now see here: I don't feel any chips or knots in your arm, but it hurts like the devil, doesn't it? We must assume it is cracked and keep it tied up for several weeks. The knee is better from what Blunk tells me—swelling may be gone in a couple of days."

"Then I can walk?"

"You can if you've a mind for screaming pain."

The patient slammed the mattress with his good fist and growled "reprehensible" and "blast" and "hell" and a few other indignant words, while Dr. Dodd regarded him intently.

"It seems strange to me," he remarked, "that you can

remember words like 'suitable' and 'nonentity' and 'reprehensible,' yet can't recall a simple thing like your own name."

The angry young man shot him a sharp look and clamped his mouth closed, obviously wanting to control the burst of temper.

"Yes, yes," said Sir John pacifically. "A man mislikes lying helpless with folk staring at him. Remember when that wine bottle fell on my head, Dodd? M'sisters nearly drove me mad with attention. One enjoys attention more if one isn't feeling a fool."

"That's it," admitted the young man. "I was a fool to go haring off alone down that wooded stretch without a weapon, but I was eager to reach—"

"Who? What? Where?" prodded the doctor. "It's coming back. You were eager to reach what?"

The young man shook his head and then grimaced as pain shot through it. He would say no more, though the doctor asked persistently if he were expected somewhere. *Who* expected him?

Blunk had been an interested spectator of all this. "It's the head, sir," he said.

"Or the will," muttered Dodd. "Well, sir," he continued to the impatient patient, "my professional opinion is that you will recover, whether you wish to or not. I recommend doses twice daily of gratitude for the kindness of helpful folk who are trying to speed your cure."

Flushing with chagrin, the young man said, "Sorry!" and sounded as if he meant it. "To be without clothing, money, or name is extremely lowering. I'm not used to such a sorry situation."

"Eh?" said the doctor. "Just what are you used to?"

"Some advantages, I think. I hope I am never slow to thank for—er—service, but I cannot recall *needing* it so desperately." He looked to Blunk, waiting alertly. "Thank you, Blunk. You have been a godsend. And you gentlemen have been kinder than I deserve."

Pursuing facts, Dr. Dodd asked what exactly he thought that he deserved, and was answered by a crooked half-smile and a shake of the head. "I hope—but don't deserve—" he admitted "—to see the pretty miss in her ball gown." By this time, all were smiling. "Has she many beaux?"

Dr. Dodd snorted. "In this small place? Not a one." He bent a piercing look upon his wan, aching patient and added severely, "But she has defenders—her father, the vicar, Hanger, Patten, myself, and half a dozen others." Seeing that the patient took his point, he continued more affably, "Well, now, as one says to little children: We'll see. Meanwhile, pray accept the fact that you cannot walk for a while. That splinted arm will throw you out of balance, and you will require a cane or crutch to take some of the weight from your leg. A fall would be disastrous at this stage."

The patient groaned, but not resentfully.

When the visitors had said adieu Blunk followed them out onto the landing to whisper that the patient was really not difficult. "Feels out of frame—who's to wonder—but truly gives me no trouble. I think he was hoping for some sort of cure from you, Dr. Dodd."

Reminding them that he was not a magician, the doctor said cheerfully, "Sometimes a needle is more effective than medicine, if you follow me."

"Oh, yes, sir. Very true, sir."

"We have just seen a needle at work," Sir John observed with a chuckle.

The two continued down the stairs, and Blunk returned to the sickroom, where he hoisted the patient onto a heap of pillows so he could look out into the stable yard. It was not an edifying view, yet more interesting than four drab walls. Blunk shifted a chair for himself so that he, too, could see that nothing was happening.

Eventually, both dozed off. They were awakened when

Patten came up with a lunch tray that smelled spicy enough to tempt both sick and well. Mrs. Patten had put her best effort into a chicken stew and apple tarts.

After the meal the injured man had no desire for more sleep. He stared into the innyard, willing something or anything to happen, but aside from a dog scratching fleas in the stable doorway, nothing did so . . . until a blue-coated gentleman rode into view on a high-stepping, showy roan. When no ostler appeared the rider stood down, offered his mount some water at the trough, and then took him into the stable.

"See that man?" hissed the patient.

"Yes sir," responded Blunk, surprised.

"Do *not*, I command you, allow him into this room!" Tensely, head raised from the pillow, he watched until the stranger reappeared and strode toward the inn. Then he fell back.

"Have *no* conversation with him, I beg. If luck is with me, he won't linger here. Wish I could stop the Pattens' tongues, but to try would only set them wagging."

Below in the taproom, the newcomer was saying haughtily to Patten, "Can you give me something decent to eat?"

"Aye. Me wife is counted a first-rate cook," he answered stolidly. He had sized up the exquisitely cut coat, the snug-fitting buff breeches, and the glossy boots, and recognized a Tulip of the ton when he saw one. A lord, very likely, though not soft-spoken as was Sir John, whom everyone esteemed. "It is past mealtime, m'lord, and will take a bit of time."

"Well, make it quick," said the stranger. "I'm sharp-set." Casting a critical eye around the taproom, he asked, "Have a private parlor?"

"Aye. Across the hall, m'lord. The fire is laid and I'll light it if you wish."

The stranger drawled, "I wish." He strolled into the parlor, laid hat and sleek leather gloves upon a table, took up a day-old London paper resting there, and sat (with attention to the skirts of his coat) on a settle beside the hearth.

Patten, having set the fire alight, departed for the kitchen, where he told his wife that the Prince Regent had arrived and wanted the banquet served at once.

Mrs. Patten, reading his mind easily, said, "Better take him some of your own brew to sweeten his wait. Roddy, stoke up the oven. It's a male failing—as well ye know—wanting to eat the instant appetite strikes!"

Patten grunted and ordered Del, who was scrubbing pots, to leave them for Roddy and check to see if the ostler was down from the loft and was seeing to the gentleman's horse. He then strode heavily into the taproom to draw a mug of his home-brewed ale, which was popular in the neighborhood. This he deposited at his lordship's elbow without comment.

Likewise, the stranger did not speak. He eyed the mug doubtfully, lifted it to take a taste, and nodded approvingly.

A hot meal can be prepared only just so quickly. A second ale followed the first with mellowing effect.

"Tolerable," admitted the guest. "Where do you buy this? London? Bristol?"

"Nay," replied Patten, pleased and annoyed all at the same time. "Brew it meself."

The gentleman looked surprised. "Well, bring me another in fifteen minutes."

Thinking his wife's work would be wasted, Patten nodded and returned to the kitchen to announce that drink was liable to spoil the meal she was preparing.

"Often does," she replied, "but we can charge him, all the same."

Later, carrying the tray of food, Patten met the stranger seeking the privy, gave him directions, and continued to the parlor, where he set out the meal upon the table and waited to uncover the dishes.

By this time his lordship's appetite had slackened, but

when he returned to the parlor he took a chair at the table and accepted a large cloth to protect his neckcloth and vest. "I don't suppose," he said, "that you have a decent port to finish this off?"

Patten hesitated. "I've a bottle or two, iffen you want it after eating, sir."

"I'll want," was the growling reply. "Fetch it now."

"Fancy taking port with 'is meat and trimmin's," Patten grumbled to himself. But shillings were shillings and added up to crowns, and crowns to pounds. Business was business.

He clomped to the cellar, dusted off a bottle of his best port, and presented it along with a clean glass. By way of thanks came an order to uncork, which he did.

Mrs. Patten listened to her spouse's complaints with a pursing of her lips. "What a waste! Well, he won't drink it all." Generally, she was right upon any matter on which she spoke. This time, however, she was wrong. The brusque diner did polish off the whole bottle, falling asleep—or dead drunk—on the table, just as Patten snatched the crockery out of the way.

The innkeeper conferred with his wife as to what to do next, so she came in to look at the spectacle in the parlor. "He's a strapping fellow," she noted. "Well-dressed and barbered, not tallow-faced. Doesn't seem a likely drunkard. Perhaps he had a late night, with little sleep. The food, the ale and wine, the warm room—maybe boredom—have made him drowsy. Leave him be."

"I don't need to call the boys and the ostler to 'elp carry 'im to a room?"

Mrs. Patten shook her head. "Snores might disturb the poor injured chap across the landing. If he wakes here, he will think he dozed a mite. If he wakes in a strange bedchamber, he will know he made a fool of himself and will take the shame out on us."

It was good advice. They left the parlor, closing the door gently.

"No one's likely to stop 'ere this time of day," Patten said, taking comfort that he seldom had in a slack hour.

At something after three-thirty the stranger awoke and rang for warm water and a towel. When Del brought it he was standing before the mirror that hung between two front windows of the parlor, comb in hand, to discipline the brutus cut of his blond hair.

"Ah," he said, more civilly than before. "I can do with a wash. Feel like I've spent the night in a cow byre."

"No, m'lord," returned Del with a straight face. "This is The Nesting Dove."

"Well, whatever it is called, the cook can *cook.*" He washed his face and hands carefully.

"Would you be wanting to stay for dinner, m'lord?"

The gentleman said he would think about it, and indicated that he had finished with the washbowl, saying Del was to leave the door open in case the taproom became interesting.

At four, it was the hallway that attracted his attention. Sir John Eland entered with his daughter via the front door of the inn, and as the parlor door stood open, their heads turned his way (as heads to openings will turn). Sir John nodded slightly. He hurried Laurel to the stairs, though not before she had seen a smashingly handsome gentleman standing indolently and gracefully before the parlor grate.

Blunk opened cautiously to their knock at the chamber door; then, seeing who they were, admitted them, saying apologetically, "Our gentleman does not wish to receive strangers."

Laurel thought it was a very odd thing to say, as they themselves had known the patient only parts of three days and had no name to attach to him.

"It has been a very long day," the patient announced surprisingly. It sounded as though he had missed her—and Papa, of course.

She walked to the bedside and smiled. "But I can see

you have used it to gather strength. Surely you are not thinking of leaving Bayley Dell so soon!"

"It does not matter what I think, for your Dr. Dodd has laid down the law to me about daring to stir an inch. You were here, Sir John. Did he not speak very sternly?"

Laurel giggled—a very delightful little sound—and her eyes danced. "Sir, I feel sure he must have had to do so in order to restrain you. The last time I was here you made a woebegone picture that stirred all our sympathies, whereas now you—you seem bright enough to leap from the bed."

"What! Dance around the inn in Patten's nightshirt? I should not dare!"

"And Blunk would not permit it," added Sir John.

"No. He is in a devilish conspiracy with Hanger, and Dodd, and the Pattens. Daresay, Sir John, you are in it, too."

Laurel's papa said he had the young man's interests at heart. "I did agree for Laurel to read to you, didn't I?"

She looked at her father in consternation, and then at Blunk to confirm what she saw in Sir John's face. "I-I've never done such a thing," she faltered. "My aunts would not let—"

The patient succeeded in seeming crushed by allowing his chin to droop upon his chest. "We thought they might come with you," he murmured. "Your father offered books. I thought we might have tea . . . on tick, of course."

The gentleman she had glimpsed in the parlor downstairs was much more alarming—and exciting—than this one, yet *he* had the advantage of her sympathies.

"If Papa says I may come to read, and if you truly want it, then of course I shall do so, or else feel like a killjoy. What should you like to hear?"

"Sir John will choose." The young man had been so taken up with their dialogue that he had neglected to watch the stable yard. He slanted a look at Blunk, who shook his head negatively. The damnable fellow was still within The Nesting Dove. "My situation is so embarrassing," he said with a compelling glance. "I hope you will not mention me to anyone."

She seemed doubtful but assented. "Papa—?"

By now the whole of Bayley Dell must know there was a man at The Nesting Dove whose wits were to let. However, Sir John obligingly said, "Yes," adding, "It will be a puzzle to locate your family or learn your name if we do not ask around widely."

The last person he wished the Elands to ask was the one somewhere below in the inn. "Oh, pieces are beginning to come back to me. I have remembered my horse; solid black. I believe I called him 'Nipper.' "

Laurel frowned skeptically. "It is very peculiar that you can recall your horse's name and not your own."

"It seems ridiculous," he admitted.

"Did you choose that because he bites?"

"No, no. I think—wait! It is coming back. I believe it is something to do with—his speed. Should have been able to outrun thieves, would you not think?"

Laurel and her father exchanged glances.

"Well, very likely he is out of the county by now," said Sir John, "but if I see an unidentified black, I will call it 'Nipper' and see if it responds."

"Thank you," said the patient faintly, realizing he had gone too far for his purposes. He allowed his eyelids to droop from exhaustion and stretched out his palm. Without conscious thought Laurel laid her hand upon it (as she did with sick and frightened children of the village) and felt his fingers close around it.

Hoping her father had not seen, she tugged gently, yet he held firm. Another, stronger tug and his hand fell open.

At once Laurel said, "We are tiring you. We will come another day with the books. What time would be best?"

He looked up into her lovely, anxious face, and said, "Two perhaps. Would that be convenient?"

"Yes, indeed."

Below, meanwhile, some regulars had begun to drift into the taproom, some only to smoke a pipe and hear the latest neighborhood tattle. It was their recreation for the day.

Seeing his chance to learn who the pretty, well-guarded damsel might be, his lordship strolled across the hall. At first his lordly appearance dried up the local talk. Then he succeeded in engaging one old, wrinkled grandpa in discussion of Patten's homebrew, and eventually, by dint of buying a round, was accepted as not so toplofty for a peer.

When Sir John and Laurel passed through the hall on their way out of the inn a chorus of "Evening, sir" and "Evening, miss" gave him the opportunity to ask if these were local landholders. Yes, they were, but living on a bootlace due to the former Eland's spendthrift ways, he learned.

"Speck they come to see the injured gent," opined one.

The stranger pricked up his ears. "Injured?"

"Aye," said another. "Set upon in the woods. Hurt bad, they say."

Patten was not present in the tap room at this time, and when he reappeared the lord, who stood out in the room like a man with two heads, slouched casually to the bar to speak for a room and bed for the night. "I let the darkness slip up on me. No time to try the woods between here and Wells that the men have been telling me about!"

"It's not a good night route," Patten agreed. He cast a glance about his taproom, seeing no one who might follow and attack this lord, as the unidentified man had been attacked. Where the scoundrels had come from was unknown. Wondering if the lord's purse was full enough to pay his shot, Patten said slowly, "I've one room empty, m'lord." He did *not* offer to lend another of his nightshirts.

Six

Neither patron of The Nesting Dove slept well that night.

Lord Harold Guinn, which was the name he had given Patten upon taking over the second chamber of the inn, had lingered a while with the locals in the taproom, hoping to learn more about the delectable Miss Eland. He nursed his own mug of ale. The results of mixing port with ale were catching up with him, and his head was beginning to throb. He thought food might ease him, but did not care to test it. When talk in the taproom swung to drain tiles and the planting of crops he said good night and went upstairs to his room to sleep in his smallclothes, which he found damnably uncomfortable.

Across the landing the injured man lay wakeful, having refused laudanum because he wished to keep his wits about him. His body ached and his mind was troubled. Why was Harry stopping here? Ordinarily he spurned such inelegant places. Did Harry know *he* was lying helpless a dozen feet away?

"Well, sir," said Blunk, finding his patient awake early the next morning, "I can see you didn't rest well. Miss Laurel and the doctor will be faulting me for letting you slump!" He rang for hot water. "We'll just have a wash before breakfast and then mayhap you can rest easy. No harm done, sir. Just a bit tiring to have so much company."

"It's not the company I've had," muttered the man in the bed, "but the company I might have."

"Don't give it a thought, sir. The door's locked and no one gets in 'less I unlock it."

When Del tapped presently Blunk opened the door a few inches, blocking the space with his body, and received the pitcher with a muted, "Thankee, boy."

It was quietly done, yet the footfalls on the landing and the tapping roused Lord Harry, who groaned and rang for his own water. That having arrived, he asked for the loan of a razor, and Patten was obliged to send up his own, as he had lent the spare three days before for Blunk to use on the patient.

"Whom could the charmer have been coming to see?" wondered Lord Harry softly to himself. "I think I would do well to discover!" He reviewed his appearance in the mirror of a wardrobe door, decided he would pass as well as any invalid, and stepped across the hall to scratch lightly.

After a moment Blunk opened the door as he had done previously, defensively.

"How-do-you-do," intoned Lord Harry with splendid cordiality. "I heard of the gentleman's unfortunate experience and wondered if I could be of service. Perhaps I might see him for a moment?"

Recognizing the horseman his patient had warned him against, Blunk replied swiftly, "I'm sorry, sir—m'lord. My gentleman is resting after a troubled night and cannot be disturbed." So saying, he quickly closed the door and leaned against it, not wanting to let Lord Harry hear the telltale sound of a key turning.

Instead, the two inside heard footsteps receding.

Lord Harry took the stairs slowly, a puzzled expression on his face. He had not known Blunk and had expected to see a different servant. He was acquainted with all his friends' valets, so who was in the bed? The servant called him "my gentleman." It stood to reason that if he did not know the servant, then the master—the injured man—was not anyone of his circle.

Entering the taproom to command some breakfast, he took a seat facing the hallway, in order to see whoever entered the inn.

Patten's pub was immaculate, yet awash with odors—malt, wood smoke, newsprint, and tobacco—which seemed pleasing or not, depending upon the state of one's digestion. Lord Harry wrinkled his nose but told Del, who was wiping tabletops, to bring him his mother's best breakfast.

"It's gammon and buttered eggs this morning, sir," Del said. "Gruel, too, if you're wanting it."

His lordship said any and all of those would do, so long as they were hot and quick. "Black coffee, too."

Del mumbled, "Yessir," and disappeared into the kitchen to give Mrs. Patten the order. "Why does someone who spends hours doing nothing want everything at once?" he asked his mother as he filled a pot from the kettle on the stove.

Beating eggs vigorously, she replied very likely he had something important to do—like have his fingernails buffed or attend a duck race.

Del said, "Aw, Ma!" and gave her a kiss on the cheek.

"Says his name is Lord Harold Guinn," she remarked, dodging her head sideways. "To my mind the one upstairs in the bed is a sounder gentleman, being not so toplofty."

Patten entered the taproom from a side door with a minimal greeting and joined his wife in the kitchen. At one point Del passed through with a covered bowl of gruel for the invalid; when he returned Lord Harry beckoned him and asked if the invalid was a very old man, wanting only gruel to eat.

"Oh, no, sir," Del told him. "A strong young man, but so beaten upon—Ma says it's a scandal—and Dr. Dodd wants him coddled for a few days."

"Set upon, eh?"

"Aye. In the woods on the road before one meets the

Wells pike. Knocked off his horse, m'lord. Dunno how he made it back here on foot."

"Traveling alone?"

"Aye."

Lord Harry reared back in his chair. "Well, let that be a lesson to me. Good thing I slept here last night. I travel alone myself. It might," he added meditatively, "be wise to send for my rig. How can I send a message?"

Del told him that the post would make a pickup at eleven at the Everything Shop, and Lord Harry asked for paper and pen, which the boy brought.

Upstairs, the patient was eating gruel with a pained expression and his left hand. Blunk offered to help, but he said at least let him do *something* for himself like a responsible Englishman. When he had finished Blunk prepared to lock him in while he returned the bowl to Mrs. Patten.

"No, no," said the patient. "Suppose there's a fire. Suppose Miss Eland should come. Yes, I know she is not expected until two, but I should feel like a felon. I'll turn my face away from the door and pretend to be asleep; you may draw the curtains. Surely that gorgeous buck won't come again so soon."

Blunk did as bid and tiptoed out. As he walked through the taproom, he saw Lord Harry eating and, being reassured that his lordship was fully occupied, he continued to the kitchen.

Immediately, Lord Harry seized the moment, sprang from his seat, mounted the steps two at a time, and threw open the Unknown's door.

"What in God's name are you up to?" he growled.

"I am trying," said the invalid bitterly, "to enjoy a bed of pain."

"Pah! You're shamming."

"No, I am not. Every inch of me hurts. Did Lady Pamela send you?"

Impatiently, Lord Harry yanked back a curtain, the better

to see the patient's condition. "Good God! You are a mess! What happened, Gordon?" He drew Blunk's chair to the bedside and dropped onto it.

"I was coming from Dunlope's, north of Nord Cross, you know. Was late getting away, so I took a shortcut through this place, and to make my tale brief, a hundred thugs attacked me in the woods between here and the Wells pike. They knocked me from my horse and made off with it—"

"Yes, I wondered why there wasn't one in the stable."

"—relieving me of everything of value."

"Would you recognize them?"

Gordon shook his head and flinched. "Scarves over their faces. But I'll tell you one thing: I had a dandy near view of the boot that kicked me in the jaw. I'll not forget *that*, though it put me out of my head for a while."

"Abominable," agreed Lord Harry.

For a few moments both were silent; then Lord Harry said, "What do I tell my sister? She was expecting you, after all."

Before the invalid could answer, poor Blunk burst into the chamber, wringing his hands in agitation. "Oh, sir, I never thought his lordship would stir from his meal. I'll never forgive myself! M'lord, you must leave. My poor sick patient will have a relapse!"

"Never mind, Blunk. What's done is done. Not your fault. I underestimated his lordship," the patient said. "The fault is really mine . . . never thought Lord Harry would be so persistent."

Lord Harry said he was driven by his sister, if the truth must be told.

"Did she send you after me?"

"N-no. Not precisely *send*. Just made things damned uncomfortable with her histrionics. Said she was *expecting* you, Gordon. If you ask me, the whole house party was planned around you. Wish you'd offer for her and make my life easier."

"Oh, the devil!" said the injured man. "Admit she has a dozen bucks hanging on her every word! Go along, Blunk. Take a rest—have an ale or two. You deserve them. Lord Harry won't bother me much longer."

"No, you are right," said his lordship, pulling out his watch. "Must send a letter to my man to bring my carriage and luggage here."

"Here!" yelped Gordon, jerking in the bed. "Don't dare bring Lady Pamela down on me!"

"Why not?"

Gordon hesitated, regarding his friend doubtfully. "I've seen an angel," he said very low.

Lord Harry nodded. "Tawny hair and eyes? Kissable lips? Just fit under your arm? I saw her."

"Damn you, Harry. Don't get in my way!"

"Cost you," said his lordship, his eyes glinting.

Gordon asked wearily, "How much?"

"Oh—a monkey. I'm a bit short just now."

"You always are. How is it your clothes are always newest and best?"

Lord Harry said he was an advertisement for his tailor, to which Gordon countered, "Then you don't need my money."

"Father keeps his strongbox tight. A man has need of many things that cost money, as you very well know. M'valet hasn't been paid this quarter. What do *you* know about pockets to let?"

Gordon laughed mirthlessly. "Just now I do not have pockets, much less money."

"The viscount will come at once when he learns your state."

"I do not want him to come—at least not yet. It is my servants I need, and how to get in touch with them without alerting Lady Pamels, I do not know."

"But," leered Lord Harry, "someone might tell *him.*"

The injured man made a sound of disgust. "Don't know why I acknowledge you as a 'friend.' Very well; a monkey if you keep your mouth shut about me. You never saw me before, don't know who I am. And all that goes for your servants, too. Clear?"

Lord Harry looked no more satisfied than Gordon. "I agree, but damned if I can go on much longer—hardly have enough silver to jingle. When can I see the color of your money?"

"Not before I'm vertical and wearing clothes. The inn-keeper is giving *me* credit, so he ought to do the same for you, as you have a handle to your name. When your red curricle and liveried servants arrive he will be glad to take a chance on you, although where he will bed two more, I do not know." Beginning to be gray-faced, he added, "I can't talk more. Please send Blunk in."

His lordship, neither pleased nor displeased, heaved himself from the chair and went off to mail his letter, remembering to tell Blunk his "master" wanted him.

The sight of the patient's wan expression told Blunk at once that all was not well. Obviously the lord had exhausted him! He insisted upon a dose of laudanum and a good sleep before lunch, even going so far as to ring for Del to put off the midday meal until one.

"You know this lord, sir?"

"I know *of* him," the patient hedged. "Too—er—lively."

"Right, sir. Too high spirits and too much talk for a sick-room. Now, if you will just take a spoonful of this, sir, and I'll draw the curtains again so you can have a nice sleep before Miss Laurel comes."

As Blunk smoothed his rumpled covers, he obediently closed his eyes, not expecting oblivion, but the laudanum did its trick.

Letter in his pocket, Lord Harold Guinn strolled up the village street, enjoying the admiring glances directed his way. He was the "gorgeous buck" that Gordon had called him, glowingly handsome in his way as his sister was ravishing in hers.

He passed some cottages from which smoke rose lazily and arrived at the Everything Shop (with his incredible luck) just as Sir John reached its doorstep from the north. He tipped his hat and said, "Good day, sir! May I introduce myself? I am Lord Harold Guinn and I think you must be acquainted with my father, the Earl of Clifton."

Slightly taken aback, Sir John touched his hat and said vaguely, "N-no, but I have heard of him. Has an estate beyond Wells, hasn't he? I live quietly here and do not mix much socially."

"Nor does he," Lord Harry said quickly, holding open the door of the shop for the older gentleman to enter. "Very busy with his crops. I've often heard him say, 'England will stand as long as her farmers farm.' Do you concur, sir?"

"Oh, yes. I have no use for life in the capital."

Harry's luck was holding. Miss Eland, the youngest and most delightful Miss Eland, was just turning from the counter, and when Harry snatched off his hat and bowed Sir John, compelled by circumstances, presented Harry to her.

Laurel had had virtually no experience with Corinthians. This one seemed quite elegant to her, although he had worn the same neckcloth for two days and his boots needed polish.

"Good day, Lord Harold. Are you shopping in *our town?*"

"Not this morning, Miss Eland. I have a letter to post." He drew it from his pocket, and Mrs. Mince, the venerable shopkeeper, reading its destination, named the charge. He was obliged to pay cash instead of forging his father's frank as he had intended. This was one extra that the earl permitted, since Harry wrote very few letters, and those of no length.

"Staying at The Nesting Dove, Lord Harold?" asked Sir John.

"Temporarily. I stopped for lunch yesterday on my way

north and thought my horse might be developing a swelling in a fetlock. It seemed prudent to see if rest for a day or two would clear up the problem."

Sir John agreed that yes, yes, that was wise. "I hope you are comfortably situated. It is a very small inn, of course, but the Pattens are well thought of here."

"Oh, yes, very comfortable . . . although there is some to-do about an injured person."

"Set upon, poor chap," elucidated Sir John, adding with a twinkle, "My daughter's patient."

Lord Harold turned to her with brows raised in surprise. "Indeed?"

Laurel blushed deliciously. "Dr. Dodd was ill, so they sent for me. You see, I sometimes help the doctor with children of the village—holding them while the doctor looks at their throats, and things like that. Del thought his mother needed support."

"Oh, yes. Del."

"There was not much for me to do, actually. Mr. Hanger sent a valet from the manor."

Lord Harry nodded. "I have seen the good Blunk . . . and visited your patient, Miss Eland. He seems stronger this morning."

"I am glad of that," she said.

"We must go, daughter," said Sir John. "Your aunts sent me to say they are waiting for the pins."

"Oh, yes. I have them in my reticule."

Lord Harry sprang to open the door again. Outside they separated, the Elands turning north and his lordship going south with his purse a bit lighter, though he did not regret the encounter.

"I think Pamela's chances have slipped somewhat," he said to himself. Their father indulged her quite a lot, and she was accustomed to getting what she wanted, especially as she did not squander money gambling (like her brother). It began to look as if she would *not* snare Gordon, though.

Alert in their bow window, the Misses Onslow saw the three part company before the shop.

"Oh, look!" said the younger Miss Onslow. "What a fine man! See his smart coat!"

"And breeches," added the elder.

"Can it be the injured man?"

"Who else?"

"But he has no broken arm! There. He is touching his hat with one hand . . ."

"And gesturing with the other," concluded the elder sister. "Who can he be?"

They stared avidly at each other for thirty seconds. Then Miss Onslow, the elder, snatched up her cloak (which was always kept handy) and an empty basket (for camouflage), and whipped out of the house to meet the Elands (with great surprise) as they reached the corner of Dr. Dodd's house.

The surveillance of the Onslow ladies was accepted as a routine fact of life by Bayley Dell, it being generally acknowledged that everything of daylight hours was known to them. Consequently, Sir John said at once, "Did you notice the tall, well-dressed gentleman just leaving the shop as we did? Staying unexpectedly at the inn on account of a sprained fetlock, or some such thing."

"His *horse's* fetlock." Laurel laughed. "Have you an errand down the street? May I help you? Papa will deliver my aunts' pins to them."

Miss Onslow fluttered that she was going to look for watercress in the ravine beyond the church property.

"It may be a bit early for cress," suggested Laurel mildly.

"Oh, yes," agreed Miss Onslow cheerfully, "earliest is best, if I find it. Tender, you know." Her effort at fabricating an excuse made her nose twitch revealingly.

"Well, you had best stay off the footbridge," warned Sir John. "Frances claims it needs mending. We would not want you to break an arm like Laurel's patient."

Miss Onslow asked if Dr. Dodd was not yet attending the stranger. Surely it was important for him to do so!

"Indeed he is," Laurel assured her. "Papa is making a little joke. And the invalid is doing better; at least that is what Lord Harold was just telling us."

"A lord!" cried Miss Onslow.

"Yes," said Sir John patiently. "Son of the Earl of Clifton, whose seat is over beyond—"

"—Wells," finished the old lady. "We must look him up in the *Peerage*. Might be a beau for Miss Laurel. Now, do not blush, my dear. I am sure he could not find a young lady more lovely. He may be single! Would that not be splendid?"

Laurel cast at her father a look of mingled embarrassment and pleasure, to which he responded in his gentle way: "Do not be in a hurry to deprive me of my daughter, Miss Onslow. Plenty of time for her to find someone who pleases *her.*"

He took the girl's arm and led her homeward, while Miss Onslow, quite forgetting watercress, trotted beside them, chattering about court presentations and ceremonies at St. Paul's—or would St. George's be more elegant?—and jewels that were sure to be fine.

"Good morning," said Sir John firmly when they reached their own doorstep.

Ahead, the younger Miss Onslow could be glimpsed watching avidly from the bow window. As far as anyone knew it was indolence as much as infirmity that kept her housebound. True, her health was not good, though it was most marvelously pampered.

"Sister will be so thrilled," chirped the elder as she left them. Her steps lagged and she looked back to be certain that they entered their home, until her sister tapped on the glass for her to come with the news.

Miss Frances and Miss Mirabelle received their pins happily and hurried their niece upstairs to stick some into her.

They did not notice that their brother looked unnaturally grim and Laurel was as red as a sunset.

Left to himself, Sir John surreptitiously took down *Debrett's Peerage* and ran his finger to the Earl of Clifton. Sure enough, Lord Harold was the heir, and it was unlikely that the earl would permit the marriage of his eldest son to the pauperized Miss Eland, late of Bayley Manor and now of Bayley Dell.

Seven

All three ladies sewed fine seams, but they fretted a bit about patterns and hesitated to cut boldly into the precious green fabric, until Laurel thought of asking if there might be an old frock in the attic that they could rip up to use its parts in place of a pattern.

"Perhaps we should have gone to a modiste in Nord Cross for one, though that would have added to our cost," said Aunt Mirabelle. "Let us look in the attic."

Up they went, quite as unnoticing of the frigid atmosphere as the cook and maidservant were obliged to be whenever they ascended to bed. Sure enough, a sacrificial gown was discovered, and it rode down a flight in the clasp of Aunt Mirabelle to Laurel's chamber, where the ladies found it would serve their purposes perfectly if they allowed half an inch width on each shoulder.

So interested were they in ripping tiny stitches and smoothing out pieces that they ignored the luncheon bell. Poor Fane had to come up and knock.

Sir John awaited them in the dining parlor with a pile of books beside his place. He had chosen a mixed assortment for the invalid to consider, and he expected they would show some interest in what Laurel was to read. But no! the conversation was anything but scholarly.

It was settled between the ladies that while Laurel was at The Nesting Dove her aunts would lay out fabric and pattern on Frances's bed, being careful to allow what was necessary for the foaming flounce.

"You approve of that, do you not, John?" asked Mirabelle.

"Eh?" said her brother, all at sea, which was where they wished to put all viewers of Laurel dancing.

"Foaming—like surf, dear. Mr. Finkleshaff suggested it, and it seems a charming new idea."

"Oh. To be sure. Like sea, I take it," he hurriedly agreed, having the utmost confidence in his sisters' taste, as he well remembered the admiration they had excited with their style of dress twenty-five years before.

"You must chaperone Laurel, John," said Mirabelle decisively. "We will be busy."

"But my nap!" he objected. "Surely one of her aunts—"

His sisters at once babbled that they would be *extremely* busy, for cutting the pieces of a ballgown was the most serious part. "She cannot be allowed to visit the gentleman alone," Frances reminded. "Her *father* must do his part."

He replied with a sigh, "Her father is willing. I will put my feet up until five minutes of two, Laurel."

"Thank you, Papa," she said. "I will be ready—unless I discover myself basted to the counterpane or cut into strips. Which books shall we carry to the inn?"

He patted the pile beside him. "I offered a choice of history or science or novels and he did not seem to care, so I have put together something of each—and one of verse, if he seems weakened enough to stand for it."

Laurel bit her lip to keep from giggling. "Perhaps one of those will drive him right out of the bed."

"Now, now," warned Aunt Mirabelle, "mustn't torment the young man." Her plans were all laid for gentlemen at Wells, but she had not dismissed possibilities nearer to home.

Sir John retreated to the drawing room, where he settled before the fire and prepared to doze. But this soon proved impossible as his mind remained alert to deal with the puzzle of the stranger at the inn, the boredom of a public assembly in Wells, the probable condition of his evening clothes, and other matters—any and all worrisome details *except* his shortage of funds, for he had long ago adjusted to that.

Chattering happily, the ladies proceeded upstairs to begin Laurel's gown. She stood back to watch her aunts unfold the lovely cloth. They had put a sheet protectively across the coverlet of the bed, and the green fabric flowed upon it, truly like a Southern Sea. It was very delicate muslin, a far cry from her everyday frocks. Laurel felt a warm glow as she observed her aunts' earnest care. They had always been good to her, so this intense interest in her garments, her welfare, her future was nothing new, but she had suddenly become aware of their *bottomless* love, and it made tears rise in her eyes.

She turned aside to whisk a forefinger at the corner of each eye and borrow Aunt Frances's hairbrush for a pretense at smoothing her hair.

The cutting of pieces was barely under way when it was time for her to join her father. She said, "Good-bye," which the aunts acknowledged by "Um-m-m," without raising their heads, as she closed the door.

"Papa," she said when she joined him, "your sisters are pearls beyond price, and you are solid gold!"

"Flummery," he retorted, handing her two of the books.

Mrs. Mince was in the window of her shop when they passed. She waved and nodded. Laurel thought the folk of Bayley Dell had endearing ways. Of course, gossip circulated with the speed of light, yet it was seldom malicious. Horrid things did not happen here, which is what made it so strange that a gentleman should have been attacked barely a mile away. The perpetrators had to have been "outsiders."

"You ought to be the one reading these books, Papa,"

she mentioned. "I haven't looked to see what you chose, but I always liked to listen to you—such a fine deep voice and an excellent way with words of many syllables."

"I like words, you know, my dear. They interest me," he answered in a modest manner.

She said it showed.

"Well-l, perhaps. But I think to hear *you* will be good medicine for your patient."

They had neared the inn. He added, "Poor fellow."

"Yes," she agreed. "It must feel horrid to have no memory or name."

"Aye—if he has none."

"Papa! Do you not believe it?"

He smiled with one half his mouth, which made the mouse on his lip seem tipsy. "You see, his memory seems so selective."

"But it is coming back—by bits and pieces!"

"So it appears," said her father calmly. "Here we are." He opened the door and they entered the hallway of The Nesting Dove. There was no sign of Lord Harold Guinn.

Blunk answered so promptly to their knock that he must have been standing by the chamber door, and the patient called, "Come in, come in" so cheerfully that they knew at once he was feeling stronger. He was well propped up, with a blue shawl about his shoulders making his eyes brighter.

"Where are my other ladies?"

His ladies, indeed!

"How many can read to you at once?" demanded Laurel, unloading books upon the dresser.

Her father added his to the pile, saying he was a substitute for his sisters, who were sewing a creation for Laurel. "Ah!" he continued, "I see a wing chair has been added."

"Yes, for an aunt—or you, sir. I asked Patten to bring up something comfortable." The invalid turned his face to the girl. "There was only the one in the parlor, but you see he has set an armchair here by me for you. Will that be satisfactory, Miss Eland?" Polite words. But was there a challenging gleam in his eyes before which Laurel hastily dropped hers, having had no experience in flirtation?

The room was crowded by the added furniture, leaving scant space for the Elands and Blunk to stand. The valet's own seat had been pushed into a corner.

A little breathlessly, Laurel handed Blunk her cloak before taking the armchair near the bed. Her father was wafted to the wing chair, and a glass of sherry was set upon a small table at his elbow. How did an Unknown with no money accomplish all this? She supposed he had wheedled Mrs. Patten, but her husband would not have been an easy mark.

"Pray, put the books here on the side of my bed where Miss Eland can reach them easily. There. Thank you, Blunk. You may take a rest until we ring." His manner was pleasant yet decisive. A man accustomed to giving orders? Whatever had passed between him and the valet, they appeared to respect each other.

Blunk bowed and departed.

Sir John sipped his wine and relaxed beside the grate that smoldered across the room.

Having never been in such a situation, Laurel asked diffidently what the gentleman wished to hear.

"Your voice," was the alarming reply.

She shot a glance at Papa, whose missed naps were beginning to catch up with him. "I mean, sir, which book?"

"Any will do," he replied amiably. "You cannot know how excruciating it is to be confined to bed with nothing to do."

"Yes, I can," said Laurel, "for I haven't forgotten the illnesses of my childhood, which turned the house upside-down. I was not allowed to do *anything* lest it delay my recovery."

"Did not your mother—"

She shook her head. "She died before I was out of the cradle."

"Mine was a wonderful nurse when I was an ailing child," he said. "She may have spoiled me a bit at those times. Father thinks me something of a trial, I fear."

Realizing the invalid was revealing things about himself, she peeked at Papa, who had drifted off to sleep, having emptied the glass of sherry.

"Are you his only son?" she probed gently.

"No," he said. "I have an older brother. Stuffy, but really sound. Good fellow to have with you in a pinch."

Then why did he not send for this brother now? It began to look as though Papa was right about her patient's elusive memory. However, she dared not ask his name directly for fear of drying up the well . . . or setting him against her, which she did not wish to do.

"What shall I read?" she asked, shuffling the volumes.

"Oh—anything."

"Scott?"

"Why not?"

She opened *Waverley* and read in the pleasing style of her father, although she did not realize it. After nine or ten pages, seeing that the invalid lay inert, relaxed, his ash-blond lashes thick on his cheeks, the uninjured hand palm up upon the coverlet, she halted.

Asleep. So quickly! Like her father.

She did not know whether to be annoyed, dismayed, or mortified by this failure to entertain. Actually, she felt drowsy herself but could not imagine sleeping in such circumstances, only to be discovered (like Papa) abandoned in a dream world.

"Do not stop," said a voice from the bed.

She said, "Well, you are not listening."

Without opening his eyes he said he was doing so. "It is like the alluring songs of the Sirens."

After a pause she suggested trying something else. As he made no answer, she changed books and began anew.

" 'A plane superficies is that in which any two points being taken, the straight line between them lies wholly in the plane. A plane angle is the inclination of two lines to one another, which meet together but are not in the same direction. If two circles cut one another, they shall not have the same center.' "

"Good God! Euclid!" His eyes snapped open. "Never say your papa allowed you to bring *him* to a sickroom!"

In his wing chair Sir John stirred, muttered something indistinguishable, and subsided. With a roguish expression, Laurel held up the volume for her listener to see: *A Guide to Scottish Castles.*

"You made it up," he accused.

"Certainly not. Make up planes and angles? I was only quoting the esteemed gentleman."

He moved restlessly in the bed. "See here! Geometry is an unlikely subject for a female. How deep did you go?"

"Oh, not far. Whatever took Papa's fancy was what he passed on to me. Mostly literature, of course. I am thankful to say he is not a reader of sermons."

"So you are sparing me those?"

"Yes. The vicar—Mr. Appleton—gives very timely little talks but avoids theological treatises that might cause some confusion in Bayley Dell. When Papa talks history he is more interesting than any book. You would do better to listen to him than to me."

"But you are more beautiful than he," said the patient, openly admiring the blush that showed upon her cheeks.

"You must not talk like that," whispered Laurel, hoping to hear more in the same vein. She thought this must be flirting, which was something she had never practiced and of which she did not know the rules. What would Papa think if he heard?

"It is difficult to be subtle when one is wearing a landlord's nightshirt and the landlady's shawl," he said, also whispering. "Your father—bless him!—is dozing. If you move your chair nearer to the head of the bed, we should be able to converse without disturbing him."

But this Laurel refused to do. In the present situation she did not fear any inappropriate overtures from her patient. Nevertheless, she sensed that to be too accommodating would lower herself in his estimation.

"Sir," she said roundly (if softly), "I think you are playing games. The plan was for me to entertain you by reading a book of Papa's choice. Either I read Mr. Scott now or next time I bring sermons . . . or not come at all."

"So cruel!" he crooned, his lips twitching.

When a knock sounded he frowned and called impatiently, "Well, what is it?"

Lord Harold Guinn entered. "I am it—or it is I. Anyway, here I am to brighten your afternoon." He bowed gracefully to Laurel. "Good afternoon, Miss Eland."

"You have met?" asked the Unknown without enthusiasm.

"This morning," nodded Laurel, smiling her welcome.

"At the Everything Store," added Lord Harry breezily. "Quite improved my day. I was mailing a note to my valet. Now, if he will come with fresh linen and assorted coats, then perhaps Miss Eland will cry 'friends' with me. Sir John presented me to his beauti—his daughter, you see."

The sound of his own name woke Sir John, who blinked and sat up straighter. "Lord Harold? Where did you come from?"

"I live here. Your patient and I share a landing."

"Landing?"

His lordship explained, "I occupy the room across the landing, sir."

"Oh, yes," said Sir John, fully awake now. "Patten's other room. Good to see you. Horse improving?"

"Hope so," Lord Harry replied. "I will be glad when my servants come. M'groom is excellent with horses." He drew

Blunk's chair from the corner in order to join the circle uninvited.

The patient's scowl did not discourage his lordship, who sat down and tossed one leg casually across the other, making it plain that *he* was in no hurry.

At this point Blunk erupted into their midst, clicking his tongue and admonishing the injured man, "Sir, this will never do! Dr. Dodd said you must be quiet for some days yet, and Mr. Hanger charged me with seeing we obey the doctor." He spoke to his patient, but his message was for the visitors.

They must go!

With civil words to the patient, who looked more disgruntled than exhausted, the guests rose to their feet and drifted toward the door, and since there were three to say farewell, the patient need not make much effort to talk.

"We will leave the books here for another session, eh?" suggested Sir John. His nap had caused him to lose all sense of time so that he did not realize they had been there less than half an hour, and Laurel did not point this out.

She was a little disconcerted by the invalid's trying to engage her in a tête-à-tête. Was this improper? Or only the easy manner of London social circles? Even with the purple and green bruise that spread from jaw to cheek, he was quite handsome, she thought. On the other hand, Lord Harold Guinn, tall and radiating good health, exuded charm that seemed impervious to snubs, determinedly affable. What a turn of events, to have brought two such gentlemen to her village.

"Come along, Laurel," said her papa.

"Come *back*," called the stranger from the bed, in a voice that sounded stronger than his condition (or valet) would indicate.

Meanwhile, Lord Harold was waiting at the top of the stairs to invite them to have tea in the parlor which he had blithely appropriated. "Follow me down. I should warn you

that Patten took two chairs from the parlor to put upstairs.
We may have to drag others from the taproom . . . ah, Mrs.
Patten! Just the lady we want! May we please have tea—and
something delicious that I can smell baking? Miss Eland is
dry from reading aloud."

Mrs. Patten rolled her eyes at Laurel. "Yessir. Cinnamon
buns, sir. Not quite done. I'll send the tea first."

Even without its armchair and wing chair the parlor was
a cozy place, kept so at this time for the pleasure of a real
live lord. Yellow curtains were drawn back to admit both
light and view. Before the hearth lay a red and yellow rug,
woven by village women and won by Mrs. Patten at a raffle
to benefit the church; and on one wall hung an oddly interesting "picture" composed by young Roddy Patten of
colorful autumn leaves glued to a fringed oblong of drab
cloth. Chairs were missing, yet there remained four straight
ones set around a deal table that was just right for a tea
party.

Lord Harold took Laurel's cloak to hang upon a peg and
seated her at the table, where she could look out upon the
small front lawn of the inn and a chestnut tree showing a
springtime haze of delicate green. Although here, as in the
taproom, an aroma of ale hung over all, it was less perme-
ating, overlaid pleasantly with wood smoke, and that not
oppressive either, as the chimney drew well. She would have
thought so simple a room in a rural tavern would be beneath
an earl's son, yet he gave no indication of it. Sitting easily
between her and her papa, he talked lightly of social trivialities, such as would have been suitable in the drawing
room of his father.

When the tea came he asked her if she would pour, which
she did in the graceful style of her aunts—as if tea parties
in country inns were something one encountered every day.
How little did she guess that the Elands' presence here was
what had inspired Mrs. Patten to supply dainty linen nap-
kins and her best china. In Bayley Dell the Elands counted

for more than unknown lords who sometimes drank too much.

They had just begun to sip their tea when teasing odors of cinnamon announced the coming of the promised buns, escorted by Mrs. Patten, whose disapproval was indicated by her offering them to his lordship last.

"Ah, Mrs. Patten, you have outdone yourself," said his lordship genially, as if his orgy with ale and port had never occurred.

Mrs. Patten, deaf to blandishments, set down the dish, curtsied, and went out. "I hope," she said to her elder son, who was peeling potatoes, "I know who is Solid Worth and who is only wearing fine feathers."

"M'pa's solid," observed Del loyally.

"Aye, but I was thinking of Sir John," she replied.

Patten came in then from the stable yard, and her tone changed. "That lord of yours is being mighty free with your parlor and food, and not a penny have you had from him. Better hide his saddle, I think."

"Can't wring a penny from the one upstairs in the best bed, either. And don't remind me I put 'im there. It's true I carried 'im up—m'ostler and m'self. Weren't you there, wringing your hands and saying 'poor chappie' and 'dear heaven'?"

"But he doesn't make trouble. I daresay Mr. Hanger will pay his keep, if need be."

Del asked, "Why is his lordship staying here?"

"Hiding from creditors," said Mrs. Patten with a sniff.

Her husband slowly shook his shaggy head, not disagreeing, only unsure. "Says 'is 'orse 'as a swelling, but I don't see it. Do you, Del?"

"No."

"Neither does m'ostler. Playing some sort of game, 'e is."

"Not with Miss Laurel, I hope!" exclaimed Mrs. Patten. "Has her and Sir John in the parlor now, plying them with *my* cinnamon buns."

"Better 'ave a word with Mr. 'Anger," said Patten heavily. " 'E'll know what to do."

"Yes, but the money's not his problem," she reminded him. "Nor Sir John's, either. I can't like anybody—whether his pockets are full of guineas or not—acting a scapegrace with our Missy, and what business is *that* of ours? It's all a tangle. Better hide his saddle, I say!"

He might do that, he might, Patten allowed. "You're soft over that invalid because 'e's been bad 'urt. About the other gent, I don't know. We don't get many like 'im 'ere."

"Thank God," said Mrs. Patten, having the last word.

Eight

By the next morning all the pieces of Laurel's ball gown had been cut and Miss Frances had volunteered to do the necessary basting, which left her sister free to count the weeds in the churchyard.

"I have told Mr. Appleton there is work to be done, you know," said Miss Mirabelle, "and he will be expecting me to show him where the verger is to prune. The fellow has a slow mind, but he has pruned in the past. Certainly tending the church does not keep him busy. And, oh, the weeds!"

"Never think Mr. Appleton notices weeds," advised Frances.

"No, but the Lord will . . . and I do *not* mean Lord Guinn."

Laurel smiled to hear them.

The three ladies were just finishing breakfast, while Sir John had already retired to his favorite chair in the drawing room with a newspaper.

"If you don't mind, Laurel," continued Mirabelle to her niece, "I would like you to accompany me, as I want to measure for the vicar's new curtains, and if he came last evening as usual from Hammish, it would not be proper for me to visit his house alone."

With a giggle, Laurel opined that a vicar should be above suspicion. Seeing that her aunt looked embarrassed, she added naughtily, "I shall enjoy playing chaperone. No whispering in corners, please! Or lingering too long. Chaperones must be strict if they are to protect the innocent." She knew, of course, that the beloved vicar was the perfect soul of goodness and had lived an exemplary fifty years, yet the temptation to tease was irresistible.

Mirabelle's eyebrows collided. She instructed Laurel to bring paper, pencil, and measuring tape.

A week of sunshine had subsided into drab March weather, although there was as yet no rain in Bayley Dell. Overhead a cloud cover, high, not ominous but cutting off Old Sol, spread a sort of grayness on the village, which the two ladies scarcely noticed. Their cloaks were warm. Miss Mirabelle was reminding Laurel that their ancestors had built the pretty stone church decades ago. Pride, Laurel understood, was one of the few things left to the Elands. It was true that Sir John still held title to Bayley Manor, yet they must enjoy it from outside its hedges, as Mr. Hanger ate their fruits, walked in their gardens, ordered the tilling of their fields, and dwelt under the passive watch of their ancestors hung upon the walls. Only the church was still theirs in its ancient sense.

They turned in at the lych-gate and halted on the flagged area where parishioners gathered sociably after Sunday service. To right and left, as well as behind the church building, were gravestones, crosses, urns, and vacant plots. Though the village was old, it was small, and had not yet filled its burial space.

Miss Mirabelle indicated a dead limb and Laurel made a note of it. They began to circle right, listing shrubs that needed trimming.

"McComb should recognize weeds by now," said Mirabelle. "If he does not, I shall stand over him like Nemesis and point them out."

When they had rounded the building and were in view of Mr. Appleton's cottage he came out, beaming, to join them. "I had thought we might get rain this morning, but you have brought sunshine," he said, his own smile creating that which he attributed to them.

Laurel and her aunt smiled back, for his amiability was contagious.

"We are making a list of what needs to be done in the churchyard before growing things run wild this spring," explained Mirabelle. "If it is convenient, we will also measure for your new curtains. I have talked with several women and they are eager to make them for you."

"Ah, so good!" he said, looking earnestly into Miss Mirabelle's face. "Everyone is so good to me—Hammish—Mendle—"

"And why not? You're our shepherd," said Mirabelle, coloring at her own choice of words.

Mr. Appleton noticed nothing untoward. "Dear ladies," he reminded gently, "the Lord said 'feed my flock,' not 'flock, feed my witness.' " He was an unassuming gentleman, two years a widower, having no children to comfort him, yet completely lacking preoccupation with Self. His three villages adored him (perhaps more than the Lord's servant should be *adored*), even the roughest farm laborers recognizing his worth.

"Come inside any time. Now? Do come now," he urged.

So passing down the path that ran from the rear door of the weathered gray church to Mr. Appleton's cottage, they entered a small vestibule. Narrow stairs led up, bending sharply, to the verger's garret. To either side were rooms, one smaller for Mr. Appleton's bedchamber, the other a most delightful hodgepodge of sink, shelves of food supplies and blue earthenware dishes, an oak table and two chairs between the front windows, and a wide fireplace with ancient but serviceable oven. At right angles to the hearth was a decrepit and comfortable couch, where the vicar invited his guests to sit. Slits and tatters of the curtains were readily visible.

"I am shocked to see your curtains in such poor shape," said Miss Mirabelle. "Is there any special sort you want?"

Mr. Appleton would admit to none, even saying mildly that these were "not so bad" for part-time use. They must not think he was *complaining*.

His main place of abode, four days a week, was a modern, forty-year-old house in Mendle, across from the church there. Six spacious rooms, very nice and bright, a desk, shelves for more books than he possessed. They must not think he expected so much here! Little Bayley Dell could not, need not provide as lavishly.

"We shall see," said Mirabelle. "White curtains like the walls, do you think, Laurel?"

Laurel did not suppose it was the part of a chaperone to decide details of her host's window-dressing, but as her aunt was waiting with an expectant expression on her face, she mentioned the possibility of blue borders. "To match the dishes across the room."

The vicar nodded appreciatively, as he would had she decreed coal black, which made Laurel wonder if he had long ago schooled himself to accept whatever came his way, or if material things simply did not matter. It was remarkable, she thought, how one so other-worldly was always ready to render whatever *practical* help was necessary to anyone.

"Let us measure, dearest," said Aunt Mirabelle resolutely.

Laurel handed over the measuring tape, and took a seat at the table, preparing to write dimensions as her auntie gave them. The vicar stood, hands in pockets, admiring the picture of feminine domesticity. When the first two windows proved to be very nearly identical, he suggested mildly, "Why not take home one curtain to copy, and save measuring so many windows?"

Arrested, Mirabelle cried, "How clever!" and Laurel, almost in the same moment, cried, "Then we would have no

excuse for mismeasures!" and their host looked as honored
as if he had been named Prime Minister.

So while he took down one half-curtain, they counted
the windows and went into the bedroom, somewhat embarrassed yet concealing it, to see if blue borders would be
suitable there also. They would, indeed, as Mr. Appleton
had a similar shade of blue coverlet for his bed and a blue
rug to keep his floor warm in winter. All was spanking-
clean and neat, due to the attentions of the unseen verger.

"Come to tea when you can," invited Miss Mirabelle as
they put on their cloaks to leave. "We are always home
afternoons."

"Except when buying ball gowns in Nord Cross," he
teased gently, to which Mirabelle replied with a sigh, "That
is only every ten or twelve years, you know."

Mr. Appleton evidently did not realize that she and
Frances were making Laurel's dress, or he would very likely
have cut his tongue off before mentioning it. He had pas-
tored the little flock at Bayley Dell long enough to remember when Eland ladies commanded every elegancy of dress.
In his eyes they continued to look lovely; he was too unworldly to notice makeshifts now.

"Set McComb to work on the weeds, Mr. Appleton, and
tell him I'll discuss the pruning when he is ready," Mirabelle said as they went outside. The vicar followed in gentlemanly fashion, and when they reached the forepart of the
churchyard they found McComb on his knees, already at
work on weeds, having read the meaning of Miss Eland's
visit astutely.

The ladies continued to the Everything Shop to consider
fabric with Mrs. Mince, who was as honestly interested in
the vicar's curtains as she was in making a sale. The selec-
tion was smaller than a draper's in Nord Cross would have
been, being only the most basic of muslins suitable for
round gowns, sheeting, and such.

"I know you said white," ventured Mrs. Mince, "but

what would you think of this?" She spread before them a bolt of palest sky blue, which harmonized perfectly with the bolder blue they had chosen for trim.

"Ideal!" exclaimed Laurel, forgetting in her admiration that her aunt must make the decision.

"Why, *yes*," agreed Miss Eland. "Charming! You have an excellent eye for colors, Mrs. Mince."

It was not Mrs. Mince's policy to argue with customers, especially not when their opinion matched hers. She permitted a slight smile to deepen the creases on her wrinkled face. "Shall I hold back the two blues until you have counted how many ells you will need? If you like, I can cut the deeper blue strips for you in my spare moments—the larger panels, too. The counter is often empty, and I have scissors attached to my waist every minute of the day, you know."

Miss Mirabelle said promptly that she would appreciate every assistance. "Laurel and I are on our way home to measure a curtain that Mr. Appleton let us carry off." She indicated the folded curtain that Laurel held. "One of us will bring you word just what lengths we require. It is good to know I can always count upon you for help, Mrs. Mince. Mr. Appleton will want to thank you, too."

As the two ladies continued up the village street, they encountered Dr. Dodd, carrying a cane and a satchel. *"Good day, ladies,"* he roared for the whole of Bayley Dell to hear. "I am on my way to see if *Miss Laurel's patient* is able to stand upright."

"Oh," she said anxiously, "do you think he is fit enough? It would be a shame for him to have a setback!"

The doctor chuckled. "Still practicing medicine, girlie?"

Laurel turned pink. "I didn't mean to interfere, sir. It is just that—that—he has suffered a great deal, and suppose it *is* too much for him?"

"Won't know until we try," was the incontestable response. Dr. Dodd and Miss Mirabelle exchanged looks. "Want to come along, Miss Laurel?"

She did not know how to answer. If the trial was a failure, the invalid would perhaps be mortified to have her witness it. Even if successful, he might object to her seeing him hanging to a cane—barefooted—in Patten's enormous nightshirt. Yet she was curious to have a *vertical* view of him for a change.

Miss Mirabelle settled the matter by saying bluntly, "Indeed not. Frances and I think once a day is enough. Laurel will be reading to the gentleman again this afternoon, will you not, dearest?"

Laurel said, "Yes," although she was not at all sure the patient would still want her to come. It just seemed best to take a firm stand on some point.

"Come to tea, if you have time," invited Mirabelle.

Dr. Dodd touched his hat and went on his way, leaving the ladies to enter their own house, where they found Miss Frances had begun to fashion short, full puff sleeves of delicious green.

Mirabelle had scarcely put off her bonnet when she began to report on the state of the vicar's curtains. "That man must be a saint," she said. "The curtains are in tatters and never a word of complaint."

"I daresay he doesn't notice them," commented Frances.

"Yes, you are probably right, but the more shame to us!"

"Us who?" demanded Frances, not wanting to take blame for something about which she knew nothing.

Mirabelle said, "Oh, all of Bayley Dell. We should not let that dear man live like a pauper!"

Laurel objected that Mr. Appleton did not dress or look like a pauper. Had they seen his home in Mendle? The way he spoke of it made it sound very comfortable indeed. "I did think," she mentioned, "that his sofa could be smarter. Not that it was *worn*—only such an uninteresting dull brown and gray stuff upholstery."

"Takes naps there, very likely," said Aunt Frances. "A perishable cover would not do at all."

"Yes, but the pillows—there were two pillows that looked quite shabby and lumpy! Could we not at least cover them?"

"Two pillows," mused Aunt Mirabelle. "I did not notice them. Mr. Appleton may like them the way they are. My father would never permit anyone to alter his cushions—do you remember, Frances?—as he said the lumps suited him perfectly."

"Well, then," persisted Laurel, "can we not simply cover them the way they are? Removable shams—*washable* ones would be most practical."

It was a word that appealed to Miss Mirabelle.

Leaving the older ladies with paper, pencil, and measure, Laurel went upstairs to her room. It seemed a little sad to her that her aunts found such happiness in the small affairs of the village. Perhaps, when they had lived in the manor house on the slope across the way, there had been more and *larger* matters to fill their days. Aunt Mirabelle played her Broadwood often then, and Aunt Frances embroidered elegantly.

Here every chair seat was well covered; none waited for Miss Frances's attention. And Mirabelle seldom opened the piano. There was no discontent that Laurel could see, yet no joie de vivre. Her own life was . . . flat; might as well admit it. This was why the arrivals in Bayley Dell of mysterious invalid and dazzling lord were so stimulating. But she was to have a visit to Wells, maybe even several visits, and a chance of making a marriage and settling in a home of her own. She had her aunts to thank for that! But what happiness could the dear aunts expect in years ahead? She must never forget them and Papa, nor be too taken up in her own affairs to include them.

At their noon meal the aunts presented Laurel with written directions for cutting Mr. Appleton's curtain and pillow fabric.

"You can take this order to Mrs. Mince on your way to see your patient, child," said Aunt Mirabelle. "Tell her I will be down in a day or two to pay. Thank heaven we have enough in the Upkeep Fund to cover it, and the village women will do the sewing gladly, I am sure."

Aunt Frances transfixed Sir John by saying, "And you, sir, will be escorting her to the inn again."

Sir John raised his brows but made no objection.

"Have you seen to the problem of the footbridge yet?" she continued.

"No," said the baronet calmly. "Mud in the shade. I am waiting for it to dry out."

Miss Frances was not to be deflected. "Have you no old boots to wear?"

"Yes," he said affably, "but I am hoping for them to become older." Papa, thought Laurel, had learned not to be pushed. His nature was amiable, but as the lone male in a household of women he must need a certain amount of backbone.

The footbridge in question was a shortcut for two families of laborers who lived in cottages beyond the ravine. How much easier they found it to reach the village via the churchyard than by a roundabout lane! Who had built the footbridge was long forgotten, and the only reason Sir John should "see to it" was because somebody must if the users did not.

When, at two o'clock, Sir John and his daughter reached the inn they met Dr. Dodd, just completing a lengthy visit that included lunch. Evidently he was recovered from his own sick spell, for no horse awaited him and he was swinging his satchel effortlessly.

"I've given your patient a tonic, missy, not that he needs it, but I have found the sick recover faster if you prescribe something nasty," he said, jamming his hat more securely on his head. "Now you must urge him to take it. Nothing will heal the arm but Time."

"What about his poor knee?" she asked.

"Oh, still painful, but the swelling is down. I expect you will be good medicine for his spirits. Good day, Laurel—Sir John."

"Come for tea, if you can," invited Sir John.

"Aye, maybe," returned the doctor as he lurched vigorously away.

They found the invalid ensconced in the wing chair, swathed in an exotic robe sent down by Mr. Hanger and shod with purple crocheted slippers. He looked up with chagrin and welcome mingled in his face.

"Behold," he said by way of greeting, sticking out his better foot. "Purchased for Patten by his boys. Never worn, of course! I am expected to be gratified."

"And you should be," reproved Laurel, handing Blunk her cloak. "They could never have bought them in Bayley Dell—they must have made a special trip to Nord Cross. A Christmas gift, do you suppose?"

"I don't know. At least they are warm," he admitted grudgingly.

"Frances made me similar ones when she was fourteen," said Sir John. "You may be sure I used them until they were worn in holes!"

The invalid laughed then, and apologized for occupying Sir John's seat. "Dr. Dodd made me walk about the room a bit." He motioned toward a cane. "Not very pleasant, but it has to be done, I suppose. Miss Eland, will you mind taking Blunk's chair so that Sir John may have the one with arms?"

"I do not mind at all," she said quickly, before her father could demur. "Shall we return to *Waverley?*"

Blunk handed her the book from the dresser, where it had waited, and she opened it, but the two men had already begun to discuss Mr. Scott, praising his talent and deploring his misplaced trust in a business partner. Since they seemed to have embarked on conversation, she sat quietly listening, liking the rumble of male voices and recognizing the congeniality of the two. Her father, she thought, was enjoying the company of a gentleman with whom to talk about books—instead of only herself.

Sir John seemed to know little of Mr. Scott's financial situation, and was interested when the invalid explained that Scott's former publisher had come to his rescue.

"I wish I could write," murmured Sir John.

"Then try," advised the younger man stoutly.

"But he *does,*" inserted Laurel.

"I mean," said her papa in a tone of heavy emphasis, "write well."

"Very likely Scott once thought the same way himself," the invalid observed, revealing that his mind was sharper than it had been. What would he remember next? Would his name be the last thing to come?

After a pause Sir John mentioned the other gentleman staying at the inn. "Lord Harold Guinn," he said, "is from over beyond Wells. It is not often Patten has guests staying overnight."

The invalid replied without enthusiasm, "I know. He stops in now and then to see me. What is keeping him here? No broken bones."

"Some problem with his horse, I think."

"So he said. Daresay he has sent for his groom," said the invalid with a frown.

Laurel was glad when the conversation returned to books. Obviously Papa, no scintillator in a drawing room, was pleased to exchange views with the younger man. Both were bright of face, even when disagreeing, and both had so much to say that Laurel was well advised to remain quiet. Upon the discussion's being interrupted by the advent of Lord Harold, however, Sir John fell silent. The invalid, also, lost his cheerful mien and developed a mulish expression.

After an outflow of polite trivialities from all present, Sir John announced that he and his daughter must go. She had time only to reclaim her cloak and departed carrying it, her papa's hand on her elbow urging her forward.

Lord Harold was all handsome civility, yet Laurel suspected that her father did not warm to him so much as to the injured gentleman in the lurid robe. He did not, she noticed, invite his lordship to his home for tea.

Nine

Miss Frances Eland herself had invited Mr. Hanger to tea, and with the perfect sense of timing that had stood him well in his business affairs, he allowed seventy-two hours to elapse before presenting himself at the Eland home in the village. Having trusted himself to his very superior valet, he set out in blue and buff, with a discreet gold pin in his mailcoach cravat. A smartly uniformed groom, driving his curricle, delivered him to the Elands' door, where he stepped down, gave instructions to be collected in thirty minutes, and proceeded to swing Sir John's knocker.

An astonished Fane admitted him, received his curly beaver and gloves, and announced him at the drawing-room door. Miss Mirabelle Eland shot her sister a startled glance yet, as elder of Sir John's sisters and his hostess, rose and came forward to greet the caller. She was followed by her smiling brother.

There were at that moment gathered in the room another gentleman, Mr. Appleton, and an abundance of ladies— Miss Frances Eland, Miss Laurel, the elder Miss Onslow, and an unknown lady of some elegance. Mr. Hanger bowed with perfect aplomb to the ones he knew, and when presented to the stranger, Mrs. Walden, who graciously extended her hand, kissed that hand lightly in a manner that the five ladies had to approve.

Sir John offered him a seat near himself, and Frances

poured him a cup of tea, which Laurel carried to him with a smile. Small talk was resumed.

When Laurel took a seat on the other side of Mr. Hanger, and Frances was engaged in conversation with Mr. Appleton, Mrs. Walden whispered to Mirabelle, "Your niece is truly lovely. You will have no difficulty in turning her off. Is the gentleman talking with her perhaps a suitor?"

Mirabelle stared at her in shock. "Suitor? N-no . . . I cannot think . . . No, no. He is the one I mentioned to you—leases my brother's manor."

The visiting lady raised her perfectly arched brows and pursed her pretty pink lips. "No? . . . Plenty of blunt, I suppose?"

"Yes," admitted Mirabelle. Not wanting to expose their tenant as a cit, she added, "But such a difference in age."

"Oh, that cannot really matter. My husband was twice my age when we married, yet we shared fifteen very happy years."

The two ladies, Miss Eland and Mrs. Walden, had been on pleasant, even intimate, terms since seminary days. Although they saw each other seldom, the affinity continued. Mirabelle could not suppose her friend would lie to her or exaggerate; she must believe in Sarah Walden's felicity. Certainly, she looked youthful, contented, and secure, in none of which conditions could Mirabelle equal her.

At this point Fane brought the heirloom urn to accommodate the unusual crowd, and Mirabelle rose to give her friend fresh tea. Having handed Mrs. Walden her cup, she began to pass a silver tray of dainty cakes. Mr. Appleton immediately moved to Mirabelle's seat to ask if Mrs. Walden was acquainted with his friend, the Dean at Wells Cathedral, which she was, claiming the Dean's wife was her "particular friend."

Frances cowered behind the urn, although no one else seemed to object to Mr. Hanger's presence among them. Before long he had brought his empty cup to Frances for a refill, contriving to bring some color to her face by saying, "I do not need to ask how you are, as I can see for myself you are flourishing."

Miss Onslow, seated nearby, said, "Indeed yes!"

Since both Frances and Mirabelle had been inspired by the arrival of Mrs. Walden an hour ago in her smart chaise to bedeck themselves in their best tea gowns, he spoke only the truth.

"The Eland ladies are always charming," said Miss Onslow with a smirk, but meaning every word. The neighborliness of the Eland family had made her partial.

"But of course!" agreed Mr. Hanger and lounged toward the interesting stranger, who looked up with a welcoming smile. She supposed him to be a gentleman, which indeed he was by nature if not birth, and assumed him to be heavy in the pocket if he could rent a handsome manor.

"Why have we never met, Mr. Hanger?" she enquired archly.

He said, "I was just asking myself that very thing."

She made a beguiling little pout, which fascinated Mirabelle, and said, "I live at Wells, you see, which is a delightful city with many diversions, so I have not had much reason to travel—except to Bath or Brighton now and then."

"Not to London, ma'am?"

"Very rarely. I have no fondness for bustle and soot—and my dressmaker in Wells can be depended upon to be au courant with fashion." Her bronze ensemble testified to the truth of this. "When I learned," she continued, with a smile to Mirabelle to include her in the conversation, "that my friend, Miss Eland, was planning to bring her niece to a Wells assembly, I could not wait to meet the dear girl, and so drove over—and here I am!"

"And what do you think of our Miss Laurel?" asked Mr. Hanger.

Mirabelle frowned slightly at "our Miss Laurel" and hoped Frances had not heard.

"Exquisite!" declared Mrs. Walden. "I shall enjoy presenting her to all my friends. Mr. Hanger, pray ask her to come and talk with me."

"Certainly, ma'am."

Miss Onslow (the elder) at once switched chairs, putting herself between Frances and the vicar, where she would hear more, and leaving free her seat on the far side of the tea table, which Mr. Hanger with relentless purpose appropriated as soon as he had delivered Mrs. Walden's message to Laurel.

"You were kind to invite me to tea, Miss Frances," said Mr. Hanger in the most civil of accents. His manner could not be described as intended to goad her at all.

At least there did not seem to be double meaning in that simple sentence. "Not at all," she said with the merest hesitancy, which he did not appear to notice. His perfect garb and restrained manner rather shook her, as she was more accustomed to seeing him in riding breeches, on his big black horse, calling jovially to anyone he encountered.

"I take it that Mrs. Walden is the lady who will grease . . . that is, *smooth* Miss Laurel's way at Wells? No need to ask if she approves Sir John's daughter: a true little lady. When will you take her to an assembly?"

"Soon, I suppose. We have not had time to discuss dates as yet."

"Egad! I would like to be there to see her dazzle the beaux," he averred, watching the girl and the visitor.

Mrs. Walden had taken Laurel's hand and was telling her in a kindly fashion that the assemblies at Wells were no match for London balls, but young gentlemen and beautiful young ladies enjoyed them, all the same. It would be *her* pleasure to introduce her to the society of Wells.

Laurel blushed but did not drop her eyes, which Mrs. Walden could consider a good sign of poise. From what Mirabelle had written, the girl was unlikely to let attention go to her head, than which nothing could be more detrimental to a debut.

The several conversations in Sir John's drawing room were interrupted by the sound of the knocker at the street door. In the lull, Fane's slow steps were heard, and his deferential voice saying, "Good afternoon, m'lord."

"Ladies receiving?" asked Lord Harry, being in no doubt of his welcome.

Fane, likewise, had no hesitancy in admitting the heir to an earl. "In the drawing room, m'lord. They are just having tea." He announced Lord Harold Guinn and turned him over to Sir John and Miss Eland, who came forward, surprised but cordial, a proper upbringing fortifying their manners, while Fane went to collect wine, ratafia, and glasses as would have been offered to peers at Bayley Manor in bygone days.

His lordship bowed to Mr. Hanger, was honored to greet Miss Frances, charmed to meet Miss Onslow, and pleased to meet Mr. Appleton.

"Ah! Is that your target?" whispered Mrs. Walden to Laurel, as Sir John escorted Lord Harold around the circle.

Laurel shook her head and looked anxiously to her Aunt Mirabelle, who had coasted to her side.

"No such thing," hissed Mirabelle.

"Very wise," replied her friend softly. "Delightful rattle, not to be relied . . . How do you do, Lord Harry? What brings you to Bayley Dell?"

"Chance, Mrs. Walden. How nice to find you here! I cannot say what brought me here, but I can explain what keeps me here." He slanted a look at Laurel. "My horse's fetlock. My groom and carriage just reached the inn and I was obliged to show the questionable leg to him, or I would have come earlier."

"Will you join us in tea?" offered Sir John. "I see Fane is bringing wine and—ratafia, Fane? Would you prefer sherry, Lord Harold?"

His lordship chose sherry, and Fane, setting down the gleaming tray, poured a glass for him. Soon Miss Onslow was happily accepting ratafia, the other ladies switching likewise.

Just as Sir John was drawing up a chair for Lord Harry beside Mrs. Walden the knocker sounded again, and Fane limped to answer it.

The voice of Dr. Dodd was heard. "Afternoon, Fane. Ladies receiving?" In another moment he was among them, and a general flurry of greetings followed.

Miss Eland presented the doctor to her friend, to whom he offered a tolerable bow. He was the eldest gentleman of the group but not past the age of noticing and admiring pretty females. He eyed her with approval.

"Tea or sherry, doctor?" asked Frances as Fane brought in another chair from the dining room.

"Oh—tea. My day's not over yet. Sorry to be so late, Miss Eland, Miss Frances. Browning's boy went through the footbridge behind the church."

"Good God!" burst out Sir John. "All my fault."

Frances demanded to know if he had never tended to the bridge. "I told you and *told* you!" she cried indignantly.

Her brother admitted his negligence.

"If you had listened—" she began, but Dr. Dodd interrupted to say, "Nonsense. Not his responsibility. No one uses the footbridge except Browning's family. He's the one who should have made repairs."

"Was Billy badly hurt?" asked Laurel with troubled eyes.

"No," answered the doctor, stirring the cup she had handed him. "Deserved worse. He and half a dozen imps had found the cracked boards and were *jumping* on them." He gave a derisive snort. "Didn't go through to the ravine; just his leg up to the knee. Bit of a problem getting him loose. Your verger, Appleton, came and helped me."

"Dear, dear," murmured the vicar. "I am glad he was useful."

"Yes. Well, we got him out. Some scratches and one bad gash that I had to close."

Mr. Hanger chuckled. "Deserved what he got, but boys will always be daredevils until they learn the hard way. My own son kicked up some larks when he was a tad."

"Just one son, Mr. Hanger?" asked Mrs. Walden with interest.

"Aye. I could have used six or eight, but one is all I got."

She deemed it best not to pursue the subject, so she asked no more. He did not mention girls.

Never had the drawing room in Bayley Dell seen so many guests for tea, all coming informally, some even unexpectedly. Several conversations sprang up as twos and threes grouped themselves and regrouped.

Mr. Hanger was first to leave, when his curricle arrived to call for him as directed. Mrs. Walden's carriage was close behind.

"I must go, dear Mirabelle. We want to reach the pike while it is still light. Is it settled, then? Frances, you and Mirabelle will bring Laurel to me? The next assembly is Friday. Can you come then? Good. I shall expect you to stay the night with me. Sir John, surely you will be coming to present your daughter?"

He said he would do so, showing less reluctance than he had theretofore.

"You must be my guest, too, sir. I have ample room. Laurel, child, it will be delightful to sponsor you."

When Mrs. Walden's carriage had rolled away Miss Onslow was sent home with the cakes that had not been eaten; and Lord Harold and the vicar set off down the street together. Only Dr. Dodd, the latecomer, lingered for a second cup of tea. Then he, too, went home, hoping to have a quiet time with his paper instead of calls to the sick in this or another village.

"I do not see," said Sir John, as the four Elands settled

again in their quiet drawing room, "why we must undergo meeting a lot of strange beaux in Wells when our house has just been full of them."

"Good God!" and "Mercy on us!" cried his sisters.

"What 'beaux' can you mean?" added Frances, horrified.

"Every man in this room was single," he pointed out.

"Yes, and not one under forty except his lordship, and Sarah Walden says *he* is a rattle," retorted Mirabelle.

"Forty is not old," Sir John said.

And Mirabelle, remembering what Mrs. Walden had said about her happy May-and-December marriage, argued no more. Her sister looked irate . . . yet thoughtful. Both turned to consider Laurel, who shook her head, half smiling. Was her papa joking, or did he actually expect to marry her off to a gentleman his own age? Which caller there would be interested in that?

Her papa, Laurel knew from long experience, was kindly disposed to everyone. It was likely that he saw the gentlemen who had been present that afternoon in a different light from the one a lady of twenty would have to illuminate her opinions. Well, for that matter, she thought Dr. Dodd was a dear old bear, Mr. Appleton a softie, Lord Guinn an exciting tease, and Mr. Hanger a jolly bluffer. She saw every reason to like them, but they were not material for *her* husband! The few romantic novels that had come her way implied something more in life than mere convenience. *Place* meant much, she understood—for a lady of birth—and money seemed necessary for even a modest style of life, yet marriage without love—or at least *affection*—would surely be dreary. She hoped for more without knowing what "more" might entail.

The aunts' insistence on her exposure to the simple society of the smallest cathedral city in England revealed their concern for her future. Life had not been generous to *them;* obviously they wished better for her. And Papa had agreed, seeing their anxiety without entirely understanding it, because what a female saw in a man was not what another man valued.

By unspoken consent the subject was dropped. At dinner the three ladies talked about Mrs. Walden.

"How charming your friend is," said Frances, delicately spooning her soup.

"Yes," replied her sister. "I enjoyed her when we were girls at school, and though we see little of each other now, our relationship is as close as ever. Did you like her, John?"

"To be sure I did. Did you finish the same year? Mrs. Walden seems so—youthful."

Mirabelle shot her brother an acid glance. "We are the same age, if that is what you are wondering. Her life has been easier, although one cannot begrudge it to her, for she is not spoiled at all."

Sir John was silenced.

"You must not be shamed by our circumstances, John dear," Frances said quickly. "They are no fault of *yours.* In fact, we would be in a sad state without you."

"I have some hope . . . in a few years we may . . ." he mumbled, to be interrupted by Laurel.

"Never mind about hopes, Papa. We are happy the way we are."

"Yes," he said in a low voice, "I am not unhappy with *my* lot but must wish for better things for you. Such a contrast! Mrs. Walden—with her *esprit,* her elegance and fine carriage and carefree life—"

Mirabelle set down her spoon and leaned forward earnestly. "Brother dear, remember Mr. Appleton has said over and over that interior is more important than exterior. Sarah Walden may have problems that we cannot guess, although I hope not, as such a generous nature deserves only happiness."

Sir John smiled slightly. "You may be right. What I *do* desire is that my three ladies will look just as splendid when we attend the Wells ball."

"Well, Papa," reminded Laurel triumphantly, "my aunts have fine pearls and diamond ear-bobs, while I shall be wearing an original couture gown of matchless cloth!"

Miss Mirabelle and Miss Frances laughed with delight.

Sir John's lips twitched. "I surrender! I surrender, miss. I may be slightly shabby in my blacks, but you ladies will make me proud. Only remember, I pray, to consider the *interior* of each dashing buck you meet."

Ten

Breakfast at Eland House on Saturday was no different from other days, covered dishes waiting on the sideboard and Fane limping to and from the kitchen to be of service. One might have the feeling that it was duty as much as anything that kept him mobile.

Miss Mirabelle was first down this day since she would be collecting the boys' choir for practice. The dear wee church had no organ. Mr. Hanger, it was generally known, had offered one, but even his money could not create space for it. After so many decades the villagers had grown accustomed to *a cappella* music—indeed, the booming of an organ would have sounded to them alarmingly like French bombardment.

"Good morning, dearest," said Mirabelle, sugaring a cup of coffee.

Laurel, who had entered a moment later, kissed her aunt's cheek and chose tea to begin her day. Out of consideration for Fane and the maid-of-all-work, the Elands did not expect an early morning beverage in bed. The small indulgence had been so long done away with that the ladies never thought about it, although Fane, attending his master in the office of valet, persisted in taking coffee to *his* bedside.

By the time they were ready for food Miss Frances had joined them. "I will need you for some fitting this morning, Laurel," she said, pouring coffee for herself but allowing Fane to set it at her place "Have you any plans?"

Laurel seldom had plans.

"Nothing until Papa takes me to read to the invalid at The Nesting Dove. When you are so dear to create a beautiful ball gown for me I can certainly make a pincushion of myself."

Aunt Frances replied that it was her dream to see Laurel presented to society—even a rural society—and that she hoped Laurel would not look homemade.

"I do not expect to look that. After all, the best modistes hire women to sew for them, and I am sure you sew as perfectly as any of those!" Laurel said with conviction.

Frances looked gratified. "I have the bodice basted and wish to be sure of its fit before I set in the sleeves," she explained. "Next Friday will be upon us before we know it."

"I have not been much help to you so far," said Mirabelle, as Fane prepared her plate.

"Yes, but the choir needs you," her sister said. "You will be an angel to line the ruffle and make the underskirt."

Mirabelle promised willingly. "When Mrs. Mince has Mr. Appleton's curtains cut I will distribute them around the village for stitching, and then I will be free for any duties, Frances. Laurel's come-out means a great deal to me, too."

Laurel at once declared that they should have halos and that she hoped she did not disappoint them.

A duet of protest and affection greeted her words.

Sir John entered then, and Mirabelle demanded to know if he thought his daughter could possibly disappoint them.

"She never has," he replied with a fond smile. "A dog doesn't change his spots."

Frances cried, "Dog!"

"A rose doesn't change its scent," he amended, helping himself to a wholesome bowl of oatmeal and then inundating it with cream. "If you are going to the church to rehearse your scraggly bunch, Mirabelle, I will walk down with you." He cast a leery eye at his other sister and added that he would see what mending the footbridge needed. Frances made no comment.

Mirabelle said she would collect her music and be ready when he was. She was wearing a becoming bonnet when she and Sir John set out a quarter of an hour later.

"It is good of you, my dear, to struggle with those careless boys," he said, as they walked along.

She turned her face to him in some surprise. "But we must have music for worship. Some of the voices are very sweet."

"I wonder *boys* will submit. How do you coerce them?"

"But I do not," she assured him. "Family pride does it. Don't you realize the villagers look upon our little choral effort as 'culture?' To have a child performing before their neighbors is a source of gratification to its parents. Just imagine how exalted Mrs. Cobb must feel with *three* sons singing before God and Mr. Appleton every other Sunday!"

Sir John replied, "Upon my soul, I had not thought of that. Even so," he added, "I stand by what I said, that you are good to make it possible."

They turned in at the church, where waiting on the front step were eight or ten lads of assorted sizes and shapes. It was obvious they found waiting there in the sun warmer than inside the stone building, which had been closed for most part of a week.

Sir John continued around the church, and Miss Eland led her gaggle of boys indoors.

"You may keep your jackets, boys," she said, "though it might be wise to unbutton them so you may expand your lungs to the fullest."

Mr. Appleton emerged from the shadows beside the altar. "Shall I be in the way if I sit quietly to listen from the last stall?" he asked.

Mirabelle said, "Of course you are welcome in your own church." His being there would eliminate the necessity of Discipline, for which she would be grateful.

"It is not *my* church," he corrected gently, sliding into a rear seat.

At Eland House the younger Miss Eland and her niece were engrossed in sewing matters. Laurel stood patiently in a state of semiundress while Frances hovered over her, pins held dangerously between her lips, which slurred her speech considerably.

When the pins had been transferred to the seams of Laurel's gown she asked, "Aunt Frances, can Papa possibly be thinking of marrying me to one of our—our old family friends?"

"He will do so over my beaten corpse!" declared Frances.

Laurel relaxed with a small sigh. "Then you think he was teasing?"

Frances said, "If you can call it teasing. My opinion, dearest, is that he does not want to relinquish you to anyone, which is not an unusual reaction from the fathers of pretty daughters. But a more selfish attitude I cannot imagine."

"Papa isn't selfish," Laurel insisted loyally. "Look how good he is to us!"

Frances shrugged. "Well, perhaps I exaggerate. He is comfortable with things as they are and has difficulty in seeing a female's point of view. Our life is satisfactory. However, your aunt and I are determined that yours shall be fuller. You will enjoy the assembly at Wells, and it should open doors to you for other affairs of Society. Promise me you will keep a steady head and look for more than sartorial splendor and flowery language in a husband!"

"That's easy." Laurel laughed."The gentlemen I know best, and like, may be more than forty, but they set an example of generosity, wisdom, and consideration that I shall use as a measure."

"Well, see how Prince Charming treats his mother before you pledge yourself," warned her aunt fiercely. "If he is loving and considerate, well and good. If he submits to her every whim, beware!"

Laurel frowned anxiously. "Now you alarm me."

Her aunt slumped on her slipper chair. "I do not mean to, child. Choose a man who pleases you. There will be no problem of fortune hunters, in view of our circumstances. Your father can be relied on to see that you will be comfortable—"

"I don't ask more," the girl said truthfully.

Frances nodded in approval. "That is an attitude that will count with suitors, but considering your looks, my dear—let me be frank—you may achieve more than a competence. Suppose we forget that for the time being."

Her face turning serious now, Laurel complained that so much talk and thought and *pursuit* of money was very discouraging. "Are men also obsessed with money? Does romance mean nothing?"

"Not a great deal," admitted Frances frankly. "A rich man can indulge his sentiments, while one with less fortune must be—er—practical."

"Uff," said Laurel expressively.

"Oh, dear," moaned Frances. "I am not putting this well. Now see here; no one chooses to marry *down.* You understand that, don't you? The most suitable marriages are the ones where there is a balance—money with money, or money matching beauty or even position."

"Do you mean each side must contribute something? How horridly calculating!"

Rather weakly Frances said, "Not really. In a good match both partners have some sense of value. Now, dearest, you may safely leave the matter to your papa. He will be fortified by your aunts, you know! Be yourself and you will attract the right sort, but pray do not set your heart on a fribble."

Laurel sighed speciously. "Who would have thought dancing could be so fraught with danger. . . ."

Her aunt reminded her that if Bayley Dell had been a larger place, with a number of families to socialize, she would have grown up learning and experiencing all these matters by degrees. "You would know which gentleman was a terror to his nurse at the age of six and which mama was a doting fool."

Laurel giggled. "And they might know I was so unlady-like as to slide on the banister and scandalize Fane when I was almost old enough to put up my hair."

Though they ended by laughing together, they knew Truth had been both spoken and heard.

"There, now," said Aunt Frances. "I hear your papa downstairs. Put on your dress, dear, and let us hear what he has to say about the footbridge."

Sir John reported that the damage was not great. "I went over and had a word with Mrs. Browning, who is worth two of her spouse. If Browning spent less time in Patten's tap and more with his duties, her lot would be easier. She looked careworn. Kneading bread for that hive of children when I saw her! Well, well, I couldn't nag the poor woman, so I left a strong message for Browning, and she said she'd pass it along. You do not expect me to take a hammer and saw to the footbridge myself, do you?"

When Laurel and her father passed through the village that afternoon on their way to the inn two different people halted them to ask if the footbridge was unsafe. "Everyone knows everything about this place," Sir John grumbled to his daughter, "but no one has the gumption to do anything without being told."

"If you were not here to tell them, Papa, what do you think would happen?" asked Laurel, curious.

"All would grind to a halt. Buildings would collapse and holes in the street would swallow wheels. They have been looking to someone else to give instructions for generations until it is like an inherited disease." He smiled his tipsy-mouse smile. "One thing I am good for."

"Now, Papa," she said in minatory accents, "essentially it is *your* village and naturally they look to you. Who else could care about Bayley Dell?"

"Hanger has become a force," he muttered.

"Oh, yes, they respect his power. I do myself. He is strong as well as rich, isn't he? But they turn to you out of affection, Papa. That is better, isn't it?"

"Maybe not 'better,' but that's the way it *is*."

Without asking aloud, she wondered if her father actually enjoyed village matters. Her own life in Eland House was all she had any real awareness of, having been a young child when the move was made. She had some dim recollections of the chill halls and spacious rooms of a manor house where the stair made two bends before it could climb to the second story. There was a shadowy figure of a grandfather who smelled excessively of tweed and leather and tobacco. Grandmother, who had not long outlived him, was a soft Voice and a comfortable Lap. The uncle, baronet before Papa, was remembered chiefly for his absence, for trailing dogs through the house when he *was* home, and snapping a crop impatiently against his boot. Thinking about that now, she supposed his valet must have deplored such treatment of his painstaking effort to impose a gleam.

Oh, Papa was a different man, an affectionate father, an able landholder. He had always enjoyed books, usually spending evenings with his nose in one or another. Other times he was in the saddle, checking hedges and fences, or tramping over fields with *his* father, learning what crops to plant and when woodlands must be thinned to keep them healthy. Even when his brother came into the title, Bayley Manor needed him to govern it, for the elder brother was interested only in the funds the manor could produce. It was Papa who decided what to sow and whether to raise pigs for market.

And when at last it came to him, its wealth, its value, was already pledged to meet another's gambling losses.

How severe was Fate! Yet Papa could accept the Inevitable as he always did—except the "loss" of his daughter, perhaps.

"Papa," she said suddenly, "do you never want to let me go—to keep me in your home like my aunts?"

Startled, he said, "I don't keep them! Surely they're contented."

"Yes, but they don't have homes and children, except me, and that is not the same as their own."

"Merciful God, are you saying they are *unhappy?*"

"Oh no. They have happy natures, which I am sure you understand, as yours is the same. But, Papa, I would like—at least I *think* I would like—a husband if I can find a friendly one."

He halted midstep. "Friendly!" Then his face cleared and he chuckled. "I imagine you will do better than that."

They had reached The Nesting Dove, and neither wished to continue the discussion. They entered.

From the hall Sir John glanced casually to the taproom, seeing Lord Harry in conversation with what could only be his groom. A smothered exclamation from the girl beside him turned his eyes leftward into his lordship's parlor, which was, astonishingly, occupied by their invalid, reunited with his breeches, boots, and shirt with one sleeve missing. The wing chair had returned to the parlor, and the gentleman sat in it, a fire and Mrs. Patten's blue shawl making him cozy.

"Surprised, Miss Eland? Afternoon, Sir John," said the apparition. Dr. Dodd's cane hung over an arm of the chair, and he moved it to the other side to be out of the way as they hurried to him.

"This is good news," said Sir John.

Laurel asked anxiously if he was sure he was wise to make the effort. "However did you come down the steps?"

"Oh, Blunk helped me. Simple enough." Evidently success had made him more confident, for he continued easily, "The old knee aches like a tooth, but it is functioning. I cannot tell you how good it feels to escape that gloomy room upstairs!"

"La," said Mrs. Patten, appearing then. "You do not appreciate my best chamber!" It was obvious she and the invalid were on excellent terms, for she beamed at him benevolently.

He riposted promptly, "But *you* are down here, dear lady!"

Laurel could scarcely believe what she was hearing.

Mrs. Patten replied with an exaggerated smirk, "Best not let Patten hear you making up to me. A fair cannibal he is when jealous."

When the mild Sir John, half Patten's size, said with a twinkle, "Never fear. I shall not allow our patient to be eaten," everyone laughed, and Lord Harry came across the hall to discover what caused the merriment. Mrs. Patten, knowing her place, curtsied and withdrew.

"Well, well. It is fine to hear laughter," said his lordship. "Feeling that well?" (to the invalid), "Sit here, Miss Eland" (to Laurel), and "Will you be too warm there?" (to Sir John). Having settled them all, himself next to the young lady, he asked, "Pray, will someone tell me what is so amusing? Is it Miss Eland's debut?"

"Debut?" echoed the wounded man.

Sir John explained: "I thought everyone must know. My sister's friend, Mrs. Walden, is to sponsor Laurel next Friday at a Wells assembly."

With all eyes upon her, Laurel colored slightly. She thought her patient gave her an accusing look, which seemed odd. What possible objection could he have to her affairs? Besides, it mortified her to admit she was twenty years old and had never been brought Out.

"Too bad," said Lord Harry to the invalid with the most irritating joviality. "You cannot dance with only one leg and one arm. I shall dance twice with Miss Eland, to make up."

"Oh, will you attend?" she asked, surprised.

"I often do. My home is not far beyond Wells, you remember. Besides, I shall want to be among the first gentlemen to 'discover' a new belle."

Laurel blushed more deeply and glanced to her patient, who was inexplicably looking like a thundercloud.

"We did not come to talk to an invalid about festivities he cannot enjoy," Sir John said gently.

His lordship ducked his head. "Oh, yes. You are reading a book. What is it, Miss Eland?"

"Waverley."

"Eh?"

"Mr. Scott's recent novel."

"Ah, I see," he said hastily. "Then I am interfering. I will leave you to it." With brief bows around he returned to the taproom.

Thereupon, Sir John crossed to the door and closed it noiselessly. To his daughter's surprise he said to the patient: "I sense that Lord Harold makes you uncomfortable, sir. Is there some reason that I should know? Any trifling with women—things like that?"

"No, sir," responded the patient quickly. "Nothing beyond the line. Seems I've heard he is accepted everywhere, though I suspect most chaperones warn their young buds not to take him seriously. Pockets often to let."

"Gambling?"

"Some. Not deeply. The earl keeps him on a short leash, they say. Jolly fellow. Popular with the ladies."

The baronet looked alert. "Then you are acquainted with him?"

"I—er—know who he is. Introduced himself . . . I have heard things."

Laurel shook her head reprovingly. "A fibber is worse than a fribble."

He replied hotly, "Are you accusing me of—"

Before either young person could say more Sir John had broken in: "Well, enough of gossip. I will perch here by the fire," he said, moving to a corner of the settle. "You will never finish *Waverley* at the present rate. How many pages have you covered?"

"Ten or so," admitted Laurel meekly.

"Barely started, in fact."

"But, Papa, you must own I have been *constantly* interrupted. As I am now."

The invalid ventured to wonder if he need hear the book at all, if it tended to put Sir John to sleep.

"You will find Laurel's voice pleasing," declared her loving parent. "Never screeches. Very soothing."

Not soothing was the loud, affable voice heard from the hall, where a newcomer was asking Lord Harry why he had been ousted from his parlor.

"Elands there? I'll have a word with them."

A knock sounded and Mr. Hanger entered.

"This is more like it!" he declared heartily. "Feeling more the thing? Afternoon, missy. Good day, Sir John. Am I in the way? I daresay our patient would rather listen to our Miss Laurel than to stodgy gents." He seized a chair and sat upon it, motioning Lord Harold to come from the doorway where he was standing.

"So Friday is your big night, Miss Laurel." Either he had heard Mrs. Walden's parting words or the whole village was spreading the news. "Egad," he said, as he had to Miss Frances, "I would like to be there to see it."

"Yes," said Sir John, "and you would see me, like a monkey, in my blacks. M'sisters say it is a 'must.' "

Laurel declared that she was relying on her papa. "I hope I do not disgrace him or the aunties. Oh, and there is Mrs. Walden, so graciously willing to introduce me to her friends."

"I have no doubts about your success," Mr. Hanger said. "Sir John, you had better use my carriage. It will give the ladies an easier and swifter ride than Patten's—if his wheel is even mended by then. Say what time pleases you."

Quicker than her father, Laurel realized that with Papa accompanying them there would be no room for Mr. Hanger to oppress her aunts by his presence.

"*Thank* you," she accepted promptly. "Using your carriage and your coachman, we will have an easy trip."

Mr. Hanger smiled, pleased to be of service.

Eleven

As Laurel and her father walked home after the visit to the invalid—which seemed somehow to be taken over by Lord Harry and Mr. Hanger, and which allowed no time for reading *Waverley* or anything else—she was not inclined to talk. Papa, too, was never one to make inconsequential chatter; if he noticed her silence, he did not comment on it.

Being honest with herself, she admitted she felt cross, for the visit in some obscure way had been a disappointment. Mr. Hanger and Lord Harold had been merry enough, and her patient *did* seem stronger, though his mouth had looked tight most of the time—she hoped it wasn't from pain. No one seemed to have the least care for his faulty memory, which must trouble him even more than it did her.

Why it should oppress *her* she could not understand. Was it because she was sorry for him? If she had lost all remembrance of her name, her home, her loved ones, she would be devastated. And certainly not equal to conviviality such as was being heaped upon her patient.

"Papa," she said, as they neared their house, "it must be very discomforting to forget one's Self!"

Sir John, who knew his name and forebears but who had had to struggle hard to bear the loss of much that should have been his, said calmly, "Aye. It would indeed, but I think he knows very well who he is."

"Papa! Then why does he not tell?"

"That is what bothers me," he said.

Feeling (like Mrs. Patten and Blunk) that the young man had some claim on her, she asked, "Not something shameful?"

"We must hope not. I like the young man."

She was silent. This was something entirely new for her to ponder. What decent reason could he have for keeping silent? Could it be a problem of money? The men who attacked him had taken every pound and shilling from his unconscious body—even a ring of some sort, for she had noticed an indentation around one finger of a hand—not a wedding ring, for it was his right hand that was marked. Though one could not assume him to be unwed, for how many smart young men burdened themselves with signals of their "shackles"? If he valued a ring enough to wear it, he must regret its loss . . . if he even missed it. And to have no funds at all must be humiliating!

"Do you think you should offer to lend money for his most pressing—" she began as they mounted to their door.

"Indeed not," interrupted Sir John. Fane admitted them. "It would be poor manners."

Laurel handed her cloak to Fane and, untying her bonnet, set it upon a Sheraton table in the hall.

"There must be a better way of finding if—er—help is needed," Sir John said. "Your aunts would say Tact is All."

She turned to him with a percipient glance. "You are funning, Papa. I know you! You will think of a way to solve the problem."

Her father said he would try.

In the drawing room they found the aunts entertaining Mr. Appleton at tea, which was not surprising, as he generally came when it was his weekend to be at Bayley Dell for Sunday Service. Such weekends he went on to Hammish for vespers, the reverse being true another week for Bayley Dell. Two other Sundays he preached morning worship service at Mendle, which was a larger town with more people to be considered. If a month had a fifth Sunday, Mr. Appleton was free to do as he pleased. He might, of course, have given himself and his horse a rest, but being a dedicated churchman, he went where sin abounded most—and it varied—but always was to be discovered somewhere.

Accepting a cup from Aunt Frances, Laurel went to sit beside the clergyman and ask what would be the subject of his sermon on the morrow. "Is it difficult to choose a topic?" she asked.

"Sometimes," he replied, balancing his cup on his knee. "If I tell you now what to expect tomorrow, you will think you need not come!"

"It is not just a matter of need," interrupted Miss Mirabelle, who had been listening. "One remembers the Sabbath Day to keep it Holy."

Mr. Appleton beamed. "Ah! Quoting right back at me! Sabbath is for Israel, Sunday is for *us*. I shall invite you to lecture at Mendle some Sunday, Miss Eland! But back to topics; tomorrow I will preach on the Prodigal Son."

Laurel wrinkled her pretty nose. "Oh, *him*. I always felt he got more good things than he deserved."

"Most of us do," said Mirabelle.

Mr. Appleton turned to her, exclaiming, "Ah! You understand!" Laurel was forgotten as the two went off into a discussion of deserving good versus bad.

Frances drew Laurel's attention away by asking how her patient seemed.

"Rather overwhelmed by Lord Harold and Mr. Hanger," she replied.

"Oh, were they there this afternoon?"

"Yes. Both," said Sir John, joining them. "I daresay they thought to make things cheerful, but they were somewhat overpowering for an invalid."

"He had come down to the parlor," Laurel added.

"Downstairs! Was he fit?"

"I do not know. It seemed to have been quite an effort for him, and we did not do a bit of reading."

Frances considered. "Tomorrow is Sunday. I will not be sewing. Suppose I accompany you in the afternoon, Laurel, and see for myself how the poor fellow is? Yes, that is what I will do."

"Do you mean I may have my afternoon nap?" asked Sir John. His sister ignored him.

"I have been busy with your ball gown, Laurel, and have not given enough thought to the Unknown Gentleman. Men can be so unobservant, although very likely Mrs. Patten is taking good care of the fellow." She lowered her voice so as not to be heard by Mr. Appleton, who was happily immersed in conversation with Mirabelle about scriptural fine points and not attentive to the Unknown's health. "We must not overlook prospective matrimonial material, Laurel, even if your patient does not appear to compare with an earl's son."

Sir John made a clearing noise in his throat. "I would not encourage Lord Harold. All flash, I fear."

Frances looked surprised. "Do you think so? He seemed charming to me, though rarely serious."

There never before having been matrimonial considerations for her, Laurel listened eagerly. Her nature was romantical, even if she did not realize it, and the attention of her father and aunts to practical matters was rather like a dousing of chill water. Always there had been the necessity of balancing cost with need with usefulness with endurance and worth. Papa was frank to his sisters about his funds, which Mirabelle more or less administered, while Frances studied to circumvent them where agreeably possible. Aunt Frances, Laurel thought, would understand her hope for a happy marriage. If such was not her destiny, she would prefer to remain single like her aunts, who did not seem *un*happy, filling their lives with various small activities.

No gentleman quite so handsome and extroverted as Lord Harold Guinn had crossed her path before now. He paid

her a good deal of flattering attention (not neglecting to
cozen her aunts), and what damsel could resist that?

As for the Unknown, her aunts were inclined to indulge
him as a helpless male. It was Papa who seemed to find
something in him—a meeting of minds?—to appreciate.
Clearly he did not value Lord Harold as highly as did the
aunts.

So few marriageable gentlemen had come her way—
none, in fact, except Mr. Appleton, Mr. Hanger, and Dr.
Dodd, whom Papa had called "beaux," scandalizing the
aunts thereby. She thought dreamily of a dance partner at
Wells who would be as stylish as Lord Harold, as appealing
as her patient, as tender as Mr. Appleton, as generous as
Mr. Hanger, as canny as Dr. Dodd, and of course as loving
as Papa. Impossible!

Mr. Appleton was urged to stay for dinner, which he usually did when he had his regular weekend in Bayley Dell.
Looking a bit shamefaced, he declined, but was easily over-
borne by Frances, who said, "Now what concoction will
your verger have made?"

"He always allows for me," Mr. Appleton said feebly.

"Yes," agreed Frances, "I believe he is faithful, but you
will enjoy dinner more with us. Certainly you will stay."
She rang for Fane and told him to add another place for
the vicar. "Cook will be pleased," she said.

This was very likely true, as Cook was one of the vicar's
admirers, though what it mattered in this case was not clear.
Mirabelle was nodding in agreement, and it was the ladies'
privilege to order a hundred extra places if they chose.

The Elands kept country hours. They dined early, unless
the occasion was formal, which it seldom was, there being
few neighboring families for social exchange. Some they
had known in palmier days, but as Sir John no longer kept
a carriage, they visited less and had less reason to invite
guests. They felt comfortable with Mr. Appleton, as did he
with them.

Sunday morning, Bayley Dell was invigorated by the arrival at Church Service of Lord Harold Guinn, complete to a shade in magnificent wine-brown coat and artfully constructed waterfall of white cravat. Mr. Hanger greeted him affably and offered to share his pew, but already Miss Frances Eland had seen and beckoned him into the Eland stall, where Miss Mirabelle Eland greeted him warmly and Miss Laurel welcomed him with a slight blush.

This was more exciting to Bayley Dell than a visit from the Archbishop of Canterbury. And, though Mr. Appleton was at his most dramatic best, it was unlikely that a single member of the congregation associated himself with the Prodigal Son—certainly Lord Harry, whose pockets were woefully light, did not. For a moment he did wonder how his father would receive *him* before quarter day, but he was really more concerned with an impression that he might be making upon Gordon's "angel." As the Elands and his lordship were seated well forward in the nave, almost under Mr. Appleton's nose, the villagers saw little of this dazzling gentleman except his golden head and a few inches of his Weston coat. He sustained no back wounds from the boring of their eyes.

A few of the choirboys, it was true, forgot to sing from time to time, but generally the music came across sweetly, so that Miss Eland was kept nodding in approval of her pupils, and parents were so puffed with pride that they sang lustily (if less harmoniously) when their turn came for hymns.

When the service had ended the congregation remained waiting for the gentry to exit first. Sir John led off smiling, with Miss Eland on his arm; Miss Frances and Laurel followed, conscious of Lord Harry at their heels. Almost a *sigh* swept across the little church as the Elands and their guest reached Mr. Appleton on the porch. Then villagers spilled into the aisle, flowing out, hoping (some) to be presented to his lordship and (others) to have a better view of Eminence.

Both Mr. Appleton and Sir John were soon busy presenting to his lordship such as should be introduced, which meant each respectable man and his wife. Lord Harold appeared to enjoy the whole business, having grown up near a small village himself, and knowing the worth of solid yeomen. Lesser persons merely nodded and smiled self-consciously as they passed; upon them Lord Harold bestowed a nod in return. He found the whole process wonderfully soothing to the penury in which his father saw fit to keep a feckless heir.

It was Mr. Appleton's habit to ride on to Hammish and have a late meal there, so they bid him good-day. Lord Harold was not invited to share the Elands' Sunday dinner, which was always served late so that the servants also had time to attend Church.

Laurel wondered if her patient could be a Prodigal Son but did not ask, preferring not to know. She and her father followed the aunts up the gentle slope to their home.

Miss Mirabelle turned her head to say, "I believe Spring is truly on its way."

"Inevitable, thank God," replied her brother. "Flowers after hoarfrost, sunshine after rain. Much as I try, I cannot be thankful for winter."

Even Mirabelle, evidently, did not expect that of him, for she made no reply. The Misses Onslow waved from their bow window as the Elands turned onto their own stoop.

It was nearer three than two when Miss Frances and her niece walked down to the inn and sent Del upstairs to see if the Unknown would receive them.

He was just waking after a rest, Del reported, and would receive them in five minutes, so they went in the vacant parlor and almost immediately were joined by Mr. Hanger, who snatched off his hat and informed them—as they already knew—that it was Spring at last.

"Always makes me think of public days," said Miss Frances nostalgically.

Mr. Hanger asked, "What are they?"

Sorry she had raised a matter that might offend her brother's benefactor, she explained, "Oh—days when Father opened the manor to the neighborhood—games and things."

"Often?"

"Once a year. He received the villagers and provided simple prizes for competitions. Old and young, you understand"

"Not exactly. I'm London born and reared, you know," he said, "and haven't experienced much in the way of play. Sort of a fête, do you mean?"

"Yes." She turned to Laurel. "It has been a long time, hasn't it, Laurel?"

"Years," agreed Laurel. "I was a small child at the last public day. What I especially remember are the cream buns at the tea tent."

Mr. Hanger pursed his mouth ruefully. "Cream buns! Makes me hungry to think of them."

Blunk came down then to say the gentleman was ready to see them, and the three of them went up to Patten's best chamber, where they found their quarry lying on his bed, fully awake but wan.

"You've overdone!" cried Laurel at once.

"Feel a perfect fool," he admitted. "Blunk told me I wasn't ready for sitting in parlors."

"Did you sleep last night?" asked Miss Frances. "Too overtired to rest, I wager. Why did you not take laudanum?"

"Because I have had enough of dependency! Mrs. Patten cleverly sent me a fine, hearty breakfast of rare steak. Then I had a nap, so I am spoiling for action, as you can plainly see." He motioned with his unbraced arm to his prone position on the bed.

Mr. Hanger chuckled. "What I can see is that Miss Laurel could finish you off with one finger. Well, I won't linger.

You will enjoy the ladies' company more than mine. Blunk, I am going to send another man down to relieve you before *you* develop a pallor yourself. Can't nurse day and night!"

"Oh, no need, sir! I want the whole credit for mending the gentleman," the servant hastened to say with a glance at the bed. It was obvious to Laurel that he admired his patient, which told a lot about that gentleman's nature. Even dear Papa, in the rare times he fell truly sick, became perfectly irascible.

Mr. Hanger trod across the room to feel the patient's forehead and neck. "No fever, missy. I will go along, then, and leave him to you ladies and Blunk." When he paused near the door to exchange words with Miss Frances the invalid whispered to Laurel:

"I hope for a private word."

Startled, she looked to her aunt, who was bidding Mr. Hanger good-day. Blunk approached them. "If you will be seated, ma'am, I will see about some tea."

The two men could be heard descending the wooden stair.

While Frances settled herself in the armchair and drew out some embroidery, the girl took a chair near the head of the bed and reached for *Waverley,* which lay upon the coverlet.

In admonitory accents she said, "In all the times I have been here we have not advanced a dozen pages. I cannot think you want to hear this book."

"But I do!" he declared fervently. "Dr. Dodd has *prescribed* it as necessary to my cure."

Frances, who may have had her own reasons for encouraging the visits, said, "It will shorten the days for one confined to bed. Pray read, Laurel."

She spread open the volume, chose a sentence at random, and willfully read alternate words. Neither hearer seemed to notice or care. It was obvious their minds were on other matters, as was her own. She continued reading in a normal fashion until Blunk reappeared.

"Beg pardon, sir," he said. "Mrs. Patten has a problem in the kitchen and wonders if Miss Frances can advise her."

Surprised, Frances said, "Well, I do not know, but I am willing to try. Will you take my place, please, Blunk?"

It was galling to Laurel that she and the invalid had to be watched like criminals, yet Blunk and the man on the bed seemed to accept the question as routine.

"Certainly, miss. Del will bring up the tea shortly and I will see to it," Blunk said.

When she had gone down the steps, Blunk, with impassive face, went quietly onto the landing, leaving the door wide open.

Alert and curious, Laurel looked to her patient.

He reached boldly for her fingers, and holding one hand firmly (as once before), he so distracted her that she let Mr. Scott drop on his head on the carpet with a faint thump.

"May I speak in confidence?" he asked softly.

She nodded, and this time did not snatch back her tingling hand, since there was no one to see.

"My name is Rand—that is, Gordon Rand, younger son of Viscount Leadenhall. Sorry, m'dear. Wish I could claim a title! By bad luck, Lord Harry landed here. He knows me, but I have stopped his mouth with a gold clamp."

She asked, "Do you mean money?"

"Aye. It's the only thing that interests him. I was on my way to a houseparty at his home on the other side of Wells when I was attacked. Unless I miss my guess, my groom and valet await me there, for that is where I sent them in my curricle. This subterfuge began when I was injured and confused. It continued. because I wished to avoid—er— things, and then because I needed an excuse to . . . stay."

Not failing to understand the meaning of his words and intent look, she colored and lowered her eyes. This was flirting of a sort to make her breathless. How much should she believe? How much assume?

"Are you truly ill—weak?"

"Oh, my arm is broken sure enough, and my knee painful. Yes, I'm damnably weak, just when I want to . . . If I send word to Father, he will come with all speed and carry me off, which is not what I wish, you understand."

Laurel was not sure what *she* wished, but she did not think she wished him to go anywhere before they became better acquainted. He was comely and—well, interesting. Not dashing and colorful like Sir Harry, yet somehow more believable, if he would just explain what things he was so anxious to avoid.

"Is this visit to Wells very important to you?" he asked. "It is to be a *debut,* isn't it?"

"Only in a small way."

"Why not London?"

She hesitated, but since he was being frank with her she owed him an honest answer. "London would be too costly."

"You have the beauty to make a sensation there."

"Oh, no. Thank you, but I can see what is in my own mirror."

"What is in the mirror is Miss Eland in *reverse.* Even flat in a bed of pain I can see the real young lady," he insisted, laughing as he spoke. "You can count on me to be an expert. Haven't I been assessing social buds for six or seven seasons?"

"Your mind is addled," Laurel said.

"Certainly not. It is the only part of me in good condition. Do you not think you would enjoy balls and routs and dinners and promenades in Hyde Park?"

"Yes—no—well, a little perhaps, and then I would think of the cost to poor Papa." She tried to draw away her hand, but his grip was as firm as the gold clamp on Lord Harry's tongue. "Besides," she continued a bit hurriedly, "the luxury and—and sophistication of the other young ladies would put me in the shade. I would be thought a hopeless quiz."

He regarded her seriously. "If you mean fresh and sweet, the jaded beaux would recognize that. In fact, perhaps I should not encourage a visit to London. You might be spoiled by attention from the dandies. Even worse, snapped up by some wealthy peer wanting to add you to his collection."

She sat back, tossing her head. "I? Care about *money* for which I have never given a thought?"

"Never?"

"Well, almost never . . . only in concern for what Papa has missed that should have been his. For what my uncle threw away recklessly in roistering about Newmarket, Epsom Downs, and this *London* that you harp on. I enjoy such things? Never!"

Gordon laughed more lightheartedly than she had yet heard.

"You almost convince me."

Subsiding, she asked more tamely, "Have I described your circuit of amusement?"

"Somewhat. But I am not chained to it. I've sampled Wells, you know. There are good people there."

"The Guinns?"

"Yes, but they prefer the attractions of the capital. You will have a true welcome from Mrs. Walden and will like the assembly. I wish I could be there to watch, if not dance. You should wear green."

"But I plan to do so!" she exclaimed. "Did you know?"

He shook his head gently, so as not to aggravate his bruised jaw. "I think it would be the perfect color for you."

On the landing Blunk coughed, and steps sounded. It was Del coming with the tea tray, not Frances. Blunk came in to shift the small table near the bedside and was beginning to pour out strong, steaming tea when Frances returned.

"Mrs. Patten was making a special sauce that tasted delicious—yes, she gave me a spoonful—but simply would not thicken. We could not imagine what caused the problem, so we decided to let it cool and see if that made a difference. Then we fell to talking, Laurel. I hope you did not mind. Did you read much?"

Amusing herself, Laurel evaded skillfully. "Not as much as I had expected. This book does not *move* enough to entertain an invalid. I must have a look over Papa's shelves to see if there is something better."

"Oh, anything will do," said the invalid to the ceiling.

"We do not want you bored," Frances assured him.

He said lovely ladies could never bore him. "My good Blunk"—here a smile to his borrowed attendant—"is always saying yes sir, you mustn't overdo, sir, be quiet, sir, it's for your own good, sir. What I need is stimulation!"

"Well, what Mrs. Patten is preparing should provide that," Frances told him firmly. "If you are restless, I believe you are recovering."

"Aye. But not fast enough to dance with Miss Laurel at Wells on Friday!"

Twelve

By Tuesday the ball gown was finished and waiting.

Another lack confronted the Eland ladies: personal maid or maids for ladies staying overnight at Wells. Laurel was so accustomed to dressing herself with a little help with back buttons from an aunt or the maid-of-all-work that she had not thought how demeaning her aunts would find it to travel without a proper abigail.

"What will Mrs. Walden think of us?" lamented Frances when the subject arose.

This was not discussed in the presence of Sir John, who might find it another cause for mortification. Mirabelle looked unhappy, yet said resolutely, "We will take Daisy. She can wear her black church frock and ride on the box with the coachman. Yes, I know she is not a proper lady's maid, but if we strictly forbid her to say 'gor' and 'wot say' and such, she will serve to lend us a little dignity and may be useful. I have told my friend why Laurel has not had a London season. She knows we live simply."

"That is true," Frances admitted. "Though it is never advisable to tell all one's business, telling what is untrue would entangle one in risky contradictions. You did right. Her invitation to stay overnight was freely extended. I noticed John did not hesitate to accept."

Daisy, when informed that she would wear her best dress and hand-me-down pelisse to ride on Mr. Hanger's splendid chaise beside Mr. Hanger's fine, teasing coachman, cried,

"Lawks!" and brought the wrath of both aunts upon he head.

Laughing until she had tears in her eyes, Laurel decide her journey into Society would have more than one inte esting aspect.

By the next day, Wednesday, all village seamstresses re ported Mr. Appleton's curtains finished, and Miss Mirabell set Thursday morning for the hanging of them, commandin McComb to be ready with a ladder at ten. By some mys terious rural communication system that did not involv post or herald, word reached Mr. Appleton, and he made special trip from Mendle to find not only new curtains bu a bevy of women cluttering his cottage, with McComb look ing harassed atop the ladder.

The Eland ladies were there, plus all who had worked upo the curtains, except Mrs. Mince, who could not leave he shop. They seemed somewhat embarrassed to be caught i good works. He, of course, had made the trip for the purpos of "catching" them and expressing his thanks. The parish ioners of all his three small churches were in the habit o doing this or that for Mr. Appleton, but seldom did he hav a chance to thank them as his heart compelled him to do.

He thanked and admired, calling each woman by name while McComb waited on his perch.

"And so many pairs to be hung!" he said. "Where woul we be without McComb?"

McComb said "Ar-r-r" and handed down the last rod.

"Look, Mr. Appleton," exclaimed Miss Mirabelle. "Lau rel had the happy idea of making covers for these two cush ions. They are removable for washing. See, she has cleverl hidden plackets in the seams!"

The vicar, who knew nothing about plackets, admire Laurel's handiwork. "And you, dear Miss Eland, I thank fo attention to my needs and for planning all this! McComb have we hot water to give the ladies tea?"

But the women murmured self-consciously that they wer

wanted at home and took their leave. While Frances saw to the hanging of the last curtain, Mirabelle went around checking windows and smoothing folds. When that was done the Eland ladies set out for home to make final preparations for their small journey the next day. The grateful vicar mounted his horse and rode back to Mendle in a thoughtful mood.

Wells was to be such a short visit that there was not a great deal to pack. One portmanteau for the ball dresses in tissue would be enough, with three bandboxes for personal items. Fane would pack for Sir John.

"Will you go with me to the inn after lunch, Papa?" asked Laurel. "It seems unkind to ignore our patient just because we are excited about our own interests. Actually, he seems to care nothing about *Waverley* and would probably prefer to talk with you."

"But I am not as ornamental as you," he replied with a glimmer in his eye. "We will go together. Two o'clock?"

It was agreed. Laurel went up to her chamber to prepare her bandbox; brush and comb would have to wait until departure on Friday.

Aunt Mirabelle was dithering about, giving Cook orders for twenty-four hours as if Cook had not managed for as many years and more. Fane wore a long face, being sure Sir John could not don formal dress without him.

"I hope, sir, there will be a well-trained footman in Mrs. Walden's establishment," he intoned pessimistically.

Sir John assured him, "There is certain to be, as Mrs. Walden lives in some elegance, which you can judge from her smart carriage and attendants."

According to plan, father and daughter went down at two to see the Unknown. He had remained in his room this day, and although they several times asked if he was suffering, he denied anything more than "some aches." They thought he looked pale, they said afterwards to each other, and . . . disgruntled? It was not a pleasant visit for Laurel and put a sort of blight on her enthusiasm for the adventure to come, so she excused him to herself by assigning him a slight setback.

"I wish you a happy evening at Wells," he said when they rose to leave the chamber. "Also many new gentlemen acquaintances—but no *particular* one." No smile accompanied the wish, and Laurel felt indignantly that it was about as helpful as no wish at all. She frowned at him and said, "Thank you, I think."

Sir John snapped a sharp look at her, but added only, "We shall expect to see improvement in you when we return. It will be at least forty-eight hours."

"How can I sleep forty-eight hours?" the young man demanded.

"Try rum," advised Sir John, which surprised himself as much as it did his hearers.

After lunch on Friday Mr. Hanger sent them off in fine style with two outriders in dark green livery to match the coachman. At daybreak there had been scattered light clouds and a weak sun; however, by trip time the clouds had dissipated and the sun was high and warm. So new was foliage in the woods that the stretch where Laurel's Unknown had been attacked did not seem threatening at all. The lane was dappled with light, the woodland quite delightful in shades of green and bronze.

Mr. Hanger's coachman made friendly conversation with Daisy, who (mindful of the aunts' strictures) managed very well by holding tightly to a low side bracket of the box and answering carefully with "La!" and "Well, I nivver!" They went on agreeably this way until they reached the Wells pike. With a better road before him, the coachman set his horses at a faster pace, which meant closer attention to them was needed. Light talk ended, although he cast Daisy an encouraging smile now and then, seeing that she was both frightened and exhilarated.

Inside the carriage, Sir John and Laurel rode on the backward-facing bench out of consideration of the aunts' delicate stomachs. He soon fell asleep, while the ladies chatted idly. With the increase of speed at the pike, talk ceased; the aunts dug in their reticules for vinaigrettes but remained healthy. Laurel continued to enjoy a backwards sort of view, so to speak. When they neared the city she was obliged to twist around to have a view of the great towers belonging to the Gothic cathedral of St. Andrew.

At the slowing of the coach for noisy city traffic Sir John awoke and observed that they had had a quick, comfortable journey. His sisters did not reply, though Laurel saw them put away their smelling bottles.

She said, "Papa, what is this water flow along the street?"

"High Street, m'dear. The water comes from St. Andrew's Well, as it has since the fifteenth century."

Presently, the carriage and outriders took a side turning where they saw narrow, well-kept houses, of which one proved to be Mrs. Walden's. It was four stories tall, severely plain yet well proportioned, set flush to a walkway, with several steps up to a slate-colored door.

One groom had tossed his reins to his partner and was dismounting to knock when the door opened and a tall, dignified butler emerged, accompanied by a young footman with an expression so nearly like his superior's as to make Laurel think he was endeavoring to duplicate him.

While Mrs. Walden's servants hurried to open the carriage door and assist the occupants to descend, Mr. Hanger's groom lifted down a breathless Daisy.

"There ye be, girlie," said the coachman from his elevated seat. "We'll pick ye up agin tomorra."

The butler turned his head to ask if Mrs. Walden could

provide stabling, but the coachman said, "Nay. We've orders to rack up at Swan 'Otel."

Leaving footman and groom to deal with the luggage, Mrs. Walden's butler conducted the guests into the house via a small entrance hall to a red-flocked stair hall. Their hostess emerged from a paneled library to the left, welcoming them with every evidence of delight, seeing that a maid took their wraps and leading them up a flight to her drawing room.

This was a charming apartment having walls and draperies of light peach with white woodwork and delicate moldings of white upon the ceiling. Tea was already set out, waiting for them, so Mrs. Walden settled them about the low table and began to pour aromatic cups, all the time saying how she had looked forward to their coming. She was wearing an afternoon gown the same color as the room, though deeper in hue. Her hair was drawn back softly to fall in studied casualness to one shoulder; as Sir John had been so unwise as to mention after her visit to Bayley Dell, she did indeed look younger than her friend Mirabelle.

Perhaps Mrs. Walden was not truly beautiful, yet her eyes were lively, her complexion perfect with the merest blush of pink on her cheeks (whether due to Nature or artful cosmetics), and her manner open and genuinely friendly. Evidently Sir John found her as delightful as did his ladies, for he was unusually lively himself, admiring her home and saying he looked forward to the evening's festivities "if your footman can assist me with my cravat."

She laughed delightedly at this wit, and then promised help was available.

"I have invited several people to dinner, as it will be more comfortable for Miss Laurel to recognize a few faces at the assembly."

Laurel murmured polite thanks.

"Yes. Well. Let me tell you about them," Mrs. Walden continued with a smile. "First, there are Mr. and Mrs. Hugh

Cottingham—he has been in foreign service and they have traveled widely and speak several languages."

"English, I hope. Ha-ha!" said Sir John. His sisters looked at him in some surprise.

"Exquisitely," replied Mrs. Walden with a smile. "With them will be their son, Albert, whom they are anxious to see established in a suitable marriage. Money is not an object with them. Now, do not be alarmed, Miss Laurel. No one is pushing him on you. I thought you would be glad of an acquaintance who is of your own generation. Besides, he is a very pleasant young gentleman, only very shy."

Laurel said at once, "If he is shy, then I may feel less so."

Nodding, her hostess added to the list of dinner guests: "There will only be ten of us. I have sent a note to Lord Harold Guinn and he has accepted. Number ten is Mr. Kilkirk."

Lord Harold's attendance was not surprising and would mean another familiar face. Mr. Kilkirk was unidentified.

The aunts exchanged looks, assuming this unknown gentleman to be Mrs. Walden's particular gallant, while Sir John remained cheerfully unaware of titillating nuances.

"The assembly is, of course, a public one, my dear," said Mrs. Walden. "There will be mushrooms present, but I will see that only ladies and gentlemen are presented to you."

"Laurel will be guided by you," said Miss Frances firmly.

"I am grateful for your aid, Mrs. Walden," Laurel added quickly.

Mrs. Walden nodded. "Yes, and I daresay Lord Harry and young Mr. Cottingham will be besieged by gentlemen wishing to be presented to so pretty a lady. You may trust their judgment, my dear."

After sipping tea and exchanging polite conversation for a while, the elder Eland ladies suggested they would like to rest before dinner, and Laurel, who was never more wide awake, knew she must withdraw when they did.

Their hostess rang for her butler to show them to their rooms.

"Do you wish to rest also, Sir John?"

But Sir John, who always enjoyed naps and who knew the evening was going to be a long one, contrarily replied that what he would truly like was to visit the library that he had glimpsed when they entered the house.

While the ladies went off up a flight behind Mrs. Walden's grand and intimidating butler, she led Sir John to the lower floor. The collection here was not nearly so large as at Bayley Manor, yet certainly more than Sir John kept in his house in Bayley Dell.

"Did your husband choose all these?"

"The shelves between the windows are his. The rest I have bought." She peeped to see if he were disapproving, but he appeared interested, so she continued: "Books are my secret consolation. The ones on the upper shelves I have bought at estate sales—and have read few. The lower shelves, easier for me to reach, are my favorites: novels— yes, *novels*—poetry, English shires and historic homes, even gardening, although I have no garden here, only a terrace behind the dining salon."

"Have you read *Waverley?*" he asked.

"Oh, yes," she replied, seeing she was not lowering herself in his eyes. "I do admire Mr. Scott."

Other than his daughter, Sir John knew no female who seriously enjoyed reading. In fact, he realized that to say a lady was "bookish" was to damn her to most men. Yet here was this charming Mrs. Walden, so lively, so socially minded, and confessing to be a—Blue Stocking! He was scandalized and intrigued.

"May I examine your choices?" he asked

Mrs. Walden replied that of course he might. "I will leave you to it. The other guests are invited for seven, so pray allow time for dressing."

"Half an hour will be enough for me," he assured her.

"Not a dandy, then, sir? Splendid. The clock on the mantel is reliable. Ring for help if your cravat misbehaves. I will send someone to replenish the fire."

With a swirl of skirts she was gone, and Sir John hardly noticed a footman's business at the grate as he was so intent on Mrs. Walden's personal selections. Very respectable. Very respectable indeed.

Meanwhile, Frances and Mirabelle were examining their connecting rooms.

"All very refined," commented Frances, admiring a pretty bed with a half-canopy.

"Money," said Mirabelle succinctly. Laurel was across the hall and could not hear. "Reeks of money . . . although I never heard Mr. Walden left Sarah *rich*. But of course a lady can live higher for less in a small city like Wells than in London, and you know Sarah said she cares nothing for that place."

"Has she no family?"

"A brother in Hampshire, I believe, and another out in India."

Frances said, "Ah! Perhaps *he* has made a fortune out there and is able to provide elegancies for his sister."

"Perhaps. We cannot accuse her of distasteful *display*."

"No, indeed. A lady to her fingertips."

"Who does not spurn us."

Frances pointed out, "Her kindness to us is a compliment to *you*, sister."

When the Elands went down a few minutes before seven all four looked as handsome and as splendid as was possible with no money and a great deal of ingenuity. Sir John's blacks, after a good brushing and damp-pressing by Fane, did not seem at all rusty, and Frances's diamond earrings and Mirabelle's pearls drew attention to their smiling faces. Their chief concern was Laurel, the focus of their existence. Everything visible about her was delightfully new, except her face (which they might be pardoned for thinking beautiful) and her gloves.

Almost at once the Cottinghams were announced, a cordial, middle-aged couple with easy manners and no pretension to style; their son, who followed, Laurel eyed with interest. He was medium-tall and undistinguished in dress and features, but he had a very amiable expression. No pink of the pinks, she thought, but undoubtedly good-tempered. He was p-pleased to meet Miss E-Eland. Poor fellow!

Lord Harry was next, at his most splendid, and as perfectly at ease as Albert Cottingham was not.

Last to arrive was the mysterious Mr. Kilkirk, a gentleman somewhere between thirty-five and forty-five years of age, tall, complete to a shade, with heavy dark brows and eyes that saw a lot and revealed nothing. Mrs. Walden received him with a calm approval in which Frances and Mirabelle could read nothing. To *them* he was punctiliously polite.

The elder Cottinghams seemed to know him, and Lord Harry said: "Ho, Kilkirk, back from Paris?"

"As you see," the gentleman replied.

"Never say it was boring."

Mr. Kilkirk said lazily, "I would never say that."

At dinner they were seated at an oval table with great silver candlesticks and an artful centerpiece of laurel leaves. Was this some sort of play on words? None of the strangers would guess, since the young lady had been introduced as "Miss Eland." The napery was handsomely embroidered; the crystal sparkled. Mr. Albert Cottingham, at Laurel's right, had nothing to say.

She cast her eyes around Mrs. Walden's dining room to find inspiration for something to discuss. The walls were hung with Chinese paper which, though exquisite, hardly seemed a topic to interest an unsophisticated gentleman, so at last she said in a mildly inquisitive tone, "Do you enjoy dancing?" They were, after all, to attend a ball.

To her surprise, he turned to her with a shy smile and said with hardly a trace of stutter, "Oh, yes! Especially waltzes. M-may I have your first waltz, Miss Eland?"

It was her turn to be shy. "I am afraid I have never learned it."

Apparently this pleased him, for he immediately asked if he might have the pleasure of teaching her.

"At the assembly?" she cried. "I would be mortified, falling all over your feet in front of everyone."

"Well, I t-trip over my tongue, don't I?"

Liking him better by the minute, she pursed her lips and tossed her head.

"I learned when Father was stationed in Vienna. It is really quite simple. I would be pleased to teach you," he urged.

"Oh, no, I could not let you. My aunts would be shocked to see me bumbling about the dance floor." He looked truly disappointed, so she suggested hurriedly: "I have an idea. Suppose I promise to sit and watch you perform with another young lady. I would learn a great deal more by watching the dance done correctly."

This was a new idea, and not unwelcome to Albert. To be *watched* by a charming young lady was almost as delightful as dancing with her. "Will you dance another dance with me?" he asked craftily.

Laurel laughed and declared she wished to do so.

It then appeared time to change partners for dinner talk. She turned to Mr. Kilkirk on her left, perfectly tongue-tied by his suavity, and thankful to have a new friend to the right.

Mr. Kilkirk, she suspected, knew all about the blunders of which newly presented debutantes were capable. Let him start the conversation if he dared!

"You do not resemble your father or your aunts, Miss Eland," he remarked unexpectedly.

"I am said to take after my mother, sir," she replied.

"Ah, yes. I believe I can see it. She was a lovely creature."

"You knew her?"

He inclined his head. "I watched her from afar. Being several years younger, you understand."

In this exchange he had not smiled once. Perhaps he was bored, annoyed to be set so far from his hostess, but Papa and Lord Harry, both of whom outranked him, were properly placed on either side of Mrs. Walden at the far end of the table.

"Are you a resident of Wells?" she asked, seeking to find a new subject.

"Now," he replied.

Impossible! she thought. If he was Mrs. Walden's Current Interest, she would be disappointed in Mrs. Walden. Surely her hostess could not be serious about such a *stick*. Was he ever animated about anything? Had he no sense of humor? She hoped he would not ask her to dance.

"Will you save the second dance for me, Miss Eland?" he asked suddenly.

She wanted to stamp a foot and declare, "Certainly not," but Aunt Frances was looking her way. She was obliged to mumble a polite lie that she would be "pleased."

To her astonishment, he turned then to Mrs. Cottingham on his left, smiled beatifically, and said she was "blooming as always."

"Blandishments!" asserted Mrs. Cottingham fondly.

Like Daisy, Laurel thought, "Well, I nivver!"

Thirteen

Laurel had no memories of a ball at Bayley Manor, for she had been a small child when the last one occurred there. She did have some hazy recollection of what seemed to her an immense room, gloomy because of drawn draperies, with strange globes, which were chandeliers swathed in muslin. By comparison, the assembly room to which Mrs. Walden took them was modest in size, yet she could see it would accommodate thirty couples. The draperies were somewhat faded, offset by the warm glow of many candles. Around the walls were gold chairs, a bit worn, but still adding a festive air. The room was a long, fairly narrow one with wide double doors, at the far end, to a refreshment room.

Mrs. Walden led the Elands to seats midway down the room, across from the orchestra. "I like to sit here where I can watch left, right, and center with equal ease. Take the chair next to me, Miss Laurel, so I can present gentlemen to you as need be." Miss Mirabelle chose the seat at her friend's left, Miss Frances took the next, and Sir John sat at the end of their group. They saw the Cottinghams enter and take seats nearby as Albert strolled over to join some young gentlemen of his acquaintance. A number of bedecked young ladies chatted animatedly in small groups like clusters of blossoms while eyeing prospective partners covertly.

The musicians were just tuning up when a gentleman in knee breeches, a long-tail coat, and a white neckcloth (quite as elegant as Lord Harry's) bowed before Laurel and asked the honor of her first dance. Considerably surprised and taken aback, she rose to her feet with a questioning glance at Mrs. Walden.

"Good evening, Mr. Hanger," said that lady cordially. "How comfortable it will be for Miss Laurel to begin with an old friend."

"My pleasure," he replied, beaming. "Couldn't miss it! Good evening, ma'am—and Miss Eland, Miss Frances, Sir John. Might not have a chance later when missy has been seen by all the bucks."

Thankful to turn her back to her family as she walked out onto the dance floor with Mr. Hanger, Laurel wondered if her cheeks were red.

The first dance was a minuet, through which he guided her firmly. Was there anything that Mr. Hanger could not do? Though he lacked some of the flourish of the younger men, he never made an error of step or timing, and like many large men he was smooth on his feet. She had every reason to be grateful for a good beginning of her simple debut.

She had a glimpse of Albert Cottingham farther along the room with a brunette who seemed to be talking constantly. Another lady appeared to be exceedingly pleased with Lord Harry as a partner. Laurel was too anxious about her own performance to notice much, except once, when she was facing the long wall of chairs, she saw Mr. Kilkirk talking with her papa. Waiting, she feared, for the second dance with her.

"Having a happy time, lass?" asked Mr. Hanger, with obvious interest in her feelings.

Her blush had subsided. She smiled up at him and said, "Oh, yes," so fervently that he was sure to be gratified for his effort (and his valet's) to bring himself there, when balls were not his favored form of relaxation.

On the sidelines talk had dwindled as the elder Elands watched their darling dance with Mr. Hanger. All seemed to be going well. Frances, in particular, was relieved to find that Mr. Hanger could be at home in a ballroom.

When the music ceased he escorted Laurel to her family, and as her seat had been taken by an elderly lady, they stood talking about inconsequential things like the polish on the floor and the quaver of the first violin, until Mr. Kilkirk came forward to be introduced by Mrs. Walden to Mr. Hanger and to lead away Laurel as his partner.

"Who is *that?*" demanded Mr. Hanger abruptly.

Mrs. Walden laughed lightly. "Stephen Kilkirk. An aide to the Bishop."

Mr. Hanger looked surprised. "Clergyman? Dancing?"

"No and yes," replied the lady. "A very astute gentleman. He handles—er—business for the Bishop. Actually, I cannot say exactly what he does. Whatever it is involves a lot of travel in Europe. He speaks nearly as many languages as the Cottinghams, whom you have not met yet."

"But does he realize our Laurel is not a—not a hanger-on at courts? Will he keep the l—"

Mrs. Walden, understanding what he was about to say, rapped him with her fan. "Yes, yes! Of course he will."

Miss Mirabelle and Miss Frances heard this exchange with some mystification. She explained to them, "Mr. Hanger supposes Mr. Kilkirk might be too sophisticated for Miss Laurel, but he is not. Otherwise I would not have included him in my dinner group."

After the dance, during which Mr. Kilkirk acquitted himself well and said little in any language, Laurel returned to her hostess, thankful to be done with such an odd-humored gentleman and to find two unalarming others waiting to make her acquaintance. Mrs. Walden introduced them as Mr. Smythe and Mr. Woodcock, both of whom begged for the next dance.

Albert Cottingham came up then to say the next dance was to be a waltz and she had promised to *watch*. As neither newcomer would yield place to the other, they carried her off down the room, where the three could sit together to watch Mr. Cottingham perform. His ease and his grace were astonishing after his awkwardness in Mrs. Walden's drawing room. They saw Lord Harry circling grandly with an incredibly beautiful golden-blonde lady, but Laurel thought she preferred Albert's fluid restraint.

When the music had ended Lord Harry delivered his partner to a merry group near the refreshment room and came at once to Laurel, saying, "Who are these dullards, not engaging you to dance?"

Her eyes were dancing, though her feet had not. She replied that she had promised the dance to Mr. Cottingham.

"Then why did I see him with the Colby chit?"

"Because I had promised to *watch,* my lord."

"Eh? Well. Your next dance is with me." He seized her hand and drew her from her chair. "Servant, Smythe. Servant, Woodcock. Come along, Miss Laurel."

Smythe was tall, with a narrow face and brown hair that was thin on his scalp; the other young man, Woodcock, was less tall and had protruding ears and shy blue eyes. As Lord Harold led Laurel away, the dismayed expressions on their faces were curiously alike. She wanted to call back that she would save each a dance, except that would draw attention to herself.

Lord Harry's style was exuberant, as she had noted, yet enjoyable for his partner, who only momentarily faltered when she saw Aunt Frances take the floor with Mr. Hanger. How had he persuaded her to that? Meanwhile, Papa had moved over a seat to be beside Aunt Mirabelle; both were smiling and nodding their heads in time to the music. Farther along, Albert Cottingham stood with Mr. Kilkirk, exchanging random comments, most of which appeared to concern *her,* as they looked her way instead of at each other. The golden-blonde also watched from her coterie near the refreshment room; she was wearing a gold silk gown that few blondes would have dared to don.

"Who is the lovely lady with whom I saw you dancing just now?" she asked his lordship.

"My sister. Lady Pamela," he replied. "Stunning, ain't she?" He did not suggest introducing her to the lady, and Laurel felt the sting of what seemed to her to be a set-down. He might amuse himself with a *rustic* but not classify her with the dashing group of Lady Pamela and her friends. Some of the glow went out of the evening, until a movement of the dance swung her to see Mrs. Walden flash her an approving smile.

If Lord Harold Guinn had some notion of amusing himself by spicing the evening for a provincial, she would make the most of it! Swaying gracefully with the music, she whirled and swooped, setting the surf of her flounce awash upon the beach of this assembly room. The effect was as beautiful and dramatic as Mr. Finkleshaff had supposed.

Although she was breathless at the dance's end, Albert Cottingham came out on the floor to claim her, so she had no opportunity to rest or meet the gentleman waiting beside Mrs. Walden to be presented to her. That gentleman, she saw, politely extended his hand to Mrs. Walden to dance, intending, it seemed, to bring her into the same set as Laurel's, but it was filled before they could reach her, and so Laurel did not at that time meet him. There were just a few moments for Albert to introduce the other members of their set. As they took their places, she saw Mr. Kilkirk lead out Aunt Mirabelle, and Papa move over beside his hostess, the stranger drifting away.

The sets being full, Sir John and Mrs. Walden remained seated, chatting twenty to the dozen.

"Well, sir, are you pleased with your daughter's success? And not surprised, either, I warrant!"

"Yes, I am pleased . . . though it makes me feel a million years old."

She slanted him a glance. "Perhaps that is why you delayed making some push to see her established."

This was speaking plainly! "True, I fear," he confessed ruefully.

"Well, the gentlemen have found her now, and I am certain they will be beating a path to Bayley Dell. Pray give no thought to your own age. Look." She began to tip her fan toward men scattered among the couples on the floor, men who were dancing happily and well, with no absence of vigor though they were obviously as old as, even older than the baronet. "I shall insist you be my partner for the next dance!"

This was even more outspoken, although Sir John felt flattered instead of shocked by her taking the lead. Without being beautiful, Mrs. Walden was handsome, having a vitality that was attractive. As if to emphasize this point, three gentleman came along to tease and compliment the widow. *They,* Sir John soon saw, plainly felt her worth their notice, and were readily cordial to him also. He quite forgot daughter and sisters and began to enjoy himself. When the three moved away Mrs. Walden reiterated that he must engage her for the next dance.

"Not a waltz!" he protested in some alarm.

"It will be a country dance, I believe," she answered.

Meanwhile, Laurel, dancing with Albert Cottingham, was unaware that she had misjudged Lord Harry. When their dance had ended he had contrived to finish not far from where his sister stood with her friends, and he had looked over Laurel's head for permission to present her to his sister. Lady Pamela had merely raised her exquisite nose and turned away, none of which Laurel saw—thank fortune—for Albert approached her eagerly at that point.

A moment later the lofty Lady Pamela was whispering with Lord Harry, "Who is the strange girl?"

"Mrs. Walden's guest from Bayley Dell."

"Bayley Dell? No one significant ever came from there."

"She may become your sister-in-law, you must realize."

Her ladyship shot him a startled look, then glanced back

over her shoulder. "Pretty. Might do for you but will never do for Father."

He muttered an oath and swung away from the elite house party group with which his sister had surrounded herself. Unfortunately, what she had said was true.

Albert's smiling lips and admiring eyes were balm to Miss Laurel Eland, who had never, in her life at Bayley Dell, met anything but kindness. Lord Harold had taught her a first lesson of Society and it was not a pleasant one: Rank was All and amiability Nothing. Why had her ladyship brought her friends to a *provincial* ball? Such high collars on the men, such jewels on the ladies! Was there not enough at the earl's estate to amuse them? She thought unhappily that Lord Harry was quite callous, for all his exuberance and suavity.

Mr. Smythe was next to claim a dance.

Farther down the room, Sir John led Mrs. Walden onto the floor. Papa! Dancing! But the music was beginning, and Laurel was obliged to think about her feet. Mr. Smythe was wonderfully tolerant of her uncertainty with the figure, which, indeed, he should be, as he was not so accomplished himself. It was a frolic of a dance and everyone was laughing and making missteps. Now and then Laurel could see Mrs. Walden performing tastefully, while some of the younger ladies were carried away with enthusiasm and overdid their whirls. When the music concluded with a flourish Laurel saw both Papa and Mrs. Walden return flushed and smiling to their chairs.

Mr. Woodcock was awaiting eagerly his turn for a contradanse, after which Lord Harry brought a Mr. Gould and a Mr. Swanson of Lady Pamela's party to introduce to her. They had requested this, but she did not know it, and so was amazed at his lordship's condescension.

Lady Pamela vanished into the refreshment room with the remainder of her party, so she failed to watch the defection of her satellites.

If one is only twenty, one has no difficulty in dancing

two hours without rest. Mrs. Walden, Miss Eland, and Miss Frances, however much they enjoyed the attention of gentlemen, were glad to sit quietly and fan themselves from time to time. They had come for the purpose of chaperoning Laurel; to be invited to the dance floor was an unexpected pleasure.

Mr. Hanger danced graciously with each of them; also with Mrs. Cottingham, Miss Colby—to whom Albert presented him—and a second time (by special permission of Sir John) with Laurel. Unmistakably, he was happily occupied with terpsichore this evening.

The guests with the Earl of Clifton's daughter departed early with her, and none of the party were missed.

When the last piece was played, the last note had sounded, and the last step been executed, a babble of voices broke out, as onlookers surged from the walls to mingle with dancers in a crush at cloak rooms. Laurel felt it had been a glorious evening, not realizing it was only a small imitation of a London ball. To make matters even finer, several gentlemen followed her to see her bestowed safely in the carriage with her family. She could still feel the music in her feet as they rode the short distance to Mrs. Walden's house, where hot chocolate awaited them in the drawing room.

"I can see my daughter is in alt," said Sir John, accepting a cup from his hostess. He was remarkably wide awake himself, although it had been nearly seven hours since his last nap.

"Did any gentlemen appeal to you, Miss Laurel? What about Mr. Kilkirk?" asked Mrs. Walden.

She was no expert at subterfuge and struggled with words to be both polite and truthful. "Very—elegant. He alarmed me a little."

"Alarmed!" Mrs. Walden tittered. "Kilkirk is a perfect lamb."

"But he looked at me so—so forbiddingly," Laurel objected.

Tolerantly, Mrs. Walden explained, "It is those dark brows that misled you, I suppose. He is really very shy, which is why I invited him with a small group."

Laurel echoed, "Shy?" doubtfully. "But for a gentleman who travels internationally on business—how can he be?"

Mrs. Walden declared that was another matter. "It is young ladies that alarm *him*. He is shier than Albert Cottingham! I am very fond of Stephen Kilkirk," she continued. "His mother was my half-sister."

Not a suitor after all.

"Your nephew!" exclaimed Miss Mirabelle and Miss Frances together. They were careful not to look at each other.

"I hope you will let Miss Laurel come to me again," said Mrs. Walden after a sip of chocolate. "The opening of the Season in London will curtail our assemblies—that is, they will be fewer and some families will go up to town. True Wellsians, such as I, don't fall into Dismals. There will continue to be private parties of all sorts. Shall I give one myself? Yes, that is a good idea. You will all be welcome."

Mirabelle and Frances acknowledged this with the vague assent that one gives to nebulous events.

"Sir John, you must not wait for formal invitations. On Sundays and Wednesdays I have informal tea parties for those interested in serious talk, which means mostly gentlemen. Do join us when you choose."

Soon after this the guests said good night and ascended to their rooms, leaving a trail of thanks as they went.

A sleepy Daisy was waiting in Miss Mirabelle's room. By common consent the aunts sent her off to tuck Laurel into bed. Taking advantage of the connecting door between their rooms, they helped each other undress and lay away their finery. It was a wonderful cozy time to compare notes . . . and plot.

"I was pleased with some of the young gentlemen Laurel met, were not you?" began Mirabelle.

"Yes, indeed," agreed her sister. "Of course we do not know much about them, but I am sure none were the mushrooms that Sarah mentioned. Did you notice some crude types—laughing too raucously and flinging themselves about the dance floor?"

"Yes, and some shocking colors on the males."

"And excessively low necklines on the females."

"I had to avert my eyes."

"After the first glimpse."

Mirabelle shook her head condemningly. "At least they kept to themselves. I think Laurel scarcely had time to notice them."

When each had got into her nightdress and a shawl they settled before the grate in Frances's room to confer about certain Possibilities.

"Sarah said the Cottinghams are looking for a match for Albert. . . ." ventured Frances.

"Yes, and money apparently is not an issue."

"But do you think—he seems a pleasant gentleman—but—"

"Not what I had in mind for Laurel," opined Mirabelle decisively.

After a pause she added, "There is Lord Harold. We found him ourselves. That is, he found *us* in Bayley Dell."

"Y-y-yes," admitted Frances, "but I am afraid that is looking too high. He did riot particularly distinguish her, do you think?"

Mirabelle, who did not know the identity of Lady Pamela and who therefore had no awareness of the snub dealt to her precious niece, was of like mind about his lordship. "Something of a rattle, I fear. Well, at least he was a familiar face, and perhaps lent her a little allure by swishing her among the dancers in a fancy style. They made a handsome pair, which other people must have noticed. A little send-off, so to speak."

"That is what I think," said Frances, crossing her arms

and running her hands inside her shawl. "She met a number of smart fellows, of course, and that is a beginning. I cannot think Mr. Smythe and Mr. Woodcock and the others are what we are looking for." Apparently she did not consider what Laurel might have in mind. "John never says much, yet I sense that he does not favor Lord Harold, and as for Mr. Kilkirk—"

"Oh, thank heaven he is Sarah's nephew, so *she* cannot throw herself away on him!" declared Mirabelle. "He is a perfect stick. I had a dance with him, you know. He may have a spectacular mind, but his personality is another matter. No, no, I would not wish him for our dear girl."

Frances ventured that he might improve upon closer acquaintance. Then she said thoughtfully, "Do you suppose the gentlemen we know in Bayley Dell seem more—agreeable—because we know them better?"

Meanwhile, in Laurel's room, Daisy, who had achieved some status belowstairs by her attendance upon a debutante, was saying, "Oh, miss, was it jist wunnerful?"

Laurel assured her that it was. "I was frightfully nervous at first for fear I world forget my steps, but then Mr. Hanger was the first to ask me to dance, and of course I am on easy terms with him."

"Mr. Hanger is a toim man," said Daisy as she removed Laurel's dress. "Do you know, miss, they has been real friendly to me here. The footman passed me the word that the lady of the house said I was to be treated nice."

Underdress and petticoat were removed and stockings untied. Soon Laurel was snug in her best sleeping gown, folded into bed. Daisy blew out Laurel's candles and traipsed off to the cot assigned to her, no sleepier than her mistress.

Like her aunts, Laurel reviewed the gentlemen she had met. Because she was a warm-hearted girl, she was inclined to like everyone she encountered whose manner was not disapproving (like Mr. Kilkirk's). The problem was that no one matched her own unsophisticated nature—except possibly Albert, who was rather young and immature, though amiable; not toplofty at all. Mrs. Walden might call Mr. Kilkirk "shy," but she thought a mature man ought to be able to say a few commonplace sentences in *some* language.

And then, of course, she thought of Gordon Rand, who did not fit in any type. His manners, except when he was feeling ill, were good, and his habit sometimes teasing in a mild way. She thought he would not hesitate to introduce her to *his* sister, if he had one. Now that she knew he was the son of Viscount Leadenhall, she could not suppose he was embarrassed for lack of money. She could not fail to notice that Papa, not one to talk of personalities, debated easily with Gordon, which surely told her he held the injured man in respect. Where Papa bestowed his friendship, Laurel thought she might do likewise.

Well, the husband-hunt (by whatever polite name) had only begun. She had enjoyed the assembly and intended to find pleasure in any other social events in which she might be included. If no compatible gentleman appeared, she resolved to make herself happy in Bayley Dell, as the aunties did!

In his chamber next door, Sir John divested himself of his clothes, which any male over six ought to be able to do. He did not ring for the footman; and thus, having no one with whom to make conversation, he climbed speedily into bed and stretched out on his back, hands knit behind his head. What he thought there was none to say. A little smile tugged at the corners of his mouth as he fell asleep.

Fourteen

In Bayley Dell on Saturday morning all was serene. Miss Laurel was known to have gone for a first public appearance at a ball in Wells, and there was a great deal of interest about this. However, immediate concerns and duties of everyday life are what have the attention of most folk in the world, so the villagers went about their small affairs, only momentarily surprised to see Mr. Appleton arrive at the church (it was not his weekend) and stroll about the graveyard, investigating what work McComb had done in his absence.

McComb was in the basement of the sanctuary polishing a candelabrum. His conscience was clear. He whistled through his teeth an unecclesiastical tune, with probably no more serious thought than what he would have for nuncheon.

Above ground, Mr. Appleton, having found only two upstart weeds on the north side of the church, walked back to examine the footbridge at the ravine. Sure enough, Miss Frances's prodding and Sir John's terse message to Browning had resulted in sound repair of broken planks.

"These ladies should be generals," he chuckled to himself. "The Eland ladies get things done."

Shortly before noon he had returned to the south garden when Mr. Hanger's carriage passed and Miss Frances waved from a window. "Why, it's Mr. Appleton," she exclaimed. "What is he doing here this week?"

Laurel, riding backwards, had the last view of the gentleman. "He is waving his hat," she said. Unobtrusively, she had been watching for some sign of Gordon Rand when they passed The Nesting Dove, yet had seen none. Now here was the vicar unexpectedly come to Bayley Dell! Was there some connection? Suppose—oh, suppose something had happened to her patient . . . yet Mr. Appleton had looked jolly, not worried.

Mr. Hanger's carriage delivered them neatly to Fane, and Cook came to collect Daisy and dampen her enthusiasm for foreign parts. As in Wells, one groom dismounted to assist Fane with the luggage.

By the time they had entered the house (glad to be safely home, as happy families always are), shed their wraps, and gone into the drawing room to await a light lunch, Mr. Appleton had walked up from the village to hear that travel agreed with them.

"You have been sorely missed," he declared, as if he had not seen them for two months or more.

"Stay for lunch," urged Frances. "It will be something simple because we had left word we might return during the afternoon. But you will not mind."

Indeed he would not.

"What brought you here this weekend?" asked Sir John.

"I—er—was anxious about leaving McComb loose with pruning to be done. Wouldn't want the shrubs hacked." In this he was maligning the verger, who had pruned conservatively for years. "And I was uneasy about the footbridge, but I see it is all right now."

"Yes," said Frances, "John laid down the law to Browning—words of one syllable that even he could understand. I am glad he responded properly. I'll have a look at the bridge myself in a day or so."

He murmured thanks and turned to Miss Mirabelle, asking if she was too tired from her travels to walk down with him after lunch to look at a holly tree that seemed to have a large dead stalk. "The Eternal Kingdom, you see, is my field; I am not very conversant with the vegetable one."

"Um-m-m," Mirabelle replied. "I did not notice anything wrong, but with so many shrubs I could have overlooked something. Yes, certainly I will walk down. I am not the least tired. Our little visit gave all of us an uplift of spirits."

Mr. Appleton's spirits were always good because he relied on the Spirit, but he said no word to correct her.

"I am glad to stretch my legs after a long carriage ride," Sir John remarked. "Shall we walk down with them, Laurel, to see your patient? Will you come with us, Frances?"

Frances said, "I think not. I will see that Daisy unpacks, and then write a note of thanks to Mrs. Walden for having so many of us as houseguests. She was a most gracious hostess, Mr. Appleton, and gave a delightful and elegant dinner before the ball. Really, we have every reason to be grateful to her."

"A charming lady," added Sir John.

"I will write, too, of course," Mirabelle said. "Since Mr. Appleton has made a special trip about the churchyard, he and I had better see to it now. The letters can go together Monday."

So it was arranged, and so it happened.

Laurel and her father went on to the inn, while Mirabelle and the vicar turned off at the lych-gate. He led her along the north side of the church building to a holly tree near the rear corner.

Mr. Appleton was scrupulously honest, so as soon as Mirabelle had agreed a stalk looked dead, he said, "This is only an excuse, dear Miss Mirabelle. I-I wished to speak to you privately, and this seemed a way to do it. You may think me an old fool—well, I *am* one—but 'nothing ventured, nothing gained,' they say."

Mirabelle looked at him in perplexity, her eyebrows turning up right angles above her nose as Frances's did, and her

brother's. But Mr. Appleton was not looking at her eyebrows; he was intent upon her eyes.

"You have been so helpful to me here," he went on.
"When I go home to Mendle, I—miss you. I wish you were
there."

Having some inkling then of what was to come, hardly
believing it possible, Mirabelle said, "Oh!" and sat abruptly
on a grave stone.

Mr. Appleton saw no incongruity in their surroundings.
He had lived amid burial grounds for twenty-five years.
"Dear Miss Mirabelle, will you come?"

"Come?" squeaked Mirabelle.

Another man would have gasped, "Dammit—come marry
me!" but swear words were not in his vocabulary. He said
gently, "Come be my wife." As Mirabelle was momentarily
speechless, he hurried on, explaining modestly, "Oh, I know
I am no match for an Eland, but I can promise your brother
to care for you in a simple and comfortable way. The house
in Mendle is a nice one, and the congregation there is recep-
tive. They will see your goodness—and kindness—and *faithfulness* as I do. They will be sure to love you—as I do."

Mirabelle raised a glowing face and stretched out her
hand. "Yes, yes, yes. I'll come . . . and *thank* you."

Mr. Appleton took the hand and released a pent breath.
"I am the thankful one," he declared.

Both were perfectly aware that they were visible to anyone passing along the village street, although his position
might shield the clasped hands from sight.

"I'll speak to your brother at once, though I must say it
will seem odd, as I am older than he is," he said with a
rueful smile.

"But not old," she corrected. "Just right for me."

"I hope Sir John will think so."

"Don't speak to him yet. Give me time to believe this,"
she begged.

"I must speak. I am obliged to return to Mendle today."

In such a small village there was no such thing as privacy. He drew her to her feet and they walked back toward the ravine and across the footbridge, passing Browning's cottage and another, slowly following a rutted lane to enter the village at its lower end. During this time their plans were made. Mr. Appleton expressed himself very well, and they discovered blissfully that Love cared nothing for Age.

The Nesting Dove came into sight, and with it a view of Laurel and Sir John sitting with the Unknown under the chestnut tree before the building. The lovers hesitated; then, finding themselves seen, schooled their expressions and went forward.

"Someone is *better*," cried Mirabelle a trifle shrilly.

Sir John, noticing nothing odd, rose to give his sister his seat on the bench. "Have you been walking?"

"We came the long way around from the church," Mr. Appleton explained calmly. "Such a beautiful day, you know; not to be wasted." Fortunately for his veracity, the weather was fine, although gray clouds were building westward toward the Bristol Channel. If Sir John and the patient noticed a certain glow in the faces of the newcomers, they attributed it, manlike, to exercise. Laurel, who had no understanding of the romance of middle-age and no personal experience of any other sort, suspected nothing.

"Is it not fine that our invalid has improved enough to venture into the fresh air?" she demanded.

"Deuced glad to breathe something besides wood smoke and ale! . . . Pardon, ladies." He shifted his wrenched knee to a more comfortable position. "I was hearing about Wells."

"Miss Mirabelle will want to add details," said Mr. Appleton. "Why don't we walk ahead to the house, Sir John? I would like your opinion on a certain matter."

The baronet, ever amiable, was willing, so they set off, speaking of inconsequentials until the parlor door had closed on them at Eland House.

At the inn Miss Mirabelle at first sat silent, and the invalid stared unspeaking at his boots. Laurel smoothed her skirts and embarked on a rambling commentary about a ballroom that she supposed Gordon Rand already well knew. "I had not guessed that dancing to an orchestra could be so delightful," she said artlessly. "Lord Harry swooped me around to a fast tune, and Albert Cottingham demonstrated a waltz, which looked charming and not at all risqué."

Rand came to life. "Harry was there, was he?"

"Yes, he said he would come, though I really did not expect him. He made quite a spectacle when he danced with his sister." Without her realizing it, her voice became wistful. "Such a beautiful and graceful lady . . ."

"Ah," said Gordon Rand with no sign of pleasure. "Lady Pamela. And did he present you to her?"

Laurel said a flat "No."

"How is this?" demanded Aunt Mirabelle, becoming more alert. "How dare he not, when he has been received as a guest in our house?"

"Perhaps there was not time," suggested Gordon.

"Only an hour or two," replied the indignant lady. "I hope I need not see him again."

The invalid said unfortunately she *would,* as his curricle and servants awaited him at The Nesting Dove. It amused him to guess that Patten did not intend the rig to leave until Lord Harold's tally was fully paid.

"He will return any time now," Gordon said.

"Then we must leave at once, Laurel. If I see that young dandy I may be tempted to speak my mind." Miss Mirabelle stood abruptly.

Laurel said, laughing, "What is Mr. Appleton's view of temptation?"

Mr. Appleton! Miss Mirabelle's startled expression surprised them. After the briefest pause she said they would go at once. "Shall we summon Blunk, sir?"

"Oh, it is not necessary. He keeps watch."

Aunt Mirabelle led Laurel briskly up the sloping street. At their own doorstep she paused to look back, but a protruding cottage blocked their sight of the Unknown and the chestnut tree. No sooner had Fane admitted them than Sir John opened the parlor door and beckoned his sister. Looking somewhere between tears and laughter, she went into the room and closed the door.

"Come with me, Laurel," said her father. "Frances is waiting for you in the drawing room." He seemed curiously elated.

Fane took Laurel's bonnet and cloak, and the two of them went in to join Frances.

Somewhat puzzled, she asked, "What is it, Auntie? Papa says you want me."

"Do I? What nonsense. I am always glad to see you, dearest, but I did not ask to do so."

"I thought," drawled the baronet, "you would like to know that Mr. Appleton has made an offer—"

"My God!" shrieked Frances. "Surely you will never give your daughter to a man more than twice her age!"

Sir John said stoutly that fifty was not *old,* which was his way of assuring himself that his own forty-seven years were not decrepitude.

Frances threw her embroidery frame to the floor. "I shall not allow it! Not until my body is bleeding on the carpet!" She cast glances right and left, as if choosing the most effective spot.

Shaking with laughter, he said, "No, no. Of course I would not permit such a match. It is *Mirabelle* he wants."

It took a minute for the fact to penetrate the ladies' turbulent minds. Then they began to crow.

"How could I refuse such an offer?" asked the happy baronet. "Or what difference would it make if I did? Mirabelle is forty-four and beyond my control. Besides, he satisfied me that he can support her. Do you know, they should, I think, be able to live as comfortably as we!" He slung himself into his favorite wing chair and listened, smiling, as his sister and daughter began to compose a rainbow of wonderful plans.

"Mendle is only a little over four miles away," he reminded them. "I should not wonder if Appleton will let Mirabelle drive his gig. Daresay she remembers how."

They had not long to wait for the betrothed couple to appear, flushed, glowing, each looking a good fifteen years younger than they were. Frances enfolded her sister in her arms, while Laurel flew to the vicar to clasp his hand and tell him it was *perfect, perfect*.

"You will be my uncle now," she cried. "I must kiss your cheek."

Mr. Appleton submitted with stumbling, grateful words that were a far cry from his fluency in the pulpit.

No one thought it was at all remarkable when Fane, with his sixth sense operating infallibly, entered with glasses and wine, including a bottle of champagne only half-dusted from the cellar.

The groom-to-be was grateful for a sip of ceremonial champagne with his new family, followed by a cup of piping hot tea to steady him. "I must, *must* get back to Mendle. Mirabelle will tell you our simple plans, but I beg that nothing be said outside this house until noon tomorrow. Mendle is my principal living and the people there deserve to hear my news first."

"Then we had better have the servants in to see if they have already spread the word to Bayley Dell," Sir John advised.

"The vicar shall quote Scripture to confound their tongues," suggested Mirabelle from her place at his side, where she had hung since entering the room.

Laurel laughed and said, "Something about avenging angels perhaps?"

Frances rang the bell.

With Fane marshaling the two females, they came in

promptly. Cook had cast off her apron; Daisy had not. All three faces were avid, because they realized Something was in the wind; they were *never* summoned to the drawing room as a group.

Sir John made a neat little speech, announcing Miss Eland's betrothal to Mr. Appleton, whom, he was sure, they revered. There was a pleased flutter from the servants and a widening of eyes, along with testimonials to guarded tongues.

"I'll speak for myself and my assistants, sir," declared Fane righteously. "Not a word has been spoke outside these walls, nor will be."

"Ah," said Laurel irrepressibly, "but has anyone come in to be spoken to?"

Assuming a pained dignity, Fane swore that no one had done so. Sir John told Fane to open a bottle of wine for the servants' use, which sent them away happy on two counts.

Mr. Appleton suggested the baronet bring the ladies to see his parsonage—Mirabelle's future home—on Wednesday, but Sir John fancied Thursday would be better, so that day was chosen, and the benedict-to-be rode away. It was thought fortunate that his horse knew the way home to Mendle.

"I am pleased for you, sister," said the baronet, taking her capable hand in his. "Appleton is an estimable man."

"I never dreamed—!" gasped Mirabelle.

"Some might say," he continued, "that a churchman of a provincial village is no match for a baronet's daughter, but we know—and the village knows—the worth of his character."

"Yes, and I, too, know it!" she averred solemnly. "Mr. Appleton is everything superior and generous."

Frances and Laurel nodded and smiled, though they were no part of the dialogue.

Sir John said to her, "Your thousand pounds from Mama

is untouched. It is possible that in a few years, when the debts are paid, I can do something more for you."

Mirabelle, who twenty-five years ago would have thought a thousand pounds paltry, now saw them as riches. "I shall want for nothing!" she declared. "To be settled so near you will be added joy."

That night it was not the sisters who whispered together while Laurel was allowed to dream of future bliss. Respecting Mirabelle's need to be alone with her sudden change in circumstances, Frances tiptoed to Laurel's room for an orgy of hugs and chortles.

"Dear Mr. Appleton will be *family,* do you realize, Auntie?" Laurel said.

"Yes, and I wonder when she will begin to call him 'James' and not 'Mr. Appleton'!"

They giggled like schoolgirls.

Then Laurel observed that management of Eland House would fall entirely upon Frances. "Shall you mind?"

Frances said, "Of course not. It is not all that onerous." It was the accepted course for an elder sister to marry first (even if a quarter century late), and Frances would now advance to the dignity of "Miss Eland," though she had never felt inferior for having been later born.

"I will help you all I can," Laurel promised.

Wedding plans, hastily formulated by Mirabelle and her James during their walk in the lane, called for banns to be read at Mendle next morning and subsequently posted at Hammish and Bayley Dell. The ceremony would naturally take place in the Elands' own little church on the first day of May. Mr. Appleton felt sure that the rector would come from Nord Cross to officiate.

May first being a Tuesday, Mr. Appleton thought he could "steal" five days for a modest wedding journey to Bath, and anything he suggested Mirabelle was sure to approve. They would not be talked into a grander affair.

"Is it not a joke?" said Laurel to Frances as they finally

separated for bed. "You aunties have designed such schemes for settling *me* but it is Aunt Mirabelle who has made a match!"

Fifteen

Laurel and Miss Mirabelle had not been long gone from the Unknown on Saturday afternoon when Dr. Dodd found him still sitting beneath the tree outside The Nesting Dove.

"Why are you moping?" growled that crusty gentleman.

Gordon started and looked up, unsmiling. "Because I am in a slump—which is something I daresay you never experience. I should like to be prancing."

"Ah!" said the doctor wisely. "Petticoat fever. No medicine for that. Well, I have said it before and I will say it again, a long face won't be of service."

Gordon said neither was Lord Harry helpful.

"I don't see him around."

"Not yet, but he ought to come caracoling along on his charger. I only hope Miss Laurel won't be here to see it. Ugh!"

Dr. Dodd clucked his tongue. "Now, now. A dandy should not be any competition for a real man."

"Competition?" challenged the invalid.

"That's what all this moping is about, isn't it?"

Gordon asked, "Who's a real man? I'm only half."

"With an overdose of feeling sorry for yourself. I don't know why I should help you, but I will: Get up and walk about."

"May I? Should I? You told me not to do so!"

Dr. Dodd snorted. "Aye, but it has been nearly two weeks

now. The arm is beyond my help, but I can tell you that knee needs exercise. Can't you take a bit of pain?"

"Of course I can, dammit." He grasped his cane and struggled to his feet. "If I fall, *you* will have to pick me up!"

"Well, I won't," replied the doctor heartlessly. "I shall leave you flat on the ground until Lord Harry comes along. *That* will get you up quick enough."

Gordon scowled and began a circuit of the tree.

"Hurt much?" asked the doctor.

"No. There is just the feeling that my leg may collapse."

Dr. Dodd settled himself on the bench. "It won't. Go around again."

After another circle the young man halted, taking his weight on both feet. "Did it!" he exulted.

The doctor grinned. "Well, now," he said, "I will just rest here while you go round the inn yard—if you have the wind."

"Of course I have it!" asserted the invalid, striking out.

Dr. Dodd watched his slow and steady plodding until he vanished from sight behind the inn, after which the doctor drew out a pipe and began to scratch in the bowl with a twig. Presently Gordon came into view on the far side of the yard, and the doctor was pleased to see that he was not limping. When, however, the young man reached the chestnut tree, Dr. Dodd said only, "Not so difficult, hey?"

Gordon eased himself to a seat and let out a huff. "End in sight, I suppose. When can I reach the Elands' house?"

"Not today, and probably not tomorrow," said the doctor sternly. "We will see how the knee looks tomorrow after this bit of walking. How does it feel after exercise?"

Gordon frowned like Vulcan with his lame leg. "Not painless," he admitted.

The doctor said they could not really expect *that*. "I'll call Blunk to get you back up to bed. See that you make another circuit of the yard in the morning before I come

down to check you. Eland House won't fly away, young
fellow! Nor Laurel, either."

Eland House did not fly away that day, but the next, Sunday, there was some flying on the Wells pike, as Mr. Smythe
and Mr. Woodcock sped toward Bayley Dell. They had exchanged some harsh words in argument over who should
lead the way and finally settled on both in Smythe's curricle
(swiftest) with Woodcock (most skillful) driving. It was
with some dismay that they reached their target only to find
Mr. Kilkirk's phaeton-and-four under guard of three ecstatic
choirboys and a bored groom. Their dismay soon gave way
to satisfaction when Miss Laurel Eland was obviously glad
to see them.

The three Eland ladies were finding it hard going to make
conversation with Mr. Kilkirk, wondering why he had come
if he had nothing to say and wishing mightily for Sir John,
who had wandered off somewhere.

Miss Frances busied herself pouring tea, and as Miss
Mirabelle smiled but seemed to drift off into space, it
obliged Laurel to create talk to fill the threatened silence.
She inquired about the gentlemen's journey and, having
compared it with what she could drag from Mr. Kilkirk
about his, was at her wits' end, when Fane announced Mr.
Hanger.

Matters took an immediate upturn.

As at his first call, Mr. Hanger was rigged out by his
valet so splendidly as to make the two young Pinks feel
shabby, yet they responded to his convivial manner.

"I wager that pair in the curricle I saw outside are snappy
goers," he boomed, and Mr. Smythe shook out his cuffs,
delighted to claim the horses as his.

"Well tooled, too," Mr. Hanger added. "Don't look over-
heated." To which Mr. Woodcock happily implied his driv-

ing of the pair by saying, "Gentle mouths, sir. Respond to the slightest signal."

Mr. Hanger said approvingly, "Ah!" and received a cup from Laurel. "Then the phaeton is yours, Mr. Kilkirk? I've heard from Lord Harry that you sport a smashing rig."

Evidently Mr. Kilkirk was not intimidated by men as he was by ladies, for he made a small cordial bow and said, "I've had a tedious time matching *four* chestnuts in color and size as well as gait. Glad you like them, Hanger. P'haps you would like to try them sometime." Somehow his visage seemed lighter.

Before Mr. Hanger could say he would or wouldn't, Lord Harry was announced, and with five gentlemen to vie for Laurel's notice there was a great deal of sociability. Sir John was not missed, though the aunts exchanged glances with raised eyebrows. The Unknown was not mentioned; and why should he be, having no name?

Eventually Mr. Hanger allowed himself to be squeezed from the inner circle and moved toward Miss Frances. "You remember speaking of Public Days of past times? I have an idea it might be pleasant to revive them. Would you allow me to drive you about the manor so that you can point out how all should be arranged?"

Frances appeared much struck with the thought, but she gave no sign of liking or disliking Mr. Hanger's holding such a fête on her brother's property. She said hesitantly, "Y-yes. I could do that." So they agreed on ten o'clock the next day, after which he punctiliously took leave of Miss Mirabelle, Laurel, and the various gentlemen.

Nothing was said of Mirabelle's betrothal to Mr. Appleton, although by this time all Mendle must know of it, and the news would percolate soon to Bayley Dell. Mirabelle might have confided in Miss Onslow, but they had not met since the wonderful event occurred, and, in any case, Sir John was the one to make formal announcements, if there were to be such.

Moving to sit beside her sister at the tea table, Mirabelle whispered, "Our Wells adventure is already bearing fruit."

Frances agreed. "Yes, but there is no sign of Albert Cottingham. I had thought him the likeliest candidate."

"So far," amended Mirabelle. "But we must remember our campaign has only begun."

There was no time for further confidences as Lord Harry came to blind them with a flowered waistcoat and to say in his light way, "This is as jolly as any Sunday I've known."

"It is delightful to have you join us," Frances murmured politely. "I thought you might have returned home."

"No, no. Horse still ailing."

"But how did you reach Wells, sir?" she persisted.

"Mr. Hanger was kind enough to lend me an excellent hack, as if he had known me from short coats. Very obliging fellow."

Frances said "Yes" faintly and offered more tea.

Mirabelle had related to her how Sir Harry had offended by failing to introduce Laurel to his sister. They were now inclined to treat him with cool civility, but it was difficult to put down a handsome buck who was blithely assured of his welcome. Besides, they had yet to hear an unpleasant word from him.

By four o'clock Sir John had not appeared, and the guests could linger no longer on the excuse of wishing to see that his health had not been imperiled by a ball. A general exodus took place. As glad to see them go as they had been to see them come, the Eland ladies flopped with sighs.

"You did not warn me how tedious ton beaux can be!" Laurel complained. "Such shallow interchange!"

Mirabelle defended by saying, "Well-l, it was a first call, and they may not have been sure of their welcome."

"Lord Harold never doubts *his*," Frances noted with a grimace.

Laurel said, "We hear much more sensible conversation from Mr. Appleton and Dr. Dodd and Mr. Hanger."

The older ladies looked at each other and raised their eyebrows. "John's 'beaux'!" gasped Frances, and burst out laughing, which made no sense to her niece.

"What an effort!" Laurel said. "At least our invalid, weary and in pain, does not spout trivialities!"

"Must not be critical of admirers, dear," cautioned Frances.

But Mirabelle said, "I understand what she means. Mr. Appleton—James—is so interesting that I could listen to him forever."

"You will! You will!" cried Frances, dissolving into giggles, which brought laughter from her niece and a self-conscious blush to Mirabelle.

"If John does not return soon to tell my tale, I swear I will run next door and confess to the Misses Onslow," Mirabelle said.

Laurel asked if she would invite them to the ceremony.

"We are agreed that there will be no formal invitations," Mirabelle replied, "but James will say everyone who wishes to come may do so. I shall feel like an idiot!"

"But a radiant one," added Frances. "No, no, I do not mean exactly that. No one will think you anything but a lovely bride who deserves such an admirable man."

"He is dear, isn't he?" Mirabelle asked with a tiny smile.

"Yes," said Laurel warmly, "but I wonder if the people of Mendle will realize how lucky *they* are," to which Frances answered quickly that they would soon find out.

"You will be cross with me for leaving you to run this household," lamented Mirabelle.

Frances said indeed she would not. "I shall be thinking how cozy you are in a home of your very own." Fane came in to see if they wished hot tea, and Frances grandly commanded him to bring sherry.

It was nearing six when Sir John returned, looking windblown but healthy, with pink in his cheeks. His eyes were bright, not sleepy at all, despite his having missed a nap.

"We have had five callers," said Frances.

"Gentleman callers," specified Mirabelle.

"Where have you been?" demanded Frances.

"Oh—" he gestured vaguely "—getting some exercise before it rains." He poured himself a sherry.

The ladies glanced to the windows and discovered just enough daylight to indicate that there was a pallid sun. Frances moaned that she had known the clear days could not last.

During the night rain clouds rolled in from the west and dropped a waterfall upon the neighborhood. Trees and budding flowers drank thirstily, and a rivulet ran through the ravine behind the church to encourage Miss Onslow's pennycress. The road through the village fared less well, sinking erratically under quagmires of mud that kept even dogs and cats sitting dejectedly on doorsteps.

By ten o'clock, when Mr. Hanger called in his curricle for Miss Frances (with a coverlet to protect her skirts from spatters), the rainfall had ended. An optimistic sun was steaming the area. No one from the three brick houses thought to walk anywhere. Consequently, strange thumps at the Elands' door were heard with some surprise. Not the knocker. What could it be?

As Fane was in the cellar, fetching vegetables for Cook, Laurel went into the hall and opened the door. At eye level she saw no one but, on looking down, discovered Mr. Rand, sitting upon the stoop with his bad leg propped upon a step.

"Good heavens!" she exclaimed. "Did you *walk?"*

"Yes, I did," he said, scraping left-handed with his cane upon his muddy boots. "This is as far as I could go. Sorry. I could not reach your knocker and had to rap with my third leg."

Laurel said anxiously, "But did the doctor say—"

"Yes, said I could come when I felt like it, though very likely he thought the mud would keep me in my prison."

"Well, you cannot stay here. You must come inside by the fire," she insisted, stooping to assist him in rising. "Fane will clean your boots."

Gordon shook his head. "It would be wasted labor, for I will have to return to the inn through the same mud. In any case, I do not think I can stand for a while."

She reached for his sound arm. "I will help you."

The expression in his eyes shook her to her toes. She had not thought blue eyes could be so . . . *fathomless.*

"Sit beside me," he ordered, and of course she did so, to hear the story of the laps that Dr. Dodd had assigned. "Mud or no mud, it feels magnificent to escape the benevolence of Patten, and Mrs. Patten, and Blunk. Such caring souls, yet Dodd's astringent commands to 'exercise' have put matters in perspective."

So they sat upon the stoop, like actors on the stage of Drury Lane, before the whole of Bayley Dell.

"Can we talk here without being overheard?" Gordon asked.

Laurel said yes and no.

"What does that mean?"

She smiled her pretty smile, revealing pearly teeth. "Do not turn your head, but the house to your left has a bow window, and I daresay we are being scrutinized now by the old ladies who live in the window."

"Live in the *window!*"

"So it seems, because they are always watching, watching. Rather sweet old ladies, but one must guard one's conduct. If we look interesting, the elder one will come out any minute to join us."

"Good God!"

"They aren't critical, you understand. Only inquisitive. It is their entertainment."

He withdrew his gaze from those perfect lips. "I'll be

quick, then. I am here without horse, clothes, or money. If I apply to Father, he will come to carry me off. I told you that. Yet to be at the moment penniless is vexing, and I have reasons for wanting to stay."

Laurel wondered if *perhaps* she was a reason, but he spoke in plural. "You mentioned a brother with affection. Could you not send word to him? Would he give you away?"

"He would come to me, yes, and bring money. But suppose he is not at home to receive a note. He may already have gone up to London for the opening of the Season. Let me think."

She waited patiently without speaking.

"You see, I am barely mobile. I want to see if I can track down those thugs who waylaid me. To do that I need good limbs and a horse."

"Mr. Hanger would lend you one."

"Yes, but he cannot furnish me with an arm and a leg." He looked down with a frown at his offending leg.

Laurel said pessimistically, "You did not actually see the men who attacked you, did you?"

"No. But I have one powerful clue. I was knocked from my horse by sudden attack, you know. When one rogue kicked me in the jaw I had a very clear view—graven in stone—of his boot. I promise you I will never forget it."

Laurel breathed, "Oh!"

"If that boot is anywhere in the county, I will recognize it. I will look—"

"Miss Onslow has come out," she warned hastily.

"I plan to begin my search in the taproom tonight," he whispered just before the peripatetic Miss Onslow reached them. Mud did not daunt her; she wore clogs.

"Good morning," she chirped sunnily. "Have you found your mind, sir? You are looking wide awake."

"This is Miss Onslow, sir," Laurel said unnecessarily.

Gordon gestured with his left arm to his injured members. "Sorry not to greet you properly, ma'am. It was my *memory* that went astray, but it is clearing by degrees, thanks to a number of people."

"Oh, yes," said Miss Onslow. "Miss Eland made excellent broth for you, did she not? Sister and I had some and found it most restorative. Very likely it has put you on your foot—feet."

"Well-l," drawled Rand, "Dr. Dodd helped, and Fane and the Pattens and Hanger—and, of course, Miss Laurel."

The old lady began to expatiate on the benefits of chamomile tea, which the invalid declared he detested. Facing the drive to Bayley Manor as she was, Laurel could see Mr. Hanger's curricle descending the slope toward them. Miss Onslow was still extolling chamomile when Mr. Hanger and Frances drew up beside them gently, with a minimum of splashing.

"Oh, Laurel," cried Frances to her niece, "the manor is as beautiful as it used to be when I was a girl."

"You are still a girl," Mr. Hanger said with a no-nonsense tone. His groom, jumping to the muddy street, sprang to hold the horses' heads, so his employer could stand down to lift his passenger to the steps of her home.

"I, too, would like to see the improvements," said Miss Onslow, blending wistfulness artfully with demand.

Mr. Hanger bluffly said, "So you shall when we have the fête."

The old lady cried, "Fête! Is there to be one? My, my, Sister will be so excited."

Frances explained that Mr. Hanger meant a Public Day.

"And I will send a carriage for both Misses Onslow," Mr. Hanger promised in his generous way. "There will be cream buns for you, missy," he added to Laurel.

Gordon asked, "What treat is there for a cripple?" And Mr. Hanger replied, "If you are still handicapped in May, there will be a goat cart at your disposal."

"*Goat* cart!"

"All you will deserve, if you are complaining when the time comes."

Miss Onslow and Frances looked amused, but Laurel chided swiftly: "Do not tease him! He is far from healed. Just walking here took tremendous effort, and I think you might offer to drive him back to the inn in your curricle."

Mr. Hanger regarded her sharply. "Do you, now, missy? So I will. Up with you, sir." He hoisted Rand from the stoop and somehow bundled him, wincing, into the curricle, muddy boots and all. "Make your lists, Miss Frances." He seized her hand, shook it violently, touched his hat to Miss Onslow, and sprang to take up the ribbons. The groom was allowed three seconds to reach his perch.

"Well!" said Miss Onslow, watching the vehicle depart.

"So much energy," said Laurel.

"Exhausting," sighed Miss Frances. "Pray excuse us, Miss Onslow. We have a thousand things to see to."

Loath to leave the scene of so much excitement, but eager to tell her sister that they would have special transportation to a revival of Public Days, the old lady headed home along the street, which was crusting in the sunshine. The younger Miss Onslow waited agog; she had seen Laurel sitting like a village girl on her doorstep, Miss Frances alighting from *Mr. Hanger's* carriage after an unexplained ride to the manor, and the Injured Man entertaining both in what was unmistakably Patten's oversize coat, splinted arm snug to his chest. Far be it from the Onslows to gossip publicly about the Elands, but privately they luxuriated in discussion of their gentry who were much more interesting than peasants, besides being beneficent to themselves.

Unaware (and heedless) of their neighbors' speculations, Frances and Laurel entered their own door to find Sir John cozy in his wing chair by the drawing room fire.

"John! John! Wake up!" cried Frances, as she flung open the drawing room door. "Mr. Hanger is going to resurrect Bayley Manor Public Days."

"What's this?" asked Mirabelle, hurrying in to join them.

Frances swung toward her. "Mr. Hanger is going to hold a Public Day, just exactly as they always were, *and* he says it is John's manor so *he* must conduct the opening ceremony!"

"Well now!" marveled Mirabelle, while Laurel clasped her hands delightedly.

Sir John roused himself to sit forward. "Demmed handsome of him, but—"

"No buts," said Frances decisively. "I admit it is generous of him, but it is exactly right, and will please the villagers as much as you." She equipped herself with paper and pencil. "Mr. Hanger said to make a list of what must be included."

They settled themselves in a small circle to combine ideas and recollections—interspersed with arrangements to visit Mr. Appleton in Mendle on Thursday. There were no callers that soggy afternoon to interrupt.

Sixteen

Gordon Rand's determined search for the criminals who had stolen his horse, which was almost a worse offense than their brutal treatment of his body, did not begin that Monday night. When Mr. Hanger delivered him to The Nesting Dove he was white and exhausted, quite willing to let Patten and Blunk hoist him up to his room. Mrs. Patten followed behind with a stream of "Mercy on us . . . overdid . . . do we need the doctor? Is there any laudanum left?"

It was not a quiet passage. Lord Harry heard the commotion and came from the taproom to investigate but was summarily ordered by a distracted Mrs. Patten to fetch a bucket of cold water from the pump. Surprised, he did as bid, muttering an oath when he splashed water on his breeches and returning to find Gordon on his bed, at which point his lordship was hustled from the room by Patten so that Mrs. Patten and Blunk could apply compresses to head and knee in peace.

After that the patient had a light lunch and, when the curtains had been drawn, a dose of laudanum.

"At least I was able to walk as far as Eland House," he mumbled to the attentive Blunk.

As the doctor had done, Blunk said, "Won't fly away, sir. You can go another time. They are saying in the village that Miss Mirabelle is going to wed the vicar, so belike there'll be much going on at the House. No one is going to vanish, sir. Rest easy."

Mr. Rand managed a lopsided grin. "I'll drift off like a babe." He worked his shoulders into the pillows and closed his eyes.

Up the street, in the middle brick house, there was a chaos of ideas, wonderings, sentiments, joy, and speculation. Naturally, Mirabelle's interest was in matrimony, though she was pleased enough at Mr. Hanger's large plans. Frances, on the other hand, was chiefly thinking of Public Days; it would be a small fête, as fêtes go, because their community was tiny, but to Frances it seemed the old life would come alive.

During lunch and dinner, and then afterwards in the drawing room, the two aunts carried on a sort of seesawing conversation, all points of which Laurel seconded enthusiastically. Sir John sat calmly, letting them chatter.

"Do you think we should include Hammish and Mendle?" asked Frances.

"I hope the weather is fine for our ceremony," Mirabelle answered.

"Mendle, especially, is going to be interested in Bayley Manor because of you, Mirabelle. I am sure Mr. Hanger would be willing to invite them."

"Bath is not a long journey. If we don't have rain, we should be able to reach there before dark."

"More people for games will make more excitement for all."

"I cannot wait to see the house in Mendle."

Even with this diversity of focus, they were able to settle on the vital matter of a date. It was Sir John who pointed out that the historic time for the fête would conflict with Mirabelle's wedding trip, and so it was decided they should propose to Mr. Hanger that the Public Day be called for the Saturday of the week following the wedding.

"That way, the twelfth, Mirabelle and James will be able to come. Mirabelle doesn't cease to be an Eland, you know," Frances said, "and the villagers will want their vicar to be present. Perhaps Laurel should be the one to obtain Mr. Hanger's approval. . . ."

Laurel was startled. "Me? He thinks me a child—calls me that infantile name 'missy'—would not think any idea of mine worth listening to."

"You could twist him around your finger," Frances said.

A shake of her head set Laurel's curls bobbing. "Not I! He did not invite *me* to ride over the manor and make plans."

"Well, you are too young to remember how it all was," countered her aunt.

"And I am still too young for a man his age to consider seriously anything I say."

Frances said, "He is only forty-three—isn't that right, John?"

"That is young," said Mirabelle, whose betrothed was fifty.

Sir John was amused at the argument. "Laurel is right, if I understand the issue. Hanger has already asked your advice, Frances. He will want to hear from you. If it makes you more comfortable, you can say *we feel* that Mr. and Mrs. Appleton must be available for such a traditional occasion."

"Very well," she said. "He is marvelously agreeable, I find, though he may have lavish plans of his own that we cannot—must not—undermine."

"In any case," opined Mirabelle, "he will talk us around to his proposals, and there will be no question of differing opinions. James says—" (the other ladies rolled their eyes at each other) "—that Mr. Hanger is very considerate of him and his clerical duties. I daresay he will want to make it possible for his vicar to attend."

"He has already said he will order a tent for tea service," Frances told them, "even if it means sending all the way to London."

"And I have a promise of cream buns to gorge on!" exulted Laurel, like the child of twelve years ago.

"Will there be flags?" wondered Sir John aloud. "Of the colonies, y'know. Might be old ones in the attics."

"I forgot those. I will put them on my list," Frances assured him, taking up her pencil.

"Do you think we might have flowers from the glasshouse for my wedding?" asked Mirabelle.

"Yes," said Frances, "but *you* must negotiate for those."

It was very likely that the only member of the family who gave any thought to the Unknown at the inn was also unaware of his relapse. When her father took her down to The Nesting Dove on Tuesday they found him dressed but keeping to his room meekly.

He admitted, disgustedly, to having overextended himself. The arm was only a dull ache, not unbearable now. "What is infuriating," he said, "is that a simple twist of a knee could put me to bed!"

The ever-attentive Blunk elucidated: "Dr. Dodd was here this morning and said a wrench is less simple than a fracture. Knees have to take the weight of his body."

"Enough of knees!" said Gordon Rand, eyes intent on Laurel.

So they told him the details of Mirabelle's venture into matrimony and asked if they could supply any wants or needs of himself. After this they went away, Laurel feeling somehow cheated of a chance for good deeds. Naturally nothing was said before Sir John and Blunk of Mr. Rand's search for an incriminating pair of boots.

Wednesday was equally disappointing. Sir John went off on business of his own, and Mirabelle dragged out her whole wardrobe for scrutiny and mending. Frances had said she would chaperone Laurel to the inn, yet before they could set out Mr. Hanger had come to discuss ideas for the fête, so that the two ladies found themselves chaperoning each other. He was going by curricle the next day to Wells to see if a tent might be ordered there for the Public Day;

if not, being tireless it seemed, he would make a run to London.

Miss Frances produced her list of details that Mr. Hanger declared to be a marvel of efficiency. He did not quibble with any point, emboldening her to suggest May twelfth as a propitious day for the celebration. He agreed promptly. By this time Frances was flushed with success and looked quite pretty, Laurel thought. Mr. Hanger's carriage was offered to the Elands for their visit to Mendle on Thursday, and such was now the cordiality between leasers and lessee that no demurral was made.

Albert Cottingham called that afternoon, but as he had brought Miss Colby "to give her a little outing," the Eland ladies could not think his visit conferred much compliment to Laurel. The girl was very petite and young, with charming manners and eyes all for Albert. He, Laurel thought, was a little more carefree, a little less poised, and enjoying the admiration that Miss Colby evinced for him. The Cottinghams should be pleased with her. Laurel suffered no pangs, only wondering how much value the ability to waltz well might add to a marital union.

She did not see Gordon Rand that day or Thursday (because of the jaunt to Mendle) and managed not to think of him while admiring the niceties of Mr. Appleton's home. With a few pieces of furniture from Eland House it would be handsome. Several chief ladies of Mendle came for tea wearing beautiful hats and lavender gloves, not looking rustic at all. Mirabelle showed herself so delighted with the elegance of them and with their cordiality that they were soon equally delighted by the vicar's choice. Very likely there had been some handkerchiefs tossed at him locally, but these caused no hard feelings toward Mirabelle, demonstrating the wisdom of a universal guide for clergy: Never marry your parishioner when you have more than one who is single.

Mr. Appleton looked blissful, seeing how completely his

Mirabelle had won over the most influential females of his church. Although he might deny it, the vicar was well aware of power struggles among the ladies of his congregation. Mirabelle's being the daughter of a baronet made her a natural object of respect; her sincerity and obvious good will clinched the matter. A *lady* who was eager to be *loved* was welcome in Mendle. Only one woman, Mrs. Crawley, might have been jealous enough to cause trouble, but Mirabelle Eland, with her uncanny perception of ringleaders, appealed to her by whispering, "I hope you are going to guide me in my new duties." In this way the skirmish was won before it began.

It was true, Laurel knew, that both the aunties were inclined to give orders to all other females, yet it was always for the purpose of setting straight their hearers' lives that they, the aunties, so perfectly understood. It was good to know that Mr. Appleton would be watching over Aunt Mirabelle while she watched over Mendle.

"You will, of course, meet all the communicants of St. Paul's Church in due time," the vicar said to Mirabelle when the ladies had gone, "and if I know you, my dear, you will be loving to all. A minister's wife cannot permit herself to be closer to some than to others as that might cause jealousy. In a way, it is a lonely situation, but you will have your family nearby . . . and me."

Mirabelle said she understood. "If I become out of—of balance, you must call me to order."

It was not an easy situation in Laurel's view, yet her aunt did not seem daunted.

They rode homeward in a haze of satisfaction.

After the first mile Frances gave a little chuckle and said, "What a zany I was, John, to think James Appleton had offered for Laurel. Next I suppose you will try to gull us into thinking Dr. Dodd or Mr. Hanger would do for her."

"Well-l, Dodd is a grandfather, but Hanger—"

"Good heavens, John!" interrupted Mirabelle, coming to life. "Hanger is too old!"

Ruffling a bit, Sir John protested, "Hanger isn't *old*. Full of vitality, Belle. Would know how to deal wisely with a young girl."

"I hope you are teasing," declared Frances. "Otherwise I shall be shocked."

Laurel also hoped he was teasing. She had already decided not to be thrust into an unwelcome match, but her intention to make a good life for herself in Bayley Dell as a spinster (like her aunts) was beginning to falter as she stared into Aunt Mirabelle's glowing face. Mirabelle's past contentment was visibly giving way to joy, which made Laurel wonder just how much real contentment there may have been. But surely there would be pleasant activities to fill her own days, and she would always be able to share a home with her father and younger aunt! Until they were gone and she had faded into another Miss Onslow . . .

What a prospect!

Her three companions in the carriage were marvelously unalarmed and clear of brow. Their view of the future suddenly seemed optimistic compared with hers.

When the carriage pulled into Bayley Dell all was tranquil, somnolent. The Onslow ladies were at their watch post, waving to them and motioning ahead to their own open door, where a servant in Mr. Hanger's livery was conversing with Fane. As the chaise drew smoothly to a halt beside their stoop, the servant stepped forward to open the chaise door.

Sir John was first out. He handed down Aunt Frances and then Aunt Mirabelle. By the time the baronet's hand had guided his daughter to the stoop Frances was already examining a note passed to her by Mr. Hanger's servant.

"Oh, yes," she said. To the footman: "Tell Mr. Hanger that tomorrow at ten will be convenient." To her kin:

"Something about the location of the tent. Mr. Hanger has found one in Wells that is a bit larger than I had described."

"If Mendle and Hammish are to be included, we will need a larger one," Mirabelle commented.

Of Gordon Rand, the Unknown, no mention was made.

At breakfast the next day, however, Sir John asked what Laurel wished to hear. "Any word on the injured man, Fane?"

"Yes, sir. Doing much better, sir. The doctor's man says he is on the mend at last. Been nearly three weeks, sir."

The ladies paused in their eating to consider this.

"His arm will take longer than that," Mirabelle said as she buttered toast. "I wonder if some herbs——"

"He is taking rare beef now, ma'am."

Mirabelle nodded. "Then he *is* better. Healthy young men are not easily overcome."

At this point the knocker sounded. Fane, who was able to recognize a gentleman as surely as Blunk, was heard to say, "Good day, sir," approvingly.

"Family receiving?" asked a voice they recognized, though it was more cheerful than they had previously heard.

It was scarcely an hour that guests might be expected, yet Fane admitted the gentleman to the hall, where the Elands, streaming from the dining parlor, greeted him warmly.

"Made it here this time with ease, though I won't refuse a chair," Mr. Rand said. His spirits as well as his knee seemed to have improved. He still carried the cane and made discreet use of it, yet he walked more confidently and spoke likewise.

They led him into the nearest room, which was the parlor, and saw him settled in an armchair. Of his family connections the elders knew nothing, yet they accepted him in friendly fashion. His manners and attitude were those of a gentleman, which really proved nothing, for upstarts and (worse) knaves might imitate them. On the other hand, his face was refined and his voice free of all ill-bred timbres.

"Feeling more the thing?" asked Sir John.

"Indeed, yes. Still some twinges, of course, but my strength is returning. Feeling more human is good for one's morale, too."

"Ah!" said Sir John with empathy. "That is always the way I react when coming out of a bout of something, isn't it, Mirabelle? Frances? Very low and then suddenly rebounding."

The young man smiled, and his hearers saw how comely his face appeared when not pulled by pain. His eyes were frank and clear, his cheeks (smoothly shaved by Blunk) pale but the horrid bruise almost gone. "You've been extraordinarily open to a stranger. I have come to believe my name is Rand—at least that will do for a start, will it not?—and I wish to thank you most heartily."

So pleasing did Frances, Mirabelle, and Sir John find the young man that they gave permission when presently he asked if Miss Laurel might walk about with him.

"It is quite dry now," he said. "There are some clouds at a distance, but rain should not reach us for several hours. Not this morning, at any rate."

The elders agreed, although Frances followed Laurel upstairs when she went to fetch bonnet and pelisse, saying, "One does not like to *pry*. See if you can discover if the young man remembers any more than the name Rand, dearest."

Feeling somewhat guilty, Laurel made a vague reply and sped downstairs.

Without conscious plan they drifted down the street at a gentle walk, Gordon seeming to have no difficulty with the pace until they passed The Nesting Dove and entered the little lane that Mirabelle and Mr. Appleton had followed in the reverse direction. Here their pace slowed. Trees were sprouting green frills and birds twittered. It was a respectable place to stroll without being overheard.

"Have you found the boots?" asked Laurel.

He admitted he had not. "I had remained upstairs for twenty-four hours weak as a cat, and during that time much of the mud had dried. When I came down at last few tipplers wore boots—and those unlike what I sought."

"The guilty man may be weeks gone from our area," she suggested, but he replied that it was logical to suppose that he had been seen and marked for robbery by a local.

"I cannot believe any of our men could be guilty. Did you ask Patten if he remembered the night—remembered if there had been any strangers present when you ordered your meal?"

"Yes, I asked," he said. "But it was several days after the fact, and Patten says men are in and out at all hours on all days, and he cannot remember precisely that fatal night."

They had slowed almost to a halt. "Did you mention the boots to Patten? He might recognize them," she suggested.

"No," said Gordon with a shake of his head. "This is my own true clue that is better kept secret." He looked at her compellingly.

Laurel colored slightly. "I will not tell."

They walked farther along the lane, weaving from side to side of it to choose the smoothest path among the ruts.

"What next?" she asked.

"Oh, I have not given up," he assured her cheerfully. "If it rains tonight, as seems likely, there may be more men wearing boots—tonight and even tomorrow. Money and wounds are nothing—well, almost nothing. To lose Nipper and think someone may be mistreating him is a lot to bear."

Laurel understood that. She knew the grief that her father felt in being separated from his manor. Of course, a horse was not the same as one's inheritance, but the *sense* of loss was similar.

"If I do not find the culprit and his cohort here, I will

widen my search. Unfortunately, black horses are not unique."

"Has he no distinguishing mark at all?"

"No. But he knows his name and he knows my voice. We must hope it rains tonight."

Believing that Mr. Rand was in no shape to pursue thieves, she urged him not to be hurried, not to push himself and perhaps receive worse injury. "If the guilty ones have lingered in the area, they must feel safe from identification," she argued reasonably. "They will have hidden the horse somewhere and are now trying to seem as normal—as natural as possible, so as not to attract undue attention. If they are near here, they will be expecting to stay."

"It is true," he admitted, "that I did not see their faces. They were at pains to prevent that. They cannot know the boots of one can convict him. But, oh! they enrage me!"

She halted him by touching his arm in a gesture of mild restraint (for she had no power to control him). "Don't be angry," she begged. "It will only cloud your thinking and sap your strength."

Rand let out his breath and smiled ruefully. "You may be right," he said. "It is sobering to find gentle words can control as tough a creature as I."

Laurel returned his smile. "You are not tough, you are recuperating."

"Loathsome word! Do at least hope it rains tonight."

But she shook her head and resumed walking. "No. I will not hope for that. You need longer to regain your strength."

When they reached the footbridge beyond Browning's cottage he would have taken her arm, but the planks were wide enough only for single file. She grasped the pole that served as a handrail on the right, turning back her head to warn that he must be careful. "You will have to twist to use the handrail with your left hand. Can you manage your cane, too? Let me carry it. It would be dreadful if you were to fall into the brook!"

Gordon Rand passed her the cane with a grin. "I will advance crab-wise," he promised, and made the crossing slowly. "You would never have been able to drag me from the ravine."

"I would not have tried," she answered, assuming a callous expression, "but would have left you as a warning to reckless young men."

"So hard of heart!" he teased, drooping with exaggerated weakness.

"Very," she agreed. "Come along now, or be left in a cemetery."

Though his knee was aching, he chuckled, and plodded beside her along the north wall of the little church until they entered the lych-gate, where a seat awaited on each side. Laurel sat across from him with a sigh.

"Sometimes," she remarked, "walking slowly is more tiring than moving briskly."

But he did not hear her; he was facing down the village street. Lord Harry was approaching lazily on foot, and beyond him Gordon could see a yellow-wheeled curricle swinging into the inn yard.

"Good God!" he exclaimed. "Lady Pamela!"

Seventeen

Within three strides Lord Harold Guinn had reached the lych-gate and slid upon the seat beside Laurel.

"What is the yelp about?" he demanded.

"Your sister! You promised not to give me away!" Gordon said angrily.

"Well, damn it, I didn't!"

Shocked at the hostile atmosphere, Laurel stared from one to the other. Gordon Rand, seated opposite her, was first to notice her expression. With some effort at control, he said, "I was *trusting* you not to give away my location."

"I tell you I didn't," his lordship answered more calmly. "Isn't it to my best interests to keep mum? What is this about Pamela, eh?"

"She has just driven into the inn yard. Did you see, Miss Eland? No, of course you didn't, for you are facing the other way. She came from the south, behind your back, Harry, but I wager she could recognize a back view of her own brother, and it is not impossible that she caught sight of me. She had a groom beside her and another standing up behind."

"Even so," sighed Harry, "she should not have driven so far from home. Stay here while I see what I can do about turning her back. Father will have *my* head if she gets in trouble, and that ain't just! Keep out of sight, Rand."

Gordon groaned, "Too late. She is down from the curricle and walking this way. Dashed determined female!"

It seemed harsh language to describe a very beautiful lady, Laurel thought, not understanding what the tension was about. The two men seemed united now in harried consideration of Lady Pamela, and Lord Harold went down to meet her along the street. Laurel and Gordon could not hear the words the siblings exchanged, which apparently were of no use in distracting her ladyship. She shrugged off Harry's hand from her arm and continued up the slope.

"I'm seen," muttered Gordon, "and it will be disgraceful if we try to conceal you, Miss Eland. An introduction will be best. Come along."

The two couples met in the dusty street, under the eyes of a passing tinker, the tinker's donkey, and a small girl holding a black-and-white cat. Lady Pamela noticed none of these.

"So. This is where you have been, Gordon," she said sharply, not impressed by his arm sling and cane (which he made a show of needing).

He said mildly, "I have had a bit of trouble. May I present Miss Eland, whose father owns Bayley Manor?"

Lady Pamela said, "How d' you do," coldly and turned her back. "If you knew Gordon was injured—and I am sure you did, Harry—why did you not tell me? You remember I was expecting him."

Lord Harry opened his mouth to make some excuse, but Gordon forestalled him. "I was ill for a while and needed quiet—not visitors. I asked Harry to say nothing, knowing you would have several gentlemen of the first stare in attendance upon you."

"But I wanted—" she began, then bit her lip. She looked very out of place in such a simple village, the long skirt of a sapphire riding dress caught up with one arm, leaving parts of it to sweep the dirt. Her jaunty hat was ornamented with sapphire plumes, of the sort which would not appear in shops of Nord Cross. Oh, yes, she was a handsome young woman much like her brother, though her upper lip was short and more enticing. But her eyes, Laurel thought, despite incredibly long lashes, were singularly cold.

Unconsciously, Laurel drew back a step.

"You need not wait, Miss—er—Eland," said the lady dismissively. "The gentlemen and I have matters to discuss."

Laurel withdrew another backward step, then turned and fled up the street. From being very chilled she began to feel extremely hot. Up ahead she could see Mr. Hanger driving off with Aunt Frances, who was clutching a handful of papers.

At Eland House no one was in evidence. Laurel pounded up the familiar stairs and shut herself into her room. Would she have felt better to know both Gordon and Lord Harry were looking very grim? But she did not know, and they, for all their grimness, followed Lady Pamela into the parlor of the inn, where they gave garbled explanations, which did not satisfy her ladyship but stopped her questions.

When he could stand no more, Gordon Rand bowed himself from the room and limped up to his room to sink upon his bed. Obviously, Lady Pamela was angry; perhaps, if he were very lucky, she would be angry enough to go away.

In the parlor Lady Pamela was saying to her brother, "So Gordon was attacked and injured. What are you doing—romping with the local milkmaid?" She was very cross and meant someone to feel it.

He flung himself into a chair. "I was earning a living."

"You?"

"Yes; five hundred pounds, if you must know. You wheedle anything you want from Father, but he keeps me damnably short. How did you find me?"

"Simple. You slipped in and out of the house without being seen by Father, but I saw you and had only to ask at the stable to learn you had come by horseback from someplace nearby. I also saw you dancing attendance upon a new girl that you, yourself, told me was from Bayley Dell. It was logical to think you have been rusticating in this

THE BEAUX OF BAYLEY DELL   197

wretched place. I did not expect to find Gordon here. You
led me to him."

"Yes, and you have cost me my monkey, for which I
have wasted days and days. You owe me what I have lost,
old girl. Hand it over."

"Certainly not. You owe *me* for concealing Gordon's
whereabouts and spoiling my plans."

Lord Harry made a disagreeable noise. "Damn your
plans. You haven't a chance with Rand or he'd be letting
you nurse him instead of these rustics. What do you want
with Rand, anyway? Not the type to dance your tune."

"Then why did he accept my invitation to a house
party?"

"How should I know? Caught him with a vacant week,
perhaps. No reason to expect an ambush in this place, at
any rate, and now that he is here, he doesn't seem eager to
leave."

"You can't think this village chit can snare *Gordon!*" she
scoffed.

Lord Harry replied, "I don't say she can, but I do say
you can't."

Lady Pamela mouthed several unladylike things that
rather awed her brother and then called for her curricle and
servants. When thwarted she was considerably less beautiful, for her mouth pinched in an unlovely manner and her
eyes had no depth. No brother and sister had less affection
for one another. She departed without farewell, and Lord
Harry slumped in the chair, wondering how he would pay
his shot to escape this place.

Presently, when he rang, Del responded.

"Where's your pa?" asked his lordship crossly.

"Gone up to the gent, m'lord."

"Oh. Well, bring me an ale. Two ales."

"Pitcher, m'lord?"

Lord Harry gestured assent, but before the ale had been

supplied, Patten came to say the gentleman wished to se
him.

Though Gordon Rand was seated on the side of his be
when Harry entered, he rose to meet him on a level, an
said to him, "I have arranged with Patten to add your ta
to mine, so you are free to leave, as I know you have wante
to do."

"Why will he give an unknown credit? Your pockets ar
lighter than mine!"

Gordon gave a little sniff of amusement. "Very true. Bu
you have a curricle and pair at present in Patten's stable—

"Wait a minute," interrupted the harassed lord. "I'm no
leaving that rig here as security! It is too valuable."

"So I told Patten. You take the rig. Your horse with th
swollen fetlock will do nicely for me to ride when I leave
I will need a horse, you know. Until then it can be securit
for my debt here, and you remember that I pay *my* debts
I'll return the animal to you eventually. You lose nothing
right?"

No clear "yes" could be wrung from the disgruntle
peer, but he mumbled something affirmative. "Damn it
Gordon. What about the days I've idled here, waiting for
monkey and keeping my mouth shut about who you are?"

"Not tightly shut," corrected the injured man. "You sai
enough to bring Lady Pam down upon us—to insult Mis
Eland. There is no saying what false tale Pamela will tak
back to her friends."

Lord Harold leaned against the doorframe. He was n
richer for the days spent in Bayley Dell, but he had eate
and drunk, been amused, and was now free to go. "It's
bargain. Are we still friends, Rand?"

"The same sort we always were, Harry," Gordon an
swered dryly. "I'll thank you to contradict any false tale
your sister spreads about me—or anyone named Eland."

Harry gave a cocky salute and turned away.

"Oh, Harry! A saddle and bridle stay with the horse."

Lord Harold nodded briefly but went away without re-
plying.

He had little cause to dawdle in such a backward settle-
ment as Bayley Dell, yet when he had ordered his servants
to pack his belongings and hitch his pair, he delayed with
a last ale in Patten's taproom. Perhaps he had some lingering
desire to vindicate his idleness, or a less admirable wish to
spoke Rand's wheel. In any case, he emptied the mug and
set it upon the counter, saying to Patten (who eyed him
with no favor), "Fine brew. Mr. Rand will settle for me.
Good-bye."

Patten inclined his head an inch. He seized the empty
mug with one large paw and swiped the counter with the
other, addressing the side door as it swung shut, "Thankee,
m'lord, thankee ve-ry much!"

However likely Gordon Rand and Mr. Patten might think
his lordship was to leave town immediately, they were
wrong. He turned his curricle up the gentle rise of the street
toward Eland House, where he reined in and passed the
lines to his groom. "Short stop," he muttered, jumping
down.

Only moments before Mr. Hanger had returned Miss
Frances to her home, and now he could be seen rolling up
his driveway at a rattling pace.

Thus it was that when Lord Harry was admitted to the
residence he found all four family members in the drawing
room, Frances in her bonnet with brown satin ribbons and
a double pelisse of brown faced with lemon yellow. Holding
his hat and gloves casually (thank you, no, he could not
sit), Lord Harry greeted the elder aunt first, then Miss
Frances, then Laurel, with a smile and little bow to each.
With Sir John he shook hands.

"I've only come to say good-bye," he said jauntily.

Miss Mirabelle exclaimed in a startled manner, "Good-
bye? Are you leaving Bayley Dell so soon?" She cast an

anxious glance at Laurel. "Why, we have just become ac quainted!"

"Well, I am certainly glad of *that*—to meet the Elan family, I mean," he responded smoothly. "Bayley Dell ha been a delightful surprise. To think it is less than twent miles from my home, yet I had not had the felicity of know ing it or this gracious family!" He cast Laurel a languishin look that was supposed to flatter without committing hir to anything serious.

Laurel asked, "Has your horse's leg mended enough fo riding?"

"Er—yes. That is, the leg is almost well. I'll leave hir here a while longer. I am traveling in my curricle, don you know. I stayed so many days in case I could be of hel to the injured gentleman." Upon turning to include Mis Frances in his display of charm, he found that she ha slipped from the room. To remove her wraps? "I must nc keep my horses waiting. Good-bye, and thank you for most kind reception. Miss Laurel, if you come to Well again, you must be sure to save me dances."

Without an excess of feeling, Sir John wished him a saf journey. It was the ladies' response that seemed to interes Harry most. They said everything cordial, and when he a last had gone their memory of him was as pleasant as h might desire.

"I declare," said Mirabelle, following her brother as h retreated to his wing chair, "who would have thought w would encounter such a fine gentleman in our village? Johr do you think we will see more of him? John! I asked i you think he will call here again."

Sir John looked up from his comfortable seat. "How cai I think any such thing, when he so obviously was overjoye to be leaving us? What I would like to know is why h lingered in Bayley Dell so long." He raised his brows quiz zically. "Wonder how his fine servants liked Patten's attic."

"What has an attic to do with anything?" said Mirabelle, frowning the Eland perpendicular frown.

While they bickered amiably, Laurel stared out into the deserted street, wondering, as her father did, what had kept Lord Harry in the village for more than two weeks. How had he borne the tedium of a small inn? The ability of a beau of the ton to squander time was beyond her ken. She had not seen him lolling in Patten's tap, willing to toss a dart if there was a game going, and finding boredom an excuse for downing ale.

She could not suppose that an interest in herself had kept his lordship here, for they saw him seldom. When they did meet him he was all admiration and courtesy, free with implied compliments. Yet neither her father nor her aunts had invited him to dine, which she had thought they might do for one clearly established as the Earl of Clifton's son. Was it possible they were ashamed for him to see the simple way they lived?

She turned from the window, seeing with a stranger's eyes the mellow drawing room, rich with fading draperies of gold and well-rubbed pieces of heirloom furniture. The carpet (if Lord Harry looked so low) was thin and ancient, yet quite lovely. Enough ornaments to grace the tables had been brought from Bayley Manor, though not enough to *clutter*, as one so often saw. Lord Harold's home might be many times larger and overwhelmingly grander, but it could not be more tasteful, she believed.

She told herself firmly that she was not going to fret over any man who was too absorbed in his own consequence to notice the refinement of a family less wealthy than himself. She did not suspect, of course, how few coins clinked in his pocket to keep him from being insolvent. His raiment was elegant, his person tall and well-proportioned, dazzling with golden good looks, and his tongue quick with facile flattery. But could she believe he was genuine in his interest in herself? "No," said her sober judgment. Yet her

experience was slight. She thought of interrupting Papa and
Aunt Mirabelle to ask their opinions but was unwilling to
reveal any eagerness for Lord Harry's attention.

He had begged her to save dances for him, had he not?
That was encouraging. Or was it polite insincerity? Papa
might know, or Aunt Mirabelle. But it had been *ages* since
they flirted with anyone. It was unlikely they could say anything helpful to her now. Yes, Harry had said, "Save
dances." But, on the other hand, he had gone from Bayley
Dell for no stated reason, and *that* suggested no serious
interest in the impecunious Miss Laurel Eland.

Mr. Rand, on the other hand, had trusted her with his
identity and his reason for lingering in the village, the two
together being, she was inclined to think, evidence that he
valued her as a trustworthy friend. The expression in the
blue pools of his eyes told her that she was . . . not under-
valued by him.

Fane opened the drawing room door to announce luncheon. Mirabelle halted in her debate with Sir John to say,
"Oh, Fane, Miss Frances went upstairs. You will have to
sound the gong."

He did so, and Frances came promptly. She was subdued,
which her siblings did not notice as Mirabelle continued
her discussion of allowing a peer to escape, and Sir John
applied himself to his plate as though he were a gourmand,
which everyone knew he was not.

When Frances had gone off that morning in Mr. Hanger's
curricle wearing a ribboned bonnet and carrying a roll of
lists and suggestions, it was intended they would drive to
the south lawn to settle the matter of where the tea tent was
to be placed. Instead, Mr. Hanger, splendid in new brown
riding coat and fawn breeches, said, "Since today is truly
a fine day, would you not like to ride about the manor? I
have business with a tenant or two; they would be pleased
to see you, I think."

Frances was torn between mortification at no longer being family-in-residence and curiosity as to how well Mr. Hanger maintained tenant cottages.

So she said, "You are right about the weather. I should enjoy a little drive." As she was forty-one and past the age of dangerous flirtations, a drive on country lanes (with a groom standing up behind) should not be compromising. Such was not suggested, and a tour of her own home lands was even more permissible. The groom would be useful for opening gates.

Though a small estate, Bayley Manor was dear to Eland eyes. As they passed orchards, beginning to bud pink and white, and crossed fields where familiar laborers were working, her vision blurred, although not so badly as to need a touch of handkerchief. By staying away these dozen years she had learned to keep control of her emotions.

Noticing nothing, Mr. Hanger said, "Isn't a farm revitalizing when it wakes for Spring? I was a city lad, you know. My friends in London tried to tell me I would sprout insensibly like a cabbage if I left the metropolis. Well, I haven't done that, but I *have* put down roots and flourished, in a manner of speaking. My bailiff tells me his pa was hard put to provide for a second son, which he was, so he trained him in land uses and sent him off to make his own way in the world. Lucky for me!"

She agreed. "John says you could not find a better man."

"Did he say that? I am glad to please him. You must let me say, Miss Frances, that I feel deeply for your brother in this situation."

"John is a man of character, which could not be said for our older brother."

"Improvident?"

"Alas, worse. John hopes—" she broke off, embarrassed.

Mr. Hanger said calmly, "Hopes to have his home again someday? Not unreasonable, you know."

"But you must not think he wants to *drive* you away!"

"Well, I don't. When his title is free and clear I will just have to buy some property for myself."

They turned into a lane lined with tenant cottages, and she leaned forward to exclaim, "Oh, there is Mrs. Dunnerd!"—which distracted them from the humiliating subject of land ownership.

"Would you like to stop?" He reined in.

Mrs. Dunnerd was a tall woman with brown hair scraped back in an untidy knot. She was lined before her time, yet smiled eagerly as she straightened from a clothes basket and hurried to the curricle, clasping a damp garment.

"Miss Frances! It's a fair treat to see you."

Frances stretched out a hand, and the woman transferred the garment to her left hand as she came forward, wiping her right hand upon her skirt. She touched the offered hand shyly.

"Mrs. Dunnerd was upstairs maid before she married Dunnerd," Frances explained to Mr. Hanger. "Many are the favors for which Mirabelle and I must thank her."

"Dunnerd upset all that?" asked Mr. Hanger with a grin.

The woman pursed her lips and jerked her head. "Dunnerd and four naughty young ones."

"Don't be misled, Mr. Hanger," said Frances. "They are bonny children."

"Indeed they are. I know them." He nodded toward Mrs. Dunnerd's clothesline. "Four keep one busy, that is sure. Where is your husband, ma'am?"

"In the east field, sir."

"Then I have missed him. Tell him to see me first thing in the morning."

The woman said, "Aye, sir." She bobbed to Frances and returned to her line, shaking out as she went the large damp smock in her hands.

"Wasted on Dunnerd," Frances observed in an undertone as they drove on.

Mr. Hanger said, "It may be so. Dunnerd is not the greatest worker. Some cuts below her, I'm afraid."

"But she is working harder than she ever did as house maid!"

"Only now she works for husband and children. Might mean more to her than someone else's home." He cast Frances an assessing look.

"You may be right," she admitted.

They completed a leisurely circuit and halted at the north door of the manor house.

"Come walk through the garden," Mr. Hanger invited. "It's dry enough. We even stirred up a bit of dust with our wheels."

He handed over the reins to the groom and stepped down.

"But we haven't settled anything. My notes—"

"Here. Pass them to me." He seized the roll of papers and thrust it into a pocket. Then he held out a large hand and commanded, "Come along, my girl."

Mr. Hanger's invitation being (as often) imperative, she allowed her small, gloved hand to rest in his palm as she descended to the gravel. Then, after he had instructed the groom to hold the curricle in readiness at the stable, he nipped her elbow between thumb and forefinger and propelled her to the garden gate, which she perfectly well knew.

He released her elbow to open the gate. "It is early yet to see mature plants, but all are thriving, I think."

Frances entered. "Norton is still in charge, is he not?"

"Yes. And cantankerous as ever. I think he keeps his sweet talk to persuade the flowers to bloom."

She laughed, adding, "And his strictest commands for vegetables. Produce or be cast out like weeds! Shall we see Norton today?"

"Oh, he is here somewhere. Turn this way, Miss Frances, so we may reach the round pool."

Beds were newly spaded and plants from the glasshouse

set out, with due attention to space for the ones that were expected to spread most. Fine pebbles made the pathways, meticulously raked. All was as Frances had known it in many bygone Aprils when she had strolled here. What was best, for both her and Mr. Hanger, was absence of anger, resentment, or even regret in her heart. The tidy garden worked its magic.

"All is perfect," she said.

"Do you think so? My orders have been to keep it as it always was. You see no errors?"

"It is just right."

"Then I beg you tell Norton so. He is at the bottom of this row now. He does not give a fiddle-dee-dee for *my* opinion . . . though it is I who pay his wages."

"Ah," she bantered, "if he disdained you he would be painfully polite. Grumbles you may take as a good sign."

They approached Norton, who, spying them, straightened somewhat and leaned upon his hoe. He was a tall, wiry man, bent a bit from age, though still vigorous.

"Good day, Norton," said Miss Frances with something of her usual verve.

He touched his hat with a grimy forefinger and said, "Ar."

"Miss Frances thinks the garden is looking as perfect as always," Mr. Hanger offered, to encourage conversation.

She followed his lead quickly: "I notice the soil is very well worked and looks rich. What manure are you using now, Norton?"

"Sheep," he growled, "when I can git it."

"I suppose that accounts for the bright foliage."

"Ar." Norton presumably agreed.

Rescuing the conversation, Mr. Hanger asked if Frances would like to walk into the shrubbery, which was near at hand.

"Damp," objected Norton, before she could reply.

Mr. Hanger said, "The weather has been dry for a while."

"Shady. Damp," said Norton, adding with surprising loquacity, "always said we needed gravel."

"It was Mama who insisted on grass in the shrubbery," Frances explained to Mr. Hanger. "She thought it would seem more natural. Of course, there were many days we could not walk there."

"Nah," concurred Norton.

"Would you prefer gravel?" Mr. Hanger asked Frances.

"We all would have done so."

"Well, why not? Sir John would not object? It sounds reasonable to me. Figure how much we will need, Norton, and I will order it."

Norton pointed the forefinger again in the direction of his hat and said, "Ar," which was understood this time to mean "Yes, sir."

Frances said, "Good-bye, Norton," and received another "Ar." Mr. Hanger returned her through the garden to the drive, which they followed idly around the house to the south lawn.

This was the area customarily chosen for activities of the Public Day, because it was wide, with scarcely any slope. Mr. Hanger drew Frances's roll of papers from his pocket to gesture with it. "The tea tent should go to the left of that oak? And the races farther out?"

"Yes. Will there be space for the larger tent that you have ordered?"

"Oh, I think so."

They drifted out onto the lawn. Nearing the splendid oak tree, Frances turned to look back at the facade of her old home.

"Would you like to see inside?" he asked with gentle awareness of her nostalgia.

"Oh—no. It would not be proper—"

"I can call my housekeeper to show you around. Perhaps only the lower rooms?"

She shook her head.

"I thought," he ventured, watching her from the corner of his eye, "you might like to see if you would want to live there again."

There was a very brief moment during which she caught her breath. His recent odd attentions suddenly illuminated, she burst out: "Mr. Hanger! Are you making me an offer?"

"Good God! You can't think I mean a slip on the shoulder!"

"But we are barely acquainted," she protested.

"And whose fault is that? Well? Well? I've had my eye on you for years, and you hardly gave me a 'how-do-you-do.' I know what I want, all right." He cast a wild look at Bayley Hall. "Good God! Twenty windows—forty eyes likely. I'm a fool to pick such a public place. Damn Norton and the damp shrubbery! What do you say?"

"I need to think."

"Another eight or ten years? Do you like me at all?"

She admitted, "I like you very well, sir, but there are problems."

"Tell me what they are and leave me to handle them."

She smiled at that. "I daresay you would try. Well, for one thing, there is Laurel. Mirabelle will be moving to Mendle when she marries James Appleton. I can't leave Laurel without a chaperone."

"She will have her father."

"Yes, but a young girl needs a woman's company and guidance."

"Simple," said Mr. Hanger. "Bring her here. Bring her here. There is nothing I would like better than to have her sweet self brightening the house."

"But that," Frances reasoned, "would leave poor John alone."

"Bring him, too," said Mr. Hanger, scenting success.

She shook her head. "He would never come as a guest."

His face fell. "No, I suppose not. There must be some

solution. You are not refusing me outright, are you, my girl?"

Miss Frances was discovering it was difficult to refuse Mr. Hanger anything to which he had set his mind. "You have paid me a beautiful compliment," she said, "but I must think."

"All right; two days."

"Oh, no. Three weeks—until Mirabelle has had her wedding."

"Three weeks! After spurning me for years already? My patience has limits. Two days ought to be enough for a thousand thoughts."

"Two weeks, at least."

In the end he agreed to wait two weeks, although he said, "There must be only one answer." He drew out his watch. "Eleven twenty-three. Two weeks from today."

Eighteen

As fair weather continued, Gordon Rand's frustration grew. Evening after evening he endured a hard settle or stool in Patten's taproom, hoping to see a particular pair of lethal boots. Seldom did he see anyone, with or without boots. While the weather was so good, men worked long hours in fields and pens to make the most of Nature's blessing. By nightfall they were too tired to congregate at The Nesting Dove; a good meal and a comfortable bed were all each wanted.

Usually Patten was behind the bar, sucking a broom straw, eyes half shut in boredom. The necessities of business and profit made him as impatient with good weather as was Rand.

The invalid took his meals there, stretching his evening meal as long as possible to fill time. Usually Del served him, although sometimes Mrs. Patten came from her kitchen to fuss over him with some idea that since she had helped to nurse him, then he must in a way belong to her.

Morning or afternoon, or both, Laurel walked with Mr. Rand, urging him to greater exercise and bearing patiently (for a while) his complaints about sunshine and balmy winds. When particularly exasperated by his wish for storms and mud, she would declare he was "unnatural." If the word "spoiled" came to her mind, she subdued it by biting her tongue.

She would say, "It is spring in England and rain will

come sooner or later. Then you will have as much mud as you will ever want to see again."

"It is not mud I want, but boots," he would reply, until she grew tired of the word. In short, he was not the best of company for a romantic young lady.

At home, at Eland House, things were not much better. Aunt Mirabelle was agitated over her wardrobe—mending and washing and ironing—and hanging things *everywhere,* as she did not wish her dresses and petticoats to muss, and it was not yet time to pack them. Aunt Frances had a sort of cloud wrapped around herself and talked little, which was certainly contradictory to her nature. Papa was no help. He was seldom at home, perhaps driven away by the female frenzy there. The ladies, busy with their own affairs, did not think to miss him.

Mr. Rand's bruises were fading, and he tried walking without his cane though continuing to carry it. Dr. Dodd still required him to keep his arm in a sling. When invited to Eland House for dinner he declined, saying the table manners produced by use of his left hand would appall the Elands.

"We won't mind," said Laurel.

"Yes you would," he replied, "and that is to say nothing about my dinner coat." He gestured to Patten's jacket, which was large enough to wrap his splinted right arm and which had the left cuff turned back several inches.

She had been right about one thing, however. It was spring and the rain did come—one night as she lay cozily in bed. Torrents of rain thundering on the roof, and making as much mud as Gordon Rand could wish.

As the downpour continued into the next day, Patten's tap had a full house. Mrs. Patten cooked so strenuously that hairs escaped from her cap and moisture beaded on her forehead. Patten himself was constantly busy behind the bar, while Del and Roddy served the tables.

Were there boots? Lots of boots! Mr. Rand applied him-

self to a study of them. Unfortunately, most were so coated
with mud that no detail could be discerned. He settled down
to watch closely as heat from a hearty fire caked the mud
and flaked it off. So busy was he with his self-imposed
duty, staring mostly about the floor and under tables, that
he failed to see Patten sling on a cape and plunge out the
side door to the stable. In fact, so intent was Mr. Rand that
he did not realize Patten had gone until mugs began to
pound upon bar and tables.

Then the side door flew open and wind blew Patten and
a splatter of water into the room.

Instinctively, Mr. Rand looked down, and there, *there* on
Patten's feet were incriminating boots. Rand stared. His
pulses jumped and blood rushed to his head. Could Patten
be the thief he sought?

The landlord of The Nesting Dove went behind the bar,
hung his cloak upon a peg, and calmly began to draw ale.

Mr. Rand's head swam.

When the villagers' wants had been met the invalid raised
his empty tankard and croaked, "Patten, another."

Patten rolled from behind the bar to take the mug. "Sorry
to be slow, sir. I had to check the horses."

"Rotten night," Mr. Rand said.

"Good for business," whispered Patten.

"But not so good for men . . . wet your feet?"

"Nah. Me boots don't leak."

Mr. Rand managed a skeptical expression. "Where did
you get boots like that?"

Patten looked bored. "Fellow in Hammish makes 'em.
Most men has got 'em. Right, Charlie?"

A nearby man turned his head. "Boots? Best damn boots
awalking. Had to save my shillings for weeks, but worth
it." He stuck out a foot and brushed away the soil clinging
to an identical boot.

Patten went away with the empty mug, and Mr. Rand
leaned an elbow on the table to catch his forehead with his

hand. Across the room, Blunk was watching. Seeing his patient's distress, and not assuming the correct cause, he came at once to say gently: "Your day has been long enough, sir. A body can take just so much. Let me help you upstairs."

Mr. Rand raised his head. "It is not my body, Blunk, but my mind. I had thought . . . well, never mind. You're right. This is no place for me."

As he lumbered to his feet, Del came with the fresh beer he had ordered. "Give that to someone, Del, and put it on my bill."

Upstairs, Blunk soon had his patient settled in bed. "I believe the rain is letting up, sir. You will feel cheerier to-morrow if the sun comes out."

"I've lost interest in rain," Mr. Rand droned.

"Very likely," said the servant in a calm and soothing manner, "but the crops will drink it up sooner than beer."

Left alone, Mr. Rand groaned and cursed himself for nearly being a fool. "Thank God I did not accuse Patten without warrant!" It did not take much thought for him to realize that Patten could never have been *before* him on the forest road that night of the attack. Nor was there a singular boot to serve as a valid clue to anyone.

In the morning there was sunlight doing its best to dry the street, and a light breeze had already made the bench under the chestnut fit for sitting. Mr. Rand settled himself there gloomily to watch the road and wonder when it would be suitable for him to walk up or Laurel Eland to walk down.

While he waited, he saw Sir John ride from the stable yard on a gray horse and head south. "What horse is that?" he asked young Roddy, who was sweeping from the inn's stoop some tender leaves that had been brought down by the rain.

"Mr. Hanger's, sir," Roddy said. "He sent it down for Sir John to use when he pleases."

"That was generous."

"Aye. M' fa says Mr. Hanger's 'most obliging' to everyone—and I gets *paid* for tending the horse!"

"That makes it a very fine horse, eh?"

Roddy grinned. "Yes, sir, it do."

In the afternoon the invalid was able to plod up the street to sit again on the Elands' doorstep and talk morosely with Laurel about the failure of his boot clue. She was not, as he had hoped and expected, sympathetic.

"Well, now you can put the whole episode out of your mind and concentrate on getting well," she said.

He looked at her reproachfully. "I thought you would feel for me."

"I have been feeling for you for days," she stated roundly. "Time to think positively. Your leg is well, isn't it? And your arm almost healed—at least it does not hurt, does it? Surely your health is more important than a *horse.*"

"I thought you understood. It was a special horse."

"Well, maybe so. I have never owned a horse, special or otherwise, but I did lose my *mother,* which is certainly worse, and I haven't gone on grieving. How can you go forward in life if you are busy being sad about something?"

Gordon Rand was silent.

"I'm sorry," she said more gently. "I don't mean to be unfeeling. You see, there is Papa. He has lost so much, and one does not see him wearing a long face. I suppose your body isn't well yet, and that keeps your spirits from being what they should."

It was impossible, of course, for him to look into those clear, amber-brown eyes and continue in absorption with Self. "Thank you, my dear Miss Eland," he said slowly, "for giving me that last excuse. You may not believe it, but I am not prone to black moods. I shall endeavor to cast this one off—"

"And look *forward?*"

"Yes, yes."

Laurel had the uncomfortable feeling that his forward-looking would mean a departure soon from Bayley Dell. There was no way for her to guess where his life belonged or where he would go.

At that point Fane opened the door to say Miss Laurel was wanted.

"I am keeping you from more important things," Gordon said, struggling to his feet. "Shall we walk tomorrow?"

A little breathlessly she answered, "Yes, if you have not left."

"Left Bayley Dell? I cannot sit a horse yet."

Fane, waiting, said again, "Miss Laurel—"

She saw Gordon start away. "Coming, Fane. Where are the ladies?"

"In the drawing room, Miss."

After one last look toward the man making his way in the direction of the village, she whisked indoors.

In the drawing room, the aunts looked up to greet her.

"I cannot like your entertaining gentlemen on the *door-step,* dearest," said Aunt Frances in a severe voice she seldom used for Laurel.

"Oh, Auntie, poor Mr. Rand has been so blue!"

Frances pursed her lips. "Once was not improper, but to make a habit of it—like a village girl with a peasant swain—"

"Now, Sister, don't fault our darling for a soft heart," objected Mirabelle, whose own heart was tender these days.

"Then she must invite him in to join us."

"When I first did so," Laurel explained, "he said he felt too shabby—and today, of course, he is muddy. Surely I cannot cause gossip when the Misses Onslow have me under constant scrutiny!"

Frances smiled forgivingly. "It is not your *behavior* that I have in mind, so much as your *seeming* like a village—well, never mind. The stranger will be gone soon."

"When he is able to ride," Laurel added. She curtsied

and escaped to her bedchamber, thinking how odd it was that her life, which had always been serene, should have become confusing in a few weeks. All was topsy-turvy. Aunt Mirabelle, who had run the household efficiently, was thinking only of her wedding. Aunt Frances, the fun-loving one of her aunts, had become downright critical. And Papa, dear Papa, was never around except for meals, and not all of those.

It had been interesting to meet someone dashing like Lord Harold Guinn, but she did not intend to fret over his leaving. If he was a sample male of the ton, she was not at all sure she wished to meet more of them. What was there to say to society beaux whose chief concern was the set of their coats?

To glide across a candlelit ballroom floor to string music was certainly pleasant, but one could not dance through life! It was more comfortable—yes, more refreshing—to stroll country lanes where sunlight filtered through new leaves.

Minutes sped by. She had only just taken out a frock for dinner when Fane's first gong sounded. She scrambled into the dress and smeared the surface of her hair with a brush.

Papa was with the aunts when she descended. He gave her a kiss and tucked her arm through his to lead her into the dining room.

When the meal had been finished the three ladies rose to leave John to his ritual port, but he accepted a glass from Fane and carried it into the drawing room in their wake.

"I grow lonely there," he said. He downed the wine and turned to poke the fire, which Fane considered his privilege.

The aunts had seated themselves and taken up needle-work in a desultory manner. He did not sit, but handed Laurel his empty wineglass and took a position before the hearth.

"I have a bit of news for you," he said. Sir John did not have an effusive manner; his ladies looked at him with only mild curiosity. "Sarah Walden has agreed to become my wife."

Frances (the talker of the family) was speechless. Mirabelle cried, "Wife!" And Laurel sank to the nearest chair.

"I must thank you, Mirabelle, for introducing Sarah into my life," he continued calmly, though the color flooded his face, as Frances and Mirabelle began a jumble of questions, the chief of which concerned how he had courted the charming widow and when the marriage was to take place.

He explained that Mr. Hanger had generously put a horse at his disposal. He had gone, as invited, to Sarah's Sunday and Wednesday teas, and then when their—ah, affinity—became noticeable, he went more often.

"You mean," queried Mirabelle, "that Hanger knew more of your business than your *sisters?*"

"He asked no embarrassing questions. Having twice seen me ride off on Patten's hack he said I needed a better mount and he would send one down to be available to me at Patten's stable. I'm obliged to him for swifter and easier trips."

"You have not said when this marriage is to take place," prodded Frances with a secret look on her face that the embarrassed lover did not notice.

"Late May or early June, perhaps. At our ages, what is the point of a long engagement? Sarah wants to take Laurel to London for the little season in the Fall. We hope she may make an eligible connection there, as Bayley Dell has nothing to offer, and Wells not much. If Laurel does not find someone to suit her, we will take her again next spring for the regular Season. Unfortunately, we are too late for this year."

"But, Papa! The cost!" exclaimed Laurel.

Her father smiled at her benignly. "Let me worry about that. A court presentation we will not consider. Otherwise, Sarah has thought it all out. She has an elderly uncle who lives in lonely splendor in Berkeley Square, and she assured me he will welcome us to his home. Sarah is eager to see Laurel settled well."

"Where will you live?" asked Frances.

Sir John smiled. "We have a plenitude of homes. In Sarah's house much of the time, but probably here in hot weather. You need not think, dear Frances, that you will have no home. This house has been, and will continue to be your dwelling."

Frances's lips twitched. "You need not fret about me. I have had an offer from Mr. Hanger."

"Hanger!" squealed Mirabelle. "Good heavens! You haven't accepted Hanger!"

"Not yet. But I must warn you that I may do so."

Mirabelle looked aghast. "But you have always said—"

"Please," interrupted Frances. "Do not pain me by recalling all the foolish and ill-natured things I may have said about Mr. Hanger. I hope I can forget them myself." She smiled warmly at Laurel. "When I suggested that I could not leave Laurel here without a lady companion he promptly invited her to join us at the manor. It was one of the lures he dangled before me."

"But Laurel will have the company of Sarah along with me," Sir John said. "After all, she is my daughter."

"Oh, Brother, you are not thinking," said Mirabelle. "Frances and I have been her *mother* since she was an infant. You must not separate her from us. Laurel must come with me to Mendle!"

Frances laughed. "Are you proposing to cut her in equal shares? Mr. Hanger may retract his offer if Laurel is not included in our marriage contract."

Laurel turned anxiously from one to another as they spoke. Suppose they asked *her* to choose? How could she? Papa or an auntie? The very prospect made her feel ill. And then Sir John asked a question that she could answer without hesitation.

"Do you want a London season, my dear?"

"No, Papa, I do not think so."

Immediately the sisters joined forces to exclaim, "Of course she does." "She must have one."

Sir John raised a hand to quiet them. "Why not, Daughter?"

"I've had a taste, Papa. The trip to Wells was exciting and I enjoyed it, but the more I think, the more I realize a debut is an artificial way to meet a husband. There is no way of telling from a dinner or a dance what a man's nature may be. If the beaux in London are all like Lord Harry, how do I distinguish between them?"

Mirabelle made a sound of distress. "My dear one, has his lordship hurt your feelings?"

She shook her head. "Not at all. It was very amusing to see him go through his repertoire of charms. One wonders if he repeats periodically."

"Good Lord!" cried Frances. "She sounds twice her age!"

"Well, I am impressed by her good sense," declared Aunt Mirabelle. "Dear child, come to James and me. There will be young ladies your age in Mendle, and very likely brothers. We will extend acquaintance to Nord Cross, and perhaps visit Bath and Bristol."

Laurel spread her hands in a helpless gesture. "How can I choose between you?"

"There is no necessity to decide tonight," Sir John said. "Will you all wish me happiness?"

His three ladies then threw themselves upon him, so that he felt smothered with femininity and affection.

When they had left him to think about his changing state and gone upstairs to a women's session in Laurel's room, Frances spoke her mind: "Why do you suppose Sarah Walden wants to marry our John? He is no sophisticate."

"Maybe because he is not," said Mirabelle. "I have known her longer and better than you. She is sound through and through. She may seem to us a bit frivolous, but she is perfectly reliable."

"Yet more lively than he is. She'll want to be *doing* much, while he likes to be quiet with some book or other."

"What difference does that make? You are livelier than I and we rub along very well. For that matter, John has been galloping around the countryside lately in an energetic fashion, although we did not know it."

"Very true," Frances agreed. "Could—could a title have something to do with it?"

"What title?"

"Lady Eland."

"Oh, because of John's impecunious 'Sir?' I doubt that carries much weight with Sarah."

"Papa has a very sweet nature," said Laurel, shocked at the question they raised. "He will make Mrs. Walden feel welcome and comfortable and loved and secure. I think that should mean a great deal to her."

They did not disabuse her of the notion, as neither could think how to do it.

"Perhaps she is lonely," Mirabelle suggested. That Sir John might also be lonely never occurred to them. After all, had he not been a contented bachelor nearly twenty years?

Nineteen

Like Laurel's mood, the sky was overcast when she awoke and lay thinking about the upheaval in her family. That she would someday be wedded had been generally understood. Talk about it had begun when she turned seventeen. At least, Aunt Frances had had much to say on the subject, more or less supported by Aunt Mirabelle, while Papa remained noncommittal. Their social life was nil. Eighteen came, and then nineteen, and now twenty. One year was like another, except the hot summer when Dr. Dodd's nephew came for a visit and gave her a slight flutter. But he was her own age and established in nothing; no one encouraged a match, least of all the doctor.

For a few weeks she dwelt in her mind on a fantasy wherein the young man went into government service, became much admired for his acumen, advanced with spectacular speed, and carried her off to live in London. None of this happened, of course, and she soon concluded that she would not like to live in a sprawling, sooty city anyway.

Now all was turned upside down, with her papa and aunts planning new homes and lives elsewhere. All were generous in offering to take her, but she sensed it would not do. New homes would be *theirs,* not hers. Yet they would never allow her to remain alone at Eland House. The manor, with Frances, might be tolerable, as it was large enough that she might not forever be in Mr. Hanger's way. To go to London with Papa and Mrs. Walden—Lady Eland!—might be better, as she would meet prospective husbands . . . if there were any less superficial than Lord Harold Guinn. As for the parsonage in Mendle, it sounded dull. She could devote herself to church work as well here as there! She was glad— yes, glad—for each of her loved ones, but her own prospects were dim indeed.

When Laurel descended to breakfast she found that Sir John had acquainted the servants with his intended marriage and assured them they would be needed to maintain Eland House in its customary condition. About Frances, apparently he had said nothing; her plans were undecided, though it seemed likely Mr. Hanger's suit would be successful.

"May I tell the Misses Onslow your news, John?" asked Mirabelle. "It will mean so much to them to be the first to know."

"Certainly you may," said her brother, his elation having spilled over into this morning. "My dears, you must find a day soon when I can take you over to Wells to welcome Sarah into our family."

There followed some discussion about inviting Sarah to visit at Bayley Dell. The perennial problem of No Guest Room was insurmountable.

"If we wait until after Mirabelle's wedding, there will be a vacant room," Frances said. "Why not invite her for the ceremony and ask her to stay until the Public Day? There is very little of interest in our village to amuse her, but she might enjoy preparations for the fête. What do you think, John?"

Sir John was quick with his opinion that the future Lady Eland would take especial interest in an Eland event.

"Papa," said Laurel, "it is really Mr. Hanger's fête, isn't it? None of us can expect to take credit for much of it."

Mirabelle look regretful. "Too true. We are hardly better than outsiders."

"Oh, in a way, in a way." He surprised them by winking at his younger sister. "If Frances can see her way clear to accepting a certain gentleman, the manor and Public Day will be all in the family."

"Don't press me," said Frances. "I am still thinking. He has given me two weeks to decide. It seems to me that the credit for a fête has very little to do with a marriage." As she seemed complacent about something, Laurel thought her aunt was in a fair way to giving in to her suitor.

Only why, wondered Laurel, was Frances keeping poor Mr. Hanger on pins and needles? Was it a game of dominance? If so, it looked as though Frances had met her match, for Mr. Hanger was not haunting their home. He had not, in fact, been heard from since bringing Frances home nearly twenty-four hours earlier.

Of the four Elands sitting at breakfast, three were plainly exhilarated. Only Laurel felt forlorn, wishing for someone to share her uncertainties. When the meal had ended she went to look out at the village street and, finding it more or less dry (at least not a total morass), decided to walk into the village in hopes of meeting *someone* who might enter into her despondent mood.

She hastened upstairs and was just returning with a hooded cloak when Fane opened the door to a huge bouquet of flowers.

"For the ladies," said a footman from the manor, and Laurel thought how clever Mr. Hanger was to include her and Mirabelle.

She threw open the drawing room door. "Aunties, Mr. Hanger has sent down beautiful flowers from the glasshouse."

They made noises of surprise and came out into the hall, where Fane was almost hidden by the bouquet. "For the ladies," he repeated.

"For all three of us?" asked Mirabelle.

"I believe so, ma'am."

"I heard Mr. Hanger's man say so," Laurel affirmed. "Do you need me to help arrange them?"

"No, dear, you're going out, aren't you? Frances and I will see to them. Aren't they lovely, Frances?"

Looking somewhat self-conscious, Frances said, "Beautiful. Take them to the kitchen, Fane. We will put them in vases right away."

Laurel let herself out the front door to encounter Miss Onslow, senior, who came racing to the Eland steps.

"Such an enormous bouquet of flowers!" she panted. "Are they from Mr. Hanger?"

"Yes. For the three of us, but enough to spread all over the house," said Laurel. "It will give us some idea of what he can furnish for Aunt Mirabelle's wedding. Is that not thoughtful of him?"

"Oh, yes. Very kind. Most kind. You will be wanting to decorate the church, won't you? Very kind of him to send a sample. I'll tell Sister."

Laurel waved to the sister in her bow window and continued down the street, amused and consequently in better spirits. At the Everything Shop she met Gordon Rand, just coming out.

"I've written Father. He will not be overjoyed to hear from me, as I have asked him to send money."

"If you explained what happened—" she began.

"Well, I did and I didn't. Said I had been robbed and had taken some nasty blows. No need to cause the old fellow to get the wind up. Just asked for money, and not as much as I had thought, now that Harry has taken himself off."

Without conscious plan they had continued to stroll down through the village.

Gordon was carrying the cane furnished by Dr. Dodd, but he was not using it. No longer talking, they passed The Nesting Dove and, upon reaching the point where the Wells road led left and the rough lane bore off to the right, they chose the lane by unspoken agreement.

"If this is too muddy, we can turn back," he said.

Laurel, whose mood was perfectly compatible with mud, merely shook her head.

"Why so quiet?" he asked, being used to her keeping his spirits on an even keel. When he was in pain she comforted; when irritated she soothed; when low she cheered; when sorry for himself she jacked him up sharply. Now, to his surprise, something was obviously depressing *her*, and it was his turn to calm and encourage.

"Feeling downcast?" he asked.

"Oh, no . . . well, a bit." She walked with her head down.

"Someone being ugly? Not missing Harry, I hope!"

"No. I had forgotten him."

"Well, that is good news. I feared you might have—er— had some interest there. He's a pretty fellow but not enduring in his attentions."

She smiled at that, a little one-sided lift at the corner of her mouth such as her papa sometimes displayed. "Lord Harry never paid me any attention that anyone could think serious—only a dance and a few routine compliments."

They rambled farther along the lane, until he demanded: "Are you going to tell me what's the matter? You've had to hear me moan and groan and rant and rave and feel sorry for myself. It's your turn. Play fair!"

The demand for fair play made her raise her head. "You will think me silly. A lot of good things are turning life upside down."

"What things?"

"Aunt Mirabelle is going to marry Mr. Appleton, for one."

"I know that. Surely you don't mind!"

"Oh, no! She is happy to be going to a home of her own in Mendle—and of course we are pleased that it is so close. Papa thinks Mr. Appleton will let her drive his gig home—I mean, here—whenever she misses us."

"Sounds propitious. You cannot be in the doldrums about that."

She hesitated. "Then Papa—"

"Your father misbehaving? You will never convince me of that!"

"No. He is the soul of honor. Well-l—no one knows this yet—he has offered for Sarah Walden. You don't know her, I suppose. A friend of Aunt Mirabelle, and very charming."

Gordon pursed his lips. "I see. Yes, I know her slightly, and you are right, she is charming. Do you feel supplanted? Is that the trouble?"

Laurel shook her head vehemently. "Not that at all. It is just so *unexpected*. We did not know he was visiting her, so it comes as a shock."

"Something of a shock to him, too, I imagine." He laughed. "Really she is a very nice lady and will never play the wicked stepmama. Is this the total of your troubles?"

There was a pause as Laurel debated with herself how much she could reveal of family secrets. He was regarding her with the warmest and most attentive of eyes. "Mr. Hanger has offered for Aunt Frances."

Her companion let out a soundless whistle. "I thought he might want—never mind. Has she accepted him?"

"Not yet." She laughed a little. "She says she is 'thinking,' but *I* think she will accept."

"Good God!" said Gordon. "More seems to have happened in Bayley Dell in the last few weeks than in fifty years!" He grinned at her. "None of this should provoke your doleful looks. Never say there is another 'problem' bothering you!"

"Well, there *is*. What is to become of me? They would never allow me to stay alone at Eland House with Fane and Cook and Daisy."

"No, of course not," he agreed. "One of them is sure to want you—at the manor, or Mendle, or wherever your father will live."

"That is just it. Papa says Mrs. Walden is eager to see me settled. She wants to move me to London for the little season, and if I don't 'take,' then we must go back in the spring."

"Oh, surely that amiable lady never said anything so callous as your not 'taking'!"

"Well, no. But that is what she meant. I don't want to go to London, anyway."

"What about your aunts?"

"They offered to have me stay with them. In fact—" she gave a watery chuckle "—they were near to dividing me in pieces. But at least I have enough sense to know I would only be in the w-way."

He stared at two tears spilling from amber-brown eyes.

"I—you—" he faltered.

The tears started down her cheeks.

He hurled down the cane violently, clasped her to him with his one good arm, and kissed her tenderly—with no violence at all but incredible sweetness. When he raised his head she opened her eyes slowly and saw in his an expression that she could not define. What he saw in hers she did not have time to guess; he kissed her again, lingering this time, holding her close, and then at last put her away from him, saying, "That settles it! Would you mind picking up my cane?"

Astonished and shaken, not knowing *what* was settled, she did as bid.

"Thank you, m'dear. I must be out of my wits—a public lane! . . . You carry the cane so I will have a hand to hold yours." Then he led her along the lane a very short distance until a curve brought them to Browning's cottage.

No one was in view there. Laurel thought thankfully that they had not been seen.

"You don't mind waiting until I hear from my father, do you, dearest? Forget the romantic relatives. Let them have their fling. I will handle everything for you, um?"

If this was a proposal, it was very odd, Laurel thought. What was "everything"? She really could not suppose he was trifling with her, for his manner was both sweet and protective. Even without experience in flirtation, she sensed he was serious. Yet she could not ask, "What is settled?" like a noddy! Not until she had mulled things over.

When they reached the footbridge across the ravine he sent her ahead of him with the cane as once before. She led him through the drowsy churchyard and thought, *thought* she heard him mutter, "Imagine courting in a grave-yard!" At least the word "courting" was clear, and that was reassuring. She smiled back at him over her shoulder.

"We will rest my blasted knee at the lych-gate," he said, wincing.

Immediately she forgot her own worries in seeing that he was seated as soon and as comfortably as possible.

"You see why I cannot ride away from Bayley Dell, even if I wanted to do so, which I do not. Do you ride? A man can manage reins with one hand, but legs are essential for anything over a walk. I should be reduced to the ignominy of a mounting block while I am in this shape."

She sat across from him. "Why do you care what figure you cut? It is not shameful to be injured."

He was not accustomed to plain speaking from young ladies of Society. "Now you are needling me!" he exclaimed with a frown. "Can I never complain?" Then he grinned and said earnestly, "Don't change. Promise me you won't change!"

She was saved having to answer this preposterous demand by the appearance of Dr. Dodd, who dropped his satchel at their feet and sat heavily beside Laurel.

"Are you needing rest?" he asked. "Young people do not know what overdoing is!" He pulled out a large square of cambric to mop his face. "I had a new baby at Diddles' and a bad ear at Jones'."

Both Laurel and Gordon sat up straighter.

"And you think you are tired! I told you, Rand, to exercise, not run a race. Surely you, Laurel, can amuse him sitting down as well as roaming." This made Mr. Rand glare with indignation, but, Laurel was used to the doctor's heavy-handed jocularity.

She said, "Pooh! A stroll isn't a race. I guess a gentleman can rest a moment without requiring amusement." She and Gordon exchanged glances, which the doctor saw.

"Old men," he said ponderously, "need rest to invigorate their blood, but young ones require cooling down."

Gordon met his eye. "Something that won't concern a lady."

The doctor nodded, as though satisfied, and got to his feet. "Now I have to see to a cut on Dunnerd's hand."

"Not Dunnerd!" said Laurel. "Oh, dear. Something else to keep him from his work."

"Aye," sighed Dr. Dodd. "I promise to sting him well when I bind him up."

Laurel said, "Good!" and the doctor went away toward Bayley Manor.

"So vengeful," said Gordon, as if surprised.

"Yes, about Dunnerd. He plays sick while his wife does the work of two or three. It makes me so cross! You see, you do not really know my nature."

"I like what I know," he replied with an insinuating little smile.

Her eyes were merry, but she said pertly as she rose to her feet, "I have wasted most of the morning with you, sir, and it behooves me to make myself useful to my aunts."

"Do that," he called after her. "Let them make the most of what time they have! Mrs. Patten will pamper *me*."

Her megrims had vanished somewhere on her walk with Gordon Rand, and she cheerfully greeted the verger, whom she saw grubbing in a corner of the churchyard as she passed. Had he heard her conversation with Mr. Rand? It did not matter, as he would never have understood a word they spoke.

That afternoon Mr. Hanger came for tea.

He bowed to the three Eland ladies and remarked that each was "blooming as usual," his manners being so evenly doled out that he could not be said to distinguish any one of them. Laurel was wide-eyed, Mirabelle puzzled, but Frances perfectly calm and casual. Actually, he talked mostly to Sir John.

"Well, sir, I have heard you contemplate matrimony. Demmed if you don't set an example for others!" He did not look at Frances as he spoke, but her family *did,* while she concentrated on pouring tea.

"I did not set out to inspire others, but I am always glad to be of use in the village," replied Sir John with a decided gleam in his eye.

"Missy will be next, I suppose," Mr. Hanger suggested roguishly as he sipped his tea in utmost tranquillity. He would have seen Frances's brows knit if he had looked, but he was watching the youngest lady.

Thinking her aunt had been punished enough, Laurel cried archly, "La, sir, are you offering for *me?* This is so sudden."

"Not sudden at all, as I am not in the market for a naughty chit," he said flatly. "Stick to your own generation, missy."

She pressed her handkerchief to her nose and sniffled. "You are trifling with my tender sentiments, sir!"

The aunts were staring at her, scandalized, but she had turned attention from poor Frances, and her papa was frankly laughing. "That is enough, Laurel," he said with some effort at discipline.

"Oh, I know a minx when I hear one," Mr. Hanger avowed easily. He did not linger long and paid Frances no particular courtesies except to ask, when he was leaving, if she cared to drive three days thence.

She accepted with polite disinterest.

It was as strange a courtship as Laurel could imagine. What was he thinking? What was Frances thinking? She saw her papa's shoulders were shaking as if he watched a traveling troupe of comedians, so it must be all right. Mr. Hanger had started life with nothing and was now a wealthy man. One could suppose he knew how to handle people and situations to his advantage.

When he had gone Frances took up her current piece of embroidery and began composedly to sew. Mirabelle raised her brows at Laurel.

Conversation died.

Twenty

After morning worship on Sunday, acting as his own curate, Mr. Appleton came from Hammish as fast as his sturdy horse would bring him. His place had already been set upon the Elands' table and some special victuals ordered by Mirabelle for his delectation.

Little they cared (any of them) about what they ate, for Sir John's engagement must be related, and Mr. Appleton's congratulations bestowed.

"Indeed!" said Mr. Appleton. "This is splendid news. How am I going to keep my mind on the lesson for Vespers this evening? Perhaps a little homily on the institution of matrimony."

"Pray, say something encouraging to spinsters like me," Laurel begged.

"A little baggage like you needs no encouragement," her father said, being very jaunty in his new status of a betrothed gentleman. "Frances, did you have something to tell Brother James?"

Her spoon rattled in her soup plate, but she replied calmly enough. "I? No, you are the one making sensations, John."

The vicar patted his napkin to his mouth. "To tell the truth, I'm glad to hear John's intentions, for it makes me feel a little less a fool."

"Fool!" cried Mirabelle.

"A fortunate fool, my dear," he amended with a sweet

smile at his fiancée. "You know what I mean. One does not feel so conspicuous in company with another whose inclinations are the same."

"To tell the truth," said Sir John, "I feel a bit like a boy who would like to go into the garden and stand on his head to get the attention of a particular girl."

"You've got it—her," said Frances drily.

Noting Laurel's expression, Mr. Appleton called them to order by saying, "I fear we are shocking our youngest lady by our frivolity."

Nothing was spoken of Frances's situation, unless Mirabelle in private hinted at another possible Connection for the family.

That evening at Vespers Gordon Rand accompanied Mrs. Patten, sitting at his insistence in the last pew, for he was still uncomfortable about his appearance. There were some whispers among the townsfolk when Mr. Patten failed to appear, though his own coat brushed shoulders with Mrs. Patten.

Monday morning Mr. Appleton paid a brief call upon his intended before prodding himself home to Mendle. When he had gone the Eland ladies were wafted by April breezes to Mrs. Mince's shop, where they examined her stock of muslins, from which they hoped to make Mirabelle modest "everyday" dresses. She must have something *new,* Frances insisted, and Mirabelle was willing, so long as nothing gaudy was chosen.

"You must have pretty colors, Auntie," Laurel decreed, reiterating her opinion until Mirabelle had selected a green-and-white stripe, a lavender for which Mrs. Mince could supply matching ribbons, and a *jonquille* sprigged in Clarence blue. These frocks would be so simple in design that the ladies thought they could easily construct them in a few days. Mirabelle was as pleased as if her wardrobe were to overflow with opera dresses and ball gowns. It would not be tactful to dress more grandly than her parishioners in Mendle, but all three wished her to be becomingly gowned for her husband's pleasure.

They went home and set to work, cutting and basting until summoned to luncheon by Fane's gong. The day had become so fair and dry that walking for pleasure was possible with only a light wrap, and Laurel could not keep herself from wondering if Gordon Rand was waiting for her at The Nesting Dove or somewhere along the village street. She both longed and dreaded to see him, for she was unsure in what light he (or she!) might consider her submission to kisses in the back lane. The aunts would be scandalized . . . even if his intentions were serious.

But she basted with good will, knowing it was right to contribute to Aunt Mirabelle's wardrobe and happiness, and she was rewarded by midafternoon by Mr. Rand's calling to ask her to walk in the fair weather.

"Of course you must go, dearest," said Mirabelle, always considerate of others. "You need fresh air to keep the bloom in your cheeks." And as Frances indicated approval, Laurel left her needle in a pincushion and ran off to fetch her cloak.

"Shall we walk toward Nord Cross for a change?" asked Mr. Rand as they stepped from the stoop. "Is there a verge to which we can leap like gazelles if traffic comes along?"

"Yes, a good one for a mile or two."

"Plenty for my recalcitrant knee."

She looked anxious. "Oh, is it bothering you today?"

"Very little," he admitted, "but I should not like to go so far that I cannot come back. You see I brought the dratted cane. If you can carry it, I will hold your hand."

"Not, if you please, until we are beyond the Onslows's house," she said, and blushed violently.

Gordon gave a shout of laughter and offered his elbow, but she shook her head, walking beside him toward the northern end of the village.

"Have you had an answer to your letter?" she asked.

"No. It is really too soon. Maybe tomorrow money will come from Father. It will be a great relief to pay off my debts to Patten."

"It is amazing he has not pressed you."

"Yes. I have been a burden for sure, but I suspect that Hanger has given them some sort of guarantee."

"Why would he do that?"

"I don't know. Likes to be helpful, I suppose. Has he not provided you with carriages more than once?"

"Yes. And Papa with horses. He has been generous."

"I thought," Gordon said, looking down at her seriously, "that he might have his eye on *you.*"

"Oh, no. It is Aunt Frances, as I told you. A very strange courtship. He does not haunt our doorstep, and she is so casual."

"It is I who haunt Eland House, and you are not—casual, I think?"

Laurel lowered her head to stare at the road.

"I cannot make you an offer," he continued softly, "until I am sure of having something to offer."

What could Laurel reply to that?

"Perhaps," he went on, as though she had encouraged him verbally, "I will have a letter tomorrow. Here. Take this blasted cane."

She accepted the cane, and they went on walking hand in hand, with no mention of a painful knee, Gordon Rand gazing left and right about the countryside.

"My little manor in Surrey lies in land much like this. Groves and gentle hills that would feel familiar to you, Laurel. It was my uncle's—Father's brother's—manor and has a small, pretty house from the time of George II. He knew there was not much to come to me from Mama's family, so he left it to me, bless him! Father thinks I do not deserve it, because I spend so little time there."

"But who manages it?" asked Laurel, shocked at such an attitude toward property.

"An excellent bailiff."

"You must keep him on his toes! *Why* do you seldom visit?"

"Because—shall I bare my soul and risk your displeasure? Because I have been trying to cut a swath in Society to prove I am just as . . . important—significant, if you prefer, as my brother, who will someday step into Father's shoes."

"Does your brother do that?" she wondered, astonished by an attitude about which she knew nothing. "Cut a swath?"

"No. He cares nothing for fripperies. He is everything a father could want in his heir."

She raised her eyes then and regarded him seriously with a steady amber-brown gaze. "You must not resent an accident of birth date. Be thankful that you had an uncle who cared enough to make you independent."

He had had sufficient lures cast at him to recognize one, or—for that matter—to notice when one was *missing*.

"You are different from the young ladies I have known," he said.

"I am just—me."

"That is what is so delightful."

She did not care to admit to knowing no young men very well. Certainly not one like Gordon Rand. Then he set an unexpected kiss upon her nearest cheek, and her heart fluttered alarmingly. Staring at her feet, walking in the dust and gravel of the lane, she thought how odd it was to feel no feet or shoes or dust.

Suddenly he thrust her onto the verge, almost into the hedge, to save her from being trampled by two speeding bucks on lathered horses who came from behind and yelled something indistinguishable as they passed.

Other occasional traffic came and went peacefully. Without speaking, they followed the verge, and when it petered out they turned back.

* * *

On Tuesday afternoon Mr. Hanger called for Frances Eland in his curricle, remaining seated at the reins while his groom knocked at the door. When Frances came out, wearing again her bonnet with brown ribbons and today a Paisley shawl, the groom assisted her into the vehicle.

Mr. Hanger tossed his servant a coin. "Have a drink at the inn," he said to the man. "I will pick you up there when I return."

Frances sat demurely beside him, making no objection. The groom stepped back, and they drove off in the same direction Gordon and Laurel had taken, northward, where there was a side road, little traveled, three miles out of town. When they returned (Day Eleven of Mr. Hanger's limit) Mr. Hanger was looking very pleased with himself, and Frances had a large emerald on her finger.

"No shilly-shallying, m'love," he said, setting her down. "I will be around to have a word with Sir John tonight, and we will settle on a date. What's there to wait for?"

Naturally Frances flew upstairs to where her sister and niece were sewing. She bit her lip, holding out her hand.

"Frances!" cried Mirabelle. "You've accepted him!"

"Y-yes," quavered the younger sister, beginning both to cry and laugh.

Immediately there was a tangle of arms and exclamations and kisses as the three Eland ladies fell into a multiple embrace.

"I did not think you would have him," said Mirabelle. "You were so cool."

"I'm not cool now." Indeed, all visible portions of her skin were rosy. "How could I have spurned his acquaintance so long? I was a fool."

Mirabelle scolded at once. "Don't say 'fool.' James calls himself that, and you must not be another! It's plain to see

Mr. Hanger knows the secret of making you happy. When can we tell?"

"Almost at once. He is coming to see John tonight—as if John would mind! He has always thought higher of Er-Ernest than you and I did, Mirabelle. Maybe we need men-folk to tell us what is what. . . ."

"Oh, no." Mirabelle was emphatic. "Only about business, perhaps, and ecclesiastical matters. Otherwise, we should heed our female senses. Men have nothing like women's intuition. They are so unromantic."

"Is James unromantic?"

It was Mirabelle's turn to blush. "I did not intend to include James."

"Well," said Frances, laughing, "I don't include Ernest Hanger. Could you mean less sentimental?"

"Yes, that is it."

"Mr. Rand is *overly* sentimental about his horse," Laurel said drolly.

At that point Fane knocked to report that Miss Onslow had called.

"Oh," gasped Mirabelle. "Surely she cannot have seen the ring from her window."

"Good heavens," whispered Frances to her sister. "Can she hear us?"

Fane supplied the answer blandly. "No, ma'am. I showed her into the drawing room and closed the door."

"Well, take in the tea and say we will be down momentarily."

Fane bowed and went out.

"Will you tell her?" asked Mirabelle.

"Might as well." Frances sighed. "If John should put his foot down, I shall defy him."

"That serious?"

"Yes. Come with me, Laurel."

But they soon found Miss Onslow was full of the news that *she* had to relay. "My dears, you will never guess! A very smart black carriage with *four* horses and postillions came past an hour ago. It turned in at the inn and I know it is still there as I could see part of a cream-colored wheel from your stoop. What do you think it can mean?"

Laurel had a horrid feeling it meant Lord Leadenhall. She ran to a front window but could see nothing from that angle.

"Did the carriage have a crest on the door?" asked Frances.

"I did not see one. Of course I could have missed it—and Sister was dozing. At any rate, it was a very handsome vehicle. When did such ever come here?"

Meanwhile, at The Nesting Dove, Patten had gone out to welcome a lady and maidservant from the carriage, whistle for his sons and stable boy, greet two smartly uniformed guards with guns, and issue orders for the accommodation of all. In answer to the lady's first question he replied that she would find Mr. Rand in the taproom.

"Indeed?" said the lady serenely. "Is this a door to that room? I will go in directly."

Mr. Rand was found to be nursing a mug near the hearth, slumped in a wooden chair, his injured leg propped upon another.

"Good God! Mama!" He knocked over his cane as he struggled to his feet, still clutching the mug, and endeavored to embrace her.

"I am glad to see you, too, dearest, but pray do not pour ale upon my cloak!" she entreated. "Surely you are not surprised to see me after that postscript to your letter. *I may have found the perfect wife.*"

"I thought it would bring Father posthaste," he explained.

"Yes, but he is in bed with a bilious attack—not made easier by your remarkable communiqué. Must we discuss private affairs in this odorous place?"

"No, the parlor will be better. Come across the hall, Mama." He led the way. "I have been befriended by everyone, but it has not been like having my adored mama to soothe my fevered brow." He shut the door, leaving her ladyship's maid to deal with luggage and everything else.

The viscountess seated herself calmly. "No need to pour butter on me. I can see you are mending from whatever happened. Your letter gave no details." She was a tall, slim woman with a mouth that hinted at firm character. Regarding him steadily from blue eyes much like his own, she threw her cloak back over her chair and prepared to hear what he had to say.

"I was on my way to Lord Clifton's place, not eager to go, but having agreed to do so in a weak moment."

"Lady Pamela pursuing you, eh?" When he did not answer she added, "I know her tricks."

"Let me say, I was in no hurry. I sent my curricle and servants on ahead—"

"And where are they?"

"Still there. I told them to wait for me."

"Still waiting? That is faithfulness!"

"Yes." He smiled a little. "My groom will have found a bed over the stable and lent a willing hand. He knows how to make himself useful. My valet is not too superior to help in service areas. It is a large establishment. I doubt the earl or Lady Pamela have any idea they are there."

"Remarkable," said the viscountess. Light from the fireplace made her *capucine* dress glow; she was a beautiful creature not more than three or four years older than Mirabelle Eland, and looking younger. "Why did you not send for your men? I am sure you needed help."

"You see, I did not wish to reveal my whereabouts. Then, damnable luck, Lord Harry happened upon me, and I was obliged to promise him a bribe to keep my location secret. Having pockets to let, he hung around and was very much in the way."

"The way of what?"

He hesitated.

"Never say he was dancing after the same girl!"

"Not dancing exactly. I was thought to have no memory of my name or circumstances, and I feared he would give me away. Besides, he is so *swashbuckling*. Look at me, Mama! I'm a mess."

"Well," she admitted, "your coat is—"

"Patten's."

"—is not the best fit, but your face is as nice as ever." If she had not been his mother, she would have said "beautiful" instead of "nice." "I hope you have not been a disagreeable patient."

"Only sometimes," he confessed.

She sat back in her chair and regarded him thoughtfully. "Suppose you describe this girl."

He ran his fingers through the blond hair that was so like his mother's. "Well-l-l, she is neither tall nor small, more small than tall, with eyes that are amber and that can see right into my head."

"Pretty?"

"Yes. Very. But blushes when complimented . . . and does not even *understand* when she is flattered. She tried to read novels like Scott's to me, though I found it hard to concentrate on written words, since I found her voice so pleasing and her expression so intent when she was reading. Will you believe she knows Euclid as well as I?"

Lady Leadenhall raised her brows.

"Not well, Mama. *As well.*" He paused. "She is as lady-like as you could want, gentle, thoughtful—"

"Oh, a paragon, I see."

He grinned. "Not always. She has combed my hair with a rake a time or two."

"Ah! For what?"

"For grouching. For feeling sorry for myself."

His mother smiled. "Always a mistake."

"Yes. Her family's problems make mine look like crumbs. Do you know anything about them?"

Her ladyship said tartly that he had never told their name.

"Didn't I? It is Eland. Her father is Sir John Eland, a true gentleman, if on hard times. Do you know the name?"

To his surprise, she said she did. "I am not acquainted with the family, but your Great-aunt Glorianna is the widow of a gentleman who was uncle to this girl's mother, who died very young, I believe."

"Good Lord! Are we *related?*"

"Not at all. A connection only. The story is that Sir John's brother ran amuck and wrecked the family fortune. There will be no dowry, I fear." But she did not appeared frightened.

He explained that the manor was leased to a Mr. Hanger, who had been extremely kind to him. "It is rumored in the village that by living frugally Sir John will pay off his brother's debts before long. It is possible, just possible, Mama, that a son of Laurel could come into a decent inheritance someday."

"One should never count on mere possibilities, Gordon."

"Oh, true. Very true. I have enough from my uncle to satisfy me. Laurel's *possibility* might comfort Father, however."

"Ring the bell for Sally," she said.

While they waited for the abigail to come, Gordon played his trump. "Laurel is a perfect lady like you, Mama."

"Oh, the butter-boat again!" She rolled her eyes toward the ceiling, but he did not think she was ill-pleased.

Sally entered and curtsied.

"Are you having any difficulties, my dear?" asked her ladyship.

"No, my lady. The only vacant room is small, so the landlord is moving Mr. Gordon there. His wife felt sure you should have the better room. Everyone is very helpful. I am not sure what they will do with the men, but the landlady says not to worry."

"Splendid. Pray order an early dinner, and then bring me pen and paper."

"Why do you need pen and paper?" Gordon asked when the girl had gone away.

She tossed her son a saucy look. "To invite myself to the Elands' house. In the village, I assume? You will understand that I must see this girl who is 'like' me. Your father is relying on my judgment."

Gordon gnawed his lip. "Father has been pressing me to settle down. Well, I have found a reason for doing so. Please do not expect her to be a toast of the town! The cats of the ton would eat her for a first course. She has no aspiration to be a belle of London. She *prefers* country to city. She is sweet and genuine—you will see!"

"I hope so," his mother said.

"You will lend me a bit of your distinction, I think," he replied fondly.

Sally brought writing materials as requested, and Lady Leadenhall wrote in her customary large, sloping hand:

> The Viscountess Leadenhall wishes to meet the Eland family and thank them for their kindness to her son, Gordon. She will call tomorrow at eleven, if that is convenient to the ladies and Sir John.

"You want it to go this evening, of course? I will send it up by one of Patten's boys." Gordon took the note and left the room, followed by Sally with pen, ink, and unused paper. Lady Margaret stared thoughtfully into the fire.

After a moment she said softly to herself, "I've had title and wealth and happiness. Plus two fine sons." She sighed. "Such a responsibility! I suppose he *will* have this girl, no matter what I say. I must hope my lord is feeling better—and not cross when I return with news he does not want to hear."

Gordon reentered then, saying cheerfully, "Mumbling,

Mama? They have put me in Harry's room, but I do not begrudge you the other. I am glad to see you, Mama. Truly I am."

"Well, that is pleasant to hear."

He sat awkwardly.

"Feeling bad?"

"No, honestly. Just tired. In another week or so I will have this arm out of the sling. I am almost well. Tell me about Father."

"Nothing serious, thank God. He is nearing sixty, you know, and I think that is depressing his spirits. Your turmoil has been a bit hard for him to take."

Gordon motioned regretfully with his serviceable hand. "It was not my intention. At least he has had several weeks without knowing about my puny condition. Did you bring the money I asked?"

"Yes." As mothers will, she offered: "If you need a bit more, I can spare it."

"We'll see—tomorrow."

After a tasty supper they retired to bed, and neither slept well, though for different reasons.

Meanwhile, at Eland House the note was received with astonishment by the three elder members of the household, who had determined Mr. Rand to be a gentleman but had no idea that his family was a titled one. Laurel, secretly, knew that much, having had it revealed to her by Gordon Rand himself.

Debrett's waited conveniently near to hand, so that, while Sir John hastily prepared a message for Del to carry back, the aunts seized upon this interesting book, so as to hunt for an entry on Leadenhall.

"Oh! Only an 'honorable' younger son!" said Frances.

"From Surrey. Maybe sixty miles," said Mirabelle.

"She will want to take him home."

"So far to come."

Laurel, listening, supposed them to mean that Gordon's

mother would be sure to carry him home, where he would
be out of easy reach of country flirts. She wondered, as she
had done many times already, if Gordon had only amused
himself with the simple young lady available in this very
small village. Certainly he had come to depend upon her
company. Was it only to fill time? Of his manner toward
her she could not complain, and his eyes, she thought, were
liquid when he looked at her. He had hinted more. Of certain stolen kisses she must not think, lest someone read her
mind.

Del was just leaving when Mr. Hanger rode down from
the manor to make a formal offer for Frances, which was
just what the Eland ladies thought he should do. Their estimation of him soared, and Frances abandoned all effort to
appear casual.

Mr. Hanger repeated his offer of a home for Laurel. He
would like, he said, to have the "pretty puss" to brighten
his household. To this Sir John made an evasive speech of
thanks, explaining that plans had not yet been determined
for his daughter.

In Eland House, just as in The Nesting Dove, there was
an excess of insomnia that night.

Twenty-one

Lady Margaret Rand, Viscountess Leadenhall, remained in her bed for a meager breakfast, while the estimable Sally, knowing her tastes perfectly, laid out a Devonshire brown morning dress that would be suitable for travel later in the day. With this was a brown straw bonnet with peach ties and peach silk blossoms under the brim to brush my lady's cheek.

Across the landing, Blunk, Del, and Roddy were in the throes of preparing a large bath for the gentleman whom Blunk, like Mrs. Patten, had somehow come to look upon as belonging to him. The viscountess had brought for her son an assortment of clothes that Mr. Hanger's superior valet would have recognized as the highest fashion, if he had seen them. So Blunk chose snug buff breeches and white-topped boots. With some patience he was able to coax a shirt sleeve over the splinted arm, but not a coat. After the splint had been supported by a scarf Mr. Rand was able to slide his left arm into the Forester's green coat, and Blunk hung the right side about his right shoulder.

"I fear, sir," lamented Blunk, "that we cannot use a cravat with the scarf knotting behind your neck."

Gordon was satisfied with what he saw in the mirror. "You are a magician, Blunk. I would like to carry you to Surrey."

"I would come, sir."

"No, no. I could not serve Mr. Hanger such a turn after he has been so obliging as to spare you to help me."

"Well, sir, I can't think he would mind so much. Mr. Hanger's valet was down to the tap last night, and he gave me a hint, you might say, that Mr. Hanger has been accepted by Miss Frances. There's the feeling at the manor that Mr. Hanger is not in a case to object to anything."

"The deuce you say! Three marriages in the Eland family!" exclaimed Mr. Rand, receiving a snuff box. He detested snuff but carried it in a pocket for offering to other gentlemen. "I wonder what will become of Miss Laurel."

Blunk smoothed the left cuff. "They all has offered her a home, sir. We'd like to have her at the manor with Miss Frances—at least until she has wed herself."

"Only Dr. Dodd is left single here," Gordon said with a snort of disapproval.

Blunk stepped back to consider the effect of his work. "There's one other at the moment, sir."

Mr. Rand turned his head from the mirror. "Is that gossip in the village?"

"Oh, no, sir. No one has mentioned it to *me.*"

"Well, see that you keep it to yourself. . . . Is there not some suggestion that the future Lady Eland wants to take Miss Laurel to London for a season?"

Blunk said, "That's known, sir. Opinions are about half and half, some saying the lady wants to get Miss Laurel off her hands as soon as possible and others saying the lady is only trying to give Miss Laurel the chance she deserves."

Gordon Rand shook his head, saying, "I had forgotten how folk gossip in villages!" Then he went down to the parlor for some breakfast.

It was there that Lady Leadenhall joined him a few minutes before eleven. She was ravishing in the ensemble that Sally had selected, and looked scarcely older than thirty-five.

"No one will believe you are my mama," he said, kissing her cheek (the one other than beside the peach flower).

"Perhaps until I am side-by-side with someone of age twenty," she wryly returned.

Gordon laughed fondly. "Shall I order the carriage? There is a bit of dust and a slight slope, but we haven't far to go."

"We must walk, of course. I am not such a decrepit creature as to ride a short distance. You remember it is my habit to walk to and from our own village and to ramble our fields."

They set out for Eland House, where the family burned with curiosity as they awaited her coming.

In bygone days, when the Elands had lived at the manor, they had been accustomed to socializing with gentry and titles in a wide circle, but poverty had made them self-conscious. No viscountess or other titled person had entered their door for a decade. They went nowhere, did nothing of note, and had nothing to say of interest (they thought) to anyone; certainly they had no knowledge of the latest *crim con* or palace rumor.

Laurel, guiltily hiding the uncertain terms on which she stood with Gordon Rand, strove to conceal her qualms by wearing a face without expression. Only her father, whose amiable nature allowed him to meet anyone on easy terms, was calm.

Frances had decreed that it was folly for country ladies to dress lavishly for the morning calls of strangers. Good grooming was what mattered. Of course, the caps of the two elder ones had been abandoned in view of their recent engagements. Fane was permitted to array Sir John as Fane was pleased to determine.

Then the moment came for which they had waited. Fane announced Lady Leadenhall. Sir John, standing nearest the drawing room door, stepped forward to have his hand compressed between two soft ones belonging to a Vision.

"Sir John," the lovely creature cried, "you cannot know how grateful I am for your attention to my poor, hurt son."

"It was no hardship for us," he said. "Let me present my sister Mirabelle—"

"Ah! The one who made nourishing soup!"

"—and my sister Frances—"

"Who brought sewing and comforted by her presence; that is what you said, Gordon, isn't it?"

Gordon drew Laurel forward. "Yes, Mama, and this is Miss Laurel Eland, who did not hesitate to accuse me of malingering."

"It is true, my lady," admitted Laurel, sketching a graceful curtsy. "I tried to be sympathetic—indeed, I *was* sympathetic, but it did not seem sensible to let him wallow in resentment."

Lady Leadenhall shot a surprised look at her son. "You are entirely right, my dear. A gentleman should never *wallow.*"

"I did not do that!" howled Gordon.

"You did! I saw it several times. Probably Blunk would say more times than that."

Mirabelle interrupted hastily. "Won't you sit down, Lady Leadenhall?"

Sir John moved a gold brocaded chair forward two inches, and the viscountess sank onto it fluidly. By this time each Eland lady had forgotten about her own appearance, so bemused were they all by Gordon's mother, who seemed entirely too young to claim this grown son. It was even more amazing when they remembered that the *Peerage* reported a son older still.

"Gordon has told me about the attack that was made upon him," said her ladyship. "What I cannot understand is how he reached the inn here after being so hurt."

Sir John suggested, "Blind luck."

"Yes," said Gordon. "When I was able to get to my feet, I just started walking. It was fortunately in this direction.

Perhaps I sensed that the bandits rode off the other way. I cannot remember."

Lady Leadenhall gave a little shudder.

"He cannot have ridden far into the wood, for he was able to reach The Nesting Dove and faint at Patten's feet," Laurel said.

Looking outraged, he cried, "I have never fainted in my life!"

"Then why did Patten and the ostler have to carry you up to bed? You were unconscious when I saw you the first time. Lady Leadenhall, I appeal to you: Would a conscious man let strange females punch upon him?"

The aunts looked shocked at such explicit talk, but Sir John wore a slight smile.

"Certainly not," agreed the lady solemnly, although her eyes sparkled as she looked toward her son. "In any case," she told him, "you were fortunate to reach Bayley Dell. Do you know, Sir John, I had never heard of Bayley Dell until Gordon's letter came, but I am bound to say he could not have received better or kinder care."

"We are chagrined to think that the attack occurred almost on our doorstep," Mirabelle said earnestly.

"We never have any crime," added Frances. "The villagers have been most distressed."

"I thought I had a clue to the culprits," said Gordon, "but it turned out I was wrong."

"Best to forget it," Sir John advised.

"That is what Laurel has been saying," admitted Gordon gloomily. If the others noticed his use of her first name, they gave no indication.

"I thought," she explained, "that it was wrong to dwell on disappointment. His spirits would never revive if he continued to do that."

"That is what James tells us regularly," said Mirabelle.

"James?" inquired her ladyship.

Mirabelle colored becomingly. "Mr. Appleton—my betrothed. He is vicar of Mendle and curate of Hammish and Bayley Dell."

It was fortunate at this slightly awkward moment that Fane opened the door to announce Mr. Hanger, who came, as usual, like a fresh breeze. He was introduced to Lady Leadenhall, who promptly thanked him for his goodness to her son. "That Blunk has been incomparable," she said.

"Yes, that is why I chose him to send down," Mr. Hanger said, agreeing with her estimate of his servant. "If I do not look sharp, Rand will steal him from me."

"Mr. Rand would never do *that!*" said Laurel, which quick defense of her son Lady Leadenhall noted with a slight pursing of her lips.

Sir John inserted pacifically, "Mr. Hanger is to wed my sister Frances, Lady Leadenhall."

"Indeed?" murmured her ladyship.

"It will be my pleasure to restore Frances to her old home," said Mr. Hanger with a benevolent look at his inamorata that caused her to blush more deeply than Mirabelle had done. "Sir John," he continued relentlessly, "is to wed also. It will be a lively spring."

"Indeed!" returned Lady Leadenhall in another tone of voice.

"Ordinarily," explained Laurel, "nothing happens in Bayley Dell of any significance."

"I understand—" said Gordon with an eye on his mother, "that Mrs. Walden intends to fire off Laurel in a season at London."

Her ladyship nodded as though the plan was admirable, if confusing. "Is Mrs. Walden kin?"

Sir John said, "My fiancée," and cleared his throat. "From Wells."

Lady Leadenhall caught herself about to use the word "indeed" again. "May I congratulate you, sir? I do not know the lady, but my friend, the Bishop of Wells, has men-

tioned her more than once. How delightful of her to take
Miss Laurel under her wing."

"But I do not wish a season," Laurel said flatly.

Her ladyship looked askance. "Nonsense. Every young
lady desires to swish through Society for a time before settling down."

Sir John's grey mouse slanted tipsily as he smiled his
little half-smile. "My daughter has had no mother to dream
about her child's capturing the ton. I am afraid we have
reared her with more serious interests."

Mr. Hanger had drawn Frances to a far corner of the
drawing room for a private talk, about what cannot be
known. Whatever he was saying to her she appeared to find
pleasing.

"You see, Lady Leadenhall," said Laurel, responding to
an imperative look from Mirabelle, "I am twenty—and a
bit old for such things as presentations. Yes, I enjoy dancing,
and very likely would enjoy opera and plays, but can you
not see I would stand out like a crow among dewy girls
three years my junior?"

"Not a 'crow,' " corrected Gordon. "A diamond."

Thinking things were beginning to get out of hand, Mirabelle opened her mouth to say her niece had nothing upon
which to judge, when Lady Leadenhall, ignoring her son's
outburst, asked, "What is wrong with being different, Miss
Laurel? I positively should prefer that to *indifference.*"

"What are you saying, Mama?"

Laurel smiled at him. "I think your mother means I may
decide some things for myself."

"Well, let us not be serious today," Sir John advised.
Neither he nor his sisters realized how far matters had pro-
gressed between his daughter and Gordon Rand.

Tea was offered. Then coffee. But Lady Leadenhall declined both. "Time to be on the way to Bath for a day or
two. Then on to Guildford." She rose. "Come, Gordon."

Frances and Mr. Hanger, hearing, rejoined the group.

Good wishes for a safe journey bounced back and forth with repeated thanks for kindnesses. With perfect tranquillity and ease, Lady Leadenhall bid each member of the Eland family and Mr. Hanger a gracious farewell and swept her son into the village street.

At first mother and son did not speak. When they neared the gate of the churchyard Gordon at last asked, "Well? Will you tell me what you think?"

"Genuine," she replied slowly. "Refined. Proud—but not too much so. Gallant—yes, I may say gallant—in adversity. Miss Mirabelle has found a safe niche with a respectable clergyman. Frances is doing somewhat better financially. I daresay Mr. Hanger will see that they want for nothing."

"He is a right one, isn't he?"

"Yes. Not a born gentleman, I suspect, yet one who has the best of instincts."

Gordon said, "I do not think they will regret the connection there."

"Nor do I. What I hear of Mrs. Walden is excellent. She will stir Sir John from the sense of family shame he has taken upon himself."

"I respect him," he said.

By this time they had reached the chestnut tree before The Nesting Dove.

"Sit on this bench, Mama," he commanded. "You have not told me what you think of Laurel. Is she not adorable?"

"Y-yes, very pretty. You quarrel delightfully, I see. She has a good deal of poise for one who knows only rustic life—"

"I don't give a damn for rusticity. Sir John has raised her with appreciation for good literature. She never gives a simper, which I, for one, would find very off-putting. You cannot say the same for the usual girl in the Marriage Mart."

Lady Leadenhall looked thoughtful. "You have been ill, dearest, and perhaps not thinking carefully—"

"My body has hurt considerably; there has been nothing wrong with my mind. Father harps on my 'settling down,' but until now I have not found a girl I would want to settle with. Will you persuade Father?"

She looked distressed. "I am not sure I should try. I want your happiness, but, Gordon, you will have to admit this is an unequal match. Your father will expect more than sweetness. Even Lady Pamela would suit him better. At least there is *distinction* there."

"Yes, and a badly spoiled temperament. I won't marry any girl just because Father likes her antecedents. You can tell him that."

Lady Margaret shook her head. "I would never tell him such a thing! Are you sure Laurel will accept an offer from you?"

"No, I cannot be sure, but I believe she is not indifferent to me."

"One cannot suppose she would be. Come home and talk to your father yourself."

He temporized. "I am not able to ride yet."

"I can squeeze you in with Sally and me."

"No, Mama dear."

"Then there is nothing more to be said." She stood and, asking him to order her carriage, went into the inn.

Gordon followed. While she was upstairs, he seized the time to write a note summoning his curricle and servants from the Earl of Clifton's seat. This, with a coin, he gave to Del to post.

When Lady Leadenhall and her maid descended, he tenderly and courteously settled them in the chaise. Standing at the open carriage door, he said, "Before you go, Mama, tell me one thing truly. What dowry did you bring to Father?"

Lady Margaret caught her breath.

"You owe it to your son to tell."

"Five hundred pounds," she whispered.

"Thank you, dearest Mama." He saluted, closed the carriage door, and waved the postillions away.

At Eland House, Laurel hid in the sanctuary of her chamber, waiting to watch the smart black carriage pass. She could not discern a gentleman inside it. And no horseman rode behind.

Trembling and hesitant, then, she descended to the lower floor, anxiously debating whether she should venture through the village. When she slipped onto the stoop she saw Gordon Rand coming from the inn yard. He waved his cane jubilantly overhead, pitched it forcefully away, and began a limping lope up the street.

ELEGANT LOVE STILL FLOURISHES—
Wrap yourself in a Zebra Regency Romance.

A MATCHMAKER'S MATCH   (3783, $3.50/$4.50)
by Nina Porter
To save herself from a loveless marriage, Lady Psyche Veringham pretends to be a bluestocking. Resigned to spinsterhood at twenty-three, Psyche sets her keen mind to snaring a husband for her young charge, Amanda. She sets her cap for long-time bachelor, Justin St. James. This man of the world has had his fill of frothy-headed debutantes and turns the tables on Psyche. Can a bluestocking and a man about town find true love?

FIRES IN THE SNOW   (3809, $3.99/$4.99)
by Janis Laden
Because of an unhappy occurrence, Diana Ruskin knew that a secure marriage was not in her future. She was content to assist her physician father and follow in his footsteps . . . until now. After meeting Adam, Duke of Marchmaine, Diana's precise world is shattered. She would simply have to avoid the temptation of his gentle touch and stunning physique—and by doing so break her own heart!

FIRST SEASON   (3810, $3.50/$4.50)
by Anne Baldwin
When country heiress Laetitia Biddle arrives in London for the Season, she harbors dreams of triumph and applause. Instead, she becomes the laughingstock of drawing rooms and ballrooms, alike. This headstrong miss blames the rakish Lord Wakeford for her miserable debut, and she vows to rise above her many faux pas. Vowing to become an Original, Letty proves that she's more than a match for this eligible, seasoned Lord.

AN UNCOMMON INTRIGUE   (3701, $3.99/$4.99)
by Georgina Devon
Miss Mary Elizabeth Sinclair was rather startled when the British Home Office employed her as a spy. Posing as "Tasha," an exotic fortune-teller, she expected to encounter unforeseen dangers. However, nothing could have prepared her for Lord Eric Stewart, her dashing and infuriating partner. Giving her heart to this haughty rogue would be the most reckless hazard of all.

A MADDENING MINX   (3702, $3.50/$4.50)
by Mary Kingsley
After a curricle accident, Miss Sarah Chadwick is literally thrust into the arms of Philip Thornton. While other women shy away from Thornton's eyepatch and aloof exterior, Sarah finds herself drawn to discover why this man is physically and emotionally scarred.